Black Borne

Warrior Slave, Volume 1

L.L. Farmer

Published by LitSpeaks Publishing, 2017.

BLACK BORNE

First edition. October 5, 2017.

Written by L.L. Farmer.

To my darling child, Nayeli, who once told me (when she was five-years-old): "I don't *want to* be an artist. I *am* an artist."

You inspire me.

Prologue

Manhattan Island
March 1741

C uffee's execution changed everything.

It started with the first fire, on the eighteenth of March, which burnt the governor's mansion to the ground.

Alarm bells clanged throughout the city, and two horse-drawn wagons carried the fire engines to Fort George. Every able-bodied man formed a brigade, but the fire spread from the barracks to the chapel to the Secretary's office.

Heavy smoke traveled through the brisk spring air, leaving the southern tip of Manhattan and blanketing both the East Ward and the Docks, forcing many of us to walk up Broad Street to escape its deadly path. Mama and I fled with the master's wife and his children while he joined the men at the fort. The fire died when the rain fell, but the damage had been done. Ft. George burnt to the ground. The next day, we learned the fire had been an accident, set by a plumber's fire pot. Or so we assumed.

A week later, another fire broke out near Fort George at the home of a sea captain. The men moved quickly and contained the fire. Although suspicion crawled beneath the surface of conversations, no one believed the fires were being set on purpose. Mama, though, got that knowing look in her eye and chanted in her native tongue. I couldn't understand her words, but I heard the worry in her voice. Trouble was stirring.

Manhattan held her breath, waiting for what might come next, but six days passed without incident. We all breathed a sigh of relief. Then, in April, the city spun out of control. That third Wednesday, on the first of April, a dockside warehouse along the East River burnt to the ground. Three days later, two separate fires broke out. This time neighbors accused each other's slaves of setting the fire. Mama's worries grew more visible, filling the kitchen with the smoke from her candles. Her prayers were for our safety and protection because she had seen death in her dreams.

On the fifth of April, two more fires blazed at a coach house, but for that fire, they arrested a slave named Quaco. Once they arrested Quaco, suspicions rose against the slaves. Whispers of a conspiracy permeated the air, terrifying both blacks and whites. White New Yorkers feared that slaves were plotting to kill them. Blacks worried that in their fear, even the mildest of whites might accuse and attack. None had forgotten that not yet thirty years had passed since a slave uprising had left several people dead.

Mama's candles and chants didn't make much difference since two more fires blazed at Ft. George. They put the first fire out easily and arrested the Spanish Negroes captured from that Spanish ship. All five of them. No sooner were they jailed and being questioned, however, when another fire broke out. Like most of the slaves, I stayed inside. I would never have been able to escape Mama's watchful eye anyhow. I was, perhaps, in the kitchen baking or in the house cleaning when white New Yorkers gathered in fear and arrested slaves in masses. And so I was safe at home when they arrested Cuffee.

WHEN I FIRST MET CUFFEE at the Market by Wall Street, I noticed his height first. Later, he told me he had noticed the same of me. I towered over most women and men, but he made me feel dainty in a way I didn't experience often. Although a slave, Cuffee hungered for freedom. He was the one who told me of the slave revolt back in 1712—that slave freedom became impossible to gain after nine whites were killed. Before the rebellion, back when there were free blacks, black men owned land by Fresh Water Pond. The Land of the Blacks, they called it.

"They stole the land from us," he told me, his voice intense in the way it got when he spoke of freedom. "Our land. My family's land, Neema. They took away our freedom. My father was born to a free man, and I aim to be free too."

Cuffee wanted freedom more than anything, maybe even more than me. And now, after those last two fires at Ft. George, he stood accused of helping to plan a great conspiracy.

"You ever dream of being free?" Cuffee asked me one day as he walked me home from the Market.

I smiled, considered the way my mother ruled the master's house, and mistook that for freedom. "What will we do in freedom?" I whispered, always mindful of the white New Yorkers that always milled around us.

"Be like them," he said, pointing to a couple that passed near us, the woman's gloved hand resting on the crook of her partner's arm. Her face turned up to his, smiling with a light-heartedness that eluded slaves.

"I wish we could," I said because I yearned to be with Cuffee without limitations. He had been walking me home for three months now. I expected him to declare for me soon, and even though I had never seen love shared freely between slaves, I knew it must be a wondrous thing.

Maybe sensing my thoughts, Cuffee, for the first time, asked me to meet him at Hughson's Tavern. I should have never gone.

Those nights I sat with him at Hughson's Tavern and listened to the talk of the slaves were strange but glorious. To watch this white tavern keeper surrounded by laughing black faces made me understand that even though my mother ruled, we were still slaves. Amidst the laughter and glowing faces, Cuffee whispered in my ear marriage and freedom and the house he wanted to build.

I took a chance, being in this place at night, but Cuffee spoke of wanting me to be a free woman. He wanted us to be free in marriage.

That was the Cuffee who sat beside me at Hughson's Tavern, not a man planning to stage a slave revolt. My Cuffee wanted freedom, but he didn't plan a revolt like the one they spoke of in the streets after his arrest. He didn't. Did he? As much as I refused to believe Cuffee would, I realized that Cuffee could. Many of us could. And the white New Yorkers knew this as well, arresting several slave women and men before the trials began. Including Caesar and Prince.

Those nights in the tavern, I often gazed at Cuffee with affection as his voice joined Caesar's with talks of casting off bondage, of owning their own land, of being treated the same as the whites. I never considered, none of us did, Hughson's sixteen-year-old indentured servant. Only two years younger than me, Mary Burton lived a long, hard life. None of us thought Mary would be used against us or cause so many to stand accused. She was an indentured servant, more like us than she was like the white women of the city, and I allowed her indentured servitude to persuade me to forget that she was nothing like the black slaves. So, so foolish of me.

Mama had warned me since I was a young child. "Neema," she often said, the sounds of Fon still adding a song to her English. "None can be your friend or your confidant. For them, you will forever be Negro and slave. You must always keep your words and feelings to yourself."

In Hughson's Tavern with so few women to talk to, I had ignored Mama's warning and occasionally talked to Mary Burton. As Mary testified first against Caesar and then against the others, her words burned my tongue with remembrance. She and I had laughed and spun tales of the men surrounding us. We had called them rebels and landowners and obsessed with being kings. We, she and I, had spun greater and greater tales, one more grandiose than the other as we painted pictures, dark and light, of slave men fighting for freedom.

I had spoken with a sixteen-year-old girl who had taken our words, my words, and used them to destroy multiple lives. A month ago, Mary Burton had taken the stand and testified against Caesar, Prince, the Hughson's and Cuffee. I couldn't attend the trial, but word spread through the city. Since slaves couldn't testify on their behalf, they saved themselves by accusing other slaves. That didn't save Caesar and Prince though. They were hanged from the gallows a few weeks ago, Caesar's body in chains for all to see what would happen to punished slaves.

Seeing Caesar hanging from the gallows made me anxious about Cuffee's fate. I know that Mary Burton only spoke because the Judge threatened her, spoke to save herself, but her words had condemned innocent men to die. Condemned Cuffee.

Even now, days later and shivering against the cool night air with a blanket clutched between my fingers, I thought of Cuffee's and Quaco's trial.

BY THE TIME CUFFEE and Quaco came to trial yesterday, Judge Horsmanden had confined over a hundred people to the prison. Although Horsmanden arrested mostly blacks, John Hughson and his wife and daughter still awaited trial. Horsmanden even called for the arrest of Peggy, a white prostitute swollen with Caesar's child.

Horsmanden called witness after witness, but the trial kept circling back to Mary Burton. She was the main attraction, spinning elaborate yarns. It was clear though, except to the most paranoid of whites, that the slave conspiracy began and ended with her.

I wanted to sit in that courtroom, watch her face and listen to her lies. But I could only hope that the trial ended soon. The news coming from the courthouse bode ill for Cuffee and the other blacks jailed and awaiting trial.

As Mary Burton's words traveled from the courtroom and into the streets of Manhattan, I recognized my own words. Our innocent speculations changed from words spoken in Hughson's Tavern filled with dreams of freedom to accusations of betrayal. Sometimes those declarations turned into impractical plans before John Hughson closed for the night, and the men wandered home. But they had been harmless declarations. In that courtroom, Mary's witty one-line comments as she served drinks at our table became a word whispered by Caesar or Prince or one of the other men in the tavern. The elaborate plots I created out of amusement, turned into Cuffee's words as Mary sacrificed slave after slave to save herself.

Guilt turned my nights sleepless. ·

And as days passed with Caesar's rotting body hanging in the wind, the guilt and worry showed in my face. I struggled to hide my concern from my mother when the image of Cuffee hanging like Caesar churned my stomach.

Mary's testimony, though, was not the only one that damned Cuffee. A firefighter claimed to have seen Cuffee fleeing that second fire at Ft. George, but I refused to doubt Cuffee. He couldn't have been involved. Even as the firefighter's testimony blamed him, I knew my Cuffee would never lead a slave plot that meant murdering masters, naming Caesar governor and making John Hughson a king. No such plot existed except in whispered confidences between me and Mary Burton. Mary Burton and me. Me.

"What have you done, Neema?" Mama asked as I quickly wrapped my clothes in a blanket the day Cuffee and Quaco stood trial.

Every time word of the trials passed near us, I pretended ignorance. I admitted only to knowing Cuffee as a passing acquaintance, and when Mama eyed me with suspicion, I pretended not to notice.

But I was a fool to think she wouldn't know. My mother was born with the gift of knowing. She healed, saw secrets, and spoke of events yet to happen. She probably knew of my part all along, but Mama always waited for me to confess before she accused.

"What have you done, Neema?" she said, again, her hands burning into my skin as she clutched my arm.

I shivered against the cool breeze and closed my eyes against the memory of my mother's disappointed face. She placed a shaking hand against my cheek, and for the first time, I watched her eyes fill with tears. "You don't realize what you have done, do you?" she said, her hand so gentle against my face. "You cost this boy his life, and so many others will die before this ends."

"I never said...." I started.

Mama shook her head and stepped back from me, the sadness on her face bringing tears to my eyes. My mother came from the Fon of Benin, a young girl on a slave ship to the Caribbean. There, she often told me, they taught us how to be slaves. My mother, though, wasn't meant to be a slave. She was born a priestess, daughter of a Dahomey woman warrior. Her ability to see the future and spirits, to heal people was one she kept hidden from the whites in our city. They only understood evil and witchcraft, she warned us. So Mama helped only the slaves, and they kept her secrets. I should have known my mother would discover my involvement.

"Go," she told me, after Cuffee was sentenced to die. He and Quaco named so many others trying to keep from death, but nothing saved them. He begged for me and in his begging, turned suspicious eyes on me.

When Mama heard Constables were coming to arrest me, she had told me, "Go to the Negro burying ground," squeezing my arms as she searched my face. "And don't leave until I come find you, Neema."

I had jerked my head forward, but something in her face spoke of the importance of her words. Through my fear, I somehow focused on her hushed voice.

"No matter what happens, Neema," she said, pressing a knotted handkerchief in my hand. "You must wait for me at the burying ground."

"Mama...."

"You wait," she said, again. Her fingers cutting into my arm. She didn't let me leave until I promised to wait for her.

And I had fled my master's house for temporary shelter in the Negro burying ground just past the Commons in the North Ward. Avoiding the busy traffic of Broadway, I walked along New Street terrified of being captured. No place was safe for any of us while they arrested slave after slave. If Horsmanden could accuse John Hughson, his wife and his daughter, if even whites weren't safe from the accusations, then none of us were safe.

IN THE COVER OF DARK, I passed through the Commons, the stench of decaying flesh drifting through the night air. I kept my gaze averted, remembering the look of Caesar's rotting body hanging from the gallows.

The burying ground was empty since slaves could not bury their dead after dark, and the White New Yorkers avoided a place many considered haunted. I understood why as I settled amongst the graves.

Huddled beneath a blanket of trees, I slept fitfully the first two nights as every sound frightened me. I had built a simple covering of the blankets Mama packed for me and fought to stay awake. Staying awake, however, proved taxing as I slept for short spells.

On the third night, however, I slept at length. I had lost the battle, and my body ceased to function. I couldn't have slept for long before I jerked awake, my heart thundering against my chest. My eyes darted around, trying to penetrate the darkness of the night, but I heard nothing.

Images of Cuffee in the Commons and Cuffee in Hughson's Tavern raged inside my head as I struggled against feelings of guilt. He had pleaded for his life, pleaded for his innocence just as Caesar had, but the belief in his guilt had been insurmountable. The memories of that night had awakened me. Or so I thought.

I jerked as I heard the crackling of branches. I had hidden deep in the cemetery, by the oldest of the graves, but that did not guarantee my safety. I heard it again, the crackling of branches and grew still. When she touched me, I jumped and almost screamed. A hand clamped over my mouth, and I stared into eyes so dark they weren't natural.

"You are the child of the priestess and the descendant of the Dahomey warrior," she said, her voice gravelly.

I tried to move away from her, but her grip only tightened. She was dark and slender, taller than even me, and her skin shone in the moonlight. Her hair coiled in a thick, silver and black braid around her head and then draped over her shoulder like a rope. She wore a wide strip of white cloth across her breasts and a wider strip across her lower region. I tried not to stare at her nakedness in shock, but the whiteness against her black skin was riveting.

"You interfered," she said, her eyes combing my face. Her other hand gripped my hair as she brought my face close to her own.

When the hand she placed over my mouth loosened some, I tried to speak, "I—"

"You interfered, and now the man is dead."

"Who are you?" I said.

She smiled, which made me tremble. "You may call me the Vodou. It matters not which one." Her head tilted as she studied me, and my heart beat against my chest so hard that I struggled to \ breathe. "He lost his life because of you," she whispered.

"I didn't mean—"

She clamped her hand over my mouth again. "You will take their place. The priestess, the hunter, the discerner. And you will live until we get back what we have lost."

I tried to speak again, but she shook her head and kept her hand pressed against my lips. "Before these trials end, many Negroes will stand accused of this rebellion. Some will be returned to Africa. Some to the Caribbean, but some will be executed. Three of the accused were chosen. You will stand in place of the chosen."

And just as suddenly, she vanished. Questions churned inside me as I struggled to understand her words, struggled to understand her existence. My mother had told me many stories of the Vodou as I was growing up, and every story had terrified me.

I JERKED AS THE WORLD around me grew louder. The crackling of branches, rumbling of men's voices and stomping of feet came closer. Grabbing the blanket from the branches, I wrapped it in my knapsack.

"I heard something," a man's voice said. "I think it's one of the Negroes."

Scared, I gathered my knapsack under my arms and ran, hoping I was heading away from the city. I had become so used to white New Yorkers avoiding the Negro burying ground I had assumed they would not venture into the graveyard. This had been a mistake.

"I see someone!" a voice said, sounding much too close.

One hand slashed at the branches slapping against my face and arms as I stumbled through the burying ground. I could hear them behind me, leading each other in my direction. Tripping on a fresh mound of dirt, I fell on my hand, my wrist bending back. I struggled to my feet again, ignoring the pain as I continued to run.

Racing out of the trees, I stumbled into a clearing and straight into the body of Caesar. I had gone the wrong way. Standing in the Commons with only the whipping post to shield me, I shoved Caesar's legs away from me. When I turned back, I found myself outnumbered and defenseless.

"Stop where you are," one man yelled, pointing a musket at me as the others fanned out into a circle. I tried to watch them all at once, but there were too many of them. Another musket pointed in my direction while others held swords, and one even had a pitchfork.

I couldn't let them catch me. I didn't want to hang, and I didn't want to be sent to Africa or the Caribbean, lands I had never known. Despite whatever the Vodou had said or meant, I hadn't betrayed Cuffee on purpose, and I refused to fall into their hands. Walking backward and keeping an eye on the men who had filled the clearing, I felt my resolve stiffen. I would not be taken alive. One of them, though, must have sensed my plan because the musket ball ripped into my throat before I had turned.

I dropped to my side, the knapsack falling beside me as I thought of Cuffee. It was only fitting I die this way after what I had done to him. If I had kept my mouth shut and if I had never spoken to Mary Burton, then Cuffee might still be alive. The surrounding sounds faded as I closed my eyes against the pain. I couldn't breathe, and the gurgling sounds coming from my throat bode ill. My final thought, as my world darkened though, was not of Cuffee but of my mother.

CHAPTER ONE

New York City

2017

I saw him from the corner of my eye, standing in front of the cooler filled with beers. He moved fast, quicker than any human eye could see. But I had become something other than human long ago. I took a single step toward the back of the bodega. Just because no one could see him didn't mean he couldn't harm them.

I laid the bag of Tostitos back on the shelf to free my hands, and released the daggers strapped to my forearms, their sharp tips hidden by the jacket sleeves. I had picked up his trail in Louisiana last week and followed him to New York—the last place I wanted to be. There was no way I would lose him now. Inching my way toward the back, I eased my hands over both daggers.

"Hey, baby girl," a voice breathed near my shoulder.

I glanced beside me to see a man much, much too old to be giving me *that* look. He wore his baseball cap turned backward, his lined face contrasting with his NY Knicks t-shirt and sagging jeans.

I looked from the Jordans on his feet to the cap perched on his head and shuddered. Old men should wear neat dress slacks and a button-down shirt. Sagging pants just didn't work after a certain age if they ever did. Too bad I didn't have time for a quick shopping spree to assuage my offended fashion sense.

He rubbed his thumb across his lips, his eyebrows moving up and down in a delusional version of sexy. Horrified, I couldn't stop looking at him, all my energy focused on keeping the *Eww* from passing my lips.

"Anybody ever tell you, you look like a delicious Hershey kiss," he said.

Holding up a finger, I shook my head. "Don't," I said, refraining from making one of my snide remarks. Frowning, I turned back to see my quarry staring straight at me, frozen.

"Damn," I muttered, right before he leaped over the shelf and bounded out the door. I so hated when they recognized me.

Moving just as fast, I raced after him. That was one of the interesting side effects of being forced to live forever: enhanced abilities. We raced down Broadway, crossing against traffic signals as he weaved in and out of pedestrian traffic. We were so quick we barely registered to the humans who felt our touch like a strong wind. When we turned up Madison Avenue, I grew angrier with each step. I hated when they made me run.

When I got close enough, I tackled him. As we landed, my daggers pressed against his neck, the holy water sealed in the blade burning his skin. He gazed up at me, the fear in his eyes palpable.

Once upon a time, I had relished in their fear. This was when the anger cut so deep I fell just shy of tormenting those

I hunted. Now, the anger had simmered to a steady bitterness, but they still remembered what I had once been.

"Why are you here?" I hissed, my knee pressed against his chest. He was a twenty-year-old human, medium in height and build. His white skin pinked with anger as he struggled against my hold. The blade nicked him, and his eyes widened as he stopped moving. His ability to take on human form meant that he was a shapeshifter, falling in the middle of the demon hierarchy. No mere possession for him when he could appear human himself.

"Just let me be," he said. "I promise. I won't fight you."

I pressed my knee harder, and he gasped for air. "You're a shapeshifter." I said. "You live to fight. I know you're here for the same reason I am. Just tell me where the death demons are."

Most demons traveled in packs, in particular death demons. That this demon had traveled so far meant something huge was happening. He had been called.

He tried to shake his head. "I don't...."

"All demons lie." I said, twisting one hand in his chin-length black hair. His charming Southern looks had become a lot less blue-eyed blonde in New York. If I had not become accustomed to his scent, I wouldn't have recognized the grungy, dark-haired young man in front of me. He had even added eye-liner to his look. "Just tell me why you're here."

"There's a woman," he swallowed as my blade nicked him. His skin bubbled black where the blade broke skin. "She's to die tonight."

"Who is she?"

"I don't know."

"Why does she matter?

"Please believe me. I.... don't....know."

"Then tell me where they are."

He tried to shake his head again. "I don't—"

I moved the dagger just a little closer until blood trickled from the cut on his neck, and the blackened and bubbled skin spread.

"Wait," he said. "I can take you there."

I smiled. He was trying to buy time. He would show me, not tell me. I moved back, daggers sliding back into place. Before he could stand, I had locked an iron collar around his neck and wrists, its link chain in my grip. At first, I had refused to use this symbol of slavery, this reminder of my capture in South Carolina, but I had needed something sturdy.

The Priest had forged the shackles into a prison for demons, and none had ever broken their hold. It had taken me many decades, several escapes, and entanglement with a mad demon before I broke down and used the shackles. I had never gotten over the churning in my stomach though when I shackled any demon. Even now I didn't want to use the chains even though I knew the demon world had relished our prolonged captivity, but I couldn't trust this young demon. I had become well-versed in the lies of demons. Trusting them was always costly.

His eyes glowed at me with hatred. "There is no need...."

I yanked at the chain and let him stumble beside me as we headed toward the street. "Show me," I said, almost tripping when he burst into a run, his wrists nestled against his chest.

THREE MINUTES LATER, we stood across the street from a brownstone blocked by police cars and yellow caution tape. Death demons swarmed the front steps, their yellow skin glowing in the moonlight, but I couldn't tell if it were murder, suicide, or something else. I needed to see the chief demon. Chief demons drawn to murder always smelled of a stronger bloodlust.

"What happened here?" I asked.

The shapeshifter struggled to wrench his gaze from the scene, drawn to it like a death demon. The chaos and tragedy surrounding violent deaths were like a drug to them, so gangs and wars were ambrosia.

His eyes glazed as he looked at me. He had gotten high. "A woman was killed. Shot."

"But why does she matter so much?"

He shrugged and turned away from me, straining to get closer to the house. Frowning, I focused my hearing on the conversations across the street.

Demons, though they gathered in clusters, only formed in numbers this big when a death meant a change that would alter several lives. The demons that fed off the assassinations of the 1960's burned into my memories.

"A teacher," I heard. "Just moved in two weeks ago."

"And you didn't hear a thing?" One woman asked.

The other woman shook her head. "That's what scares me. I was just upstairs watching TV, and you know how I do. The volume wasn't loud. I should have heard something."

"You have to go to your sister's tonight."

"Tonight?! Girl, I'm thinkin bout packin my stuff and not coming back at all."

"Might even wanna sell."

"My nephew's girlfriend *is* a realtor."

"I feel ya girl."

I shook my head as I tugged the demon's chain.

"Tell me everything you know about the victim."

He pulled away from me as far as he could go. "I can't tell you anything. Do you know what will happen if he finds out I spoke to you? I can't go into the Abyss."

I shrugged. "Then I kill you here."

When he met my gaze with an unflinching waver, I realized that his fear of this demon was much greater than his fear of me. That wasn't good. At all.

"Do what you must," he responded.

I frowned. I wasn't ready to deal with what his response revealed. Wanting to get closer to the house, I stepped forward as the chief demon came to the bottom of the steps, hoping to get a closer look. And then I wished that I hadn't. I might have little choice in this battle against demons, but there were a few demons I had learned to avoid over the years. Baal was one of them.

YANKING THE CHAIN OF the demon in my grasp, I dragged him away from the scene even though he struggled against the chains. His high from the tragedy made him sway just a little. When they were drunk like this, killing them was no challenge. Not bothering to hide my disgust, I pulled him roughly behind me. I had no reason to feel sympathy for him. Two teenagers in New Orleans were dead because of the trouble he brought. As soon as I returned him to the spiritual world, I would come back to the house. By then, Baal and his legion of demons should be gone.

"I can help you," the young demon said, putting both hands up.

I smiled. "If you know who I am, then you know I allowed a demon to help me once before."

"I am not..."

"You're right. You aren't." I said, my daggers poised above him.

"But I can help you," he said, his voice steady, but his eyes pleading. "I... I can tell you whatever you need to know."

"I can find out on my own."

"Just don't send me back. It takes so long to get here. I don't want to start at the bottom again."

"I don't need you. I already know Baal is the chief demon." I said, my blades moving so swiftly that his startled expression didn't register until after he vanished. I didn't waste my time wondering if I imagined the look on his face. His surprise at Baal's name had been obvious. Unfortunately, sometimes I moved too swiftly even for me. Now, even though he had not expected Baal to be there, I couldn't ask him why.

Annoyed, I sheathed my daggers and went inside of the brownstone I called home. These blades were forged for me many years ago after I, with much difficulty, sent several demons back to the spiritual realm. They were made from holy water and blessed by a blacksmith slash priest, along with my sword. Not only had Priest saved my life, but he helped me to become the demon hunter. Not *a* demon hunter. *The* demon hunter.

The daggers and my sword worked like any exorcism, sending demons back into the underworld. They had been taken from me only once during the two hundred plus years I wielded them. That was a time I never wanted to remember or relive.

WHEN I WALKED INTO the house, Raina sat on the couch, her hands crafting more arrows for my bow.

"You find the demon?" she asked, without glancing at me.

I nodded, grabbing a bottle of water from the refrigerator before dropping on the love seat opposite her. While Raina's hands were skilled, I could see that the shaking in them had grown more intense. I didn't like to think of Raina as getting older, but all of them did. She and I had been together for fifty years now, the longest of the women and men I called my allies or partners—never, per Raina, sidekicks.

"I also saw Baal tonight," I told her.

She gave me a sharp look. "Someone was murdered?"

"A young woman," I said. "I have to go back tonight and have a look around."

She set the arrows aside and directed her full gaze on me. "You need a better set of eyes and ears than I have, Neema."

My heart thundered as Raina brought up our old conversation yet again. I wasn't ready for a new partner. I never was even though I have done this multiple times.

"Raina," I said. "You're fine."

Usually Raina will back down and return to her task, but this time she held my gaze until I realized that we were having *that* conversation. Of the many partners that had worked beside me over the years, Raina ranked high—if not the highest.

"My sister has a grandchild I've been watching these past few years. I've sent for her to come to New York. I think she's the right one for you, Neema."

"Raina..."

"It's time, Neema. I can no longer give you the help you need. She'll be here in the morning."

Her tone was final, and I knew nothing I said would matter. Raina was right. For the last ten years, she had been speaking of her replacement. My last hunt in New Orleans had been tough on her. She would do as most of my partners/allies had done before her: find her replacement.

I WAITED UNTIL ALMOST two in the morning before I returned to Allison's brownstone. Police had cordoned off the crime scene, but I slipped inside. The line between the human world and the spiritual world was thin enough for demons and angels to walk on our side. Sometimes, a human can also enter the spiritual realm. It wasn't the safest place for us to be, but I often had to move between worlds if I wanted to move freely. I slipped into the brownstone by traveling beyond human sight.

Once inside the foyer, the smell of the demons overwhelmed me, and I hadn't even gone into the victim's apartment. I placed a hand against the wall and took deep, fortifying breaths. Almost a minute passed before I could find the strength to move again. The pain and anguish of the victim still filled the rooms and seeped into the walls. The demons had enjoyed a feast tonight.

Walking upstairs, I was swift even though the brownstone stood empty. The upstairs apartment was locked, but I made quick work of both locks. Taking a deep breath, I drew an arrow just in case. The brownstone may be empty now, but demons could surprise me. Not easily but it could happen. Although I was deadlier with the blades, the arrows would allow me to slow a demon down until I had a better position.

The living room was destroyed, but the victim had fought back. I went over to the corner desk, which had been searched thoroughly. A framed picture hanging on the wall showed the victim standing next to a couple who must've been her parents. A brunette with olive skin and hazel eyes, the victim had been a lovely woman. Work related items covered her desk: the copy of a lesson plan, a grade book, a thank you card from a student. Allison Stevens had been in her fifth year of teaching.

I glanced at her lesson plan, noting that she taught history at a Brooklyn high school nearby. Rifling through the desk drawer, I found nothing of interest so I moved to the bedroom. The queen size bed took up most of the room, and a chair sat in one corner. Clothes, yanked from the dresser and closet, were strewn across the floor.

I had no way of knowing what her killer was searching for or whether anything had been found. I should have gotten more information from that demon before I sent him back.

I went into the kitchen last, but I didn't learn much else about Allison Stevens. I would have to pay a visit to her job tomorrow to find out more information.

Letting myself out of the brownstone, I walked the short distance back to the house. Raina's bedroom downstairs was quiet, and I knew she already slept. What more could I say to her, anyway?

I considered going down to the basement to work out my frustrations, but I needed sleep. Opening the door to my bedroom, I avoided glancing at the mirror that Raina insisted I place by the door. I looked the same as I had centuries ago, and that wasn't as wonderful as it sounded. Every scratch, every scar on my body was one I had worn before that night in the Negro burying ground. Seeing my youthfulness only reminded me of the curse and thinking of the curse sparked my anger.

I took a quick shower before settling into bed. Tomorrow, I would go back to high school. For that I needed all the rest I could get. I also needed to deal with the young lady that Raina was considering as her replacement. So I slept, but I didn't sleep well.

CHAPTER TWO

Since most of the inner-city high schools had students who rarely, if ever, showed up to school, it wasn't too difficult to become a student who hadn't been seen since the first week of classes. Raina gelled down my short natural, glued weave to a wig cap, and I sported shoulder-length waves. I put on jeans and a black midriff top that would probably get me sent home. Tossing on a fitted Pink hoodie, I slipped into my sneakers before heading out the door. The bag I carried held paper and a notebook, and my daggers hid in the lining.

I had to sneak past security when I saw students walking through the scanners. Once inside, I thought I would have to sit through classes all day, but the announcement was made early that morning. A somber air traveled through the school as news of Ms. Stevens' death went from classroom to classroom. By mid-morning, many students and several teachers had become distraught, attesting to her popularity. Additional guidance counselors had come in to handle the volume of upset students and teachers.

One student separated herself from the others, and I watched her as we sat in the guidance suite. When she slipped out of the suite, I followed her to the top floor. She glanced up the hallway, but with so many students walking around, changing classes, no one noticed her go into an empty room.

I slipped in after the girl and found her in the corner of a book room, hidden by the bookshelves. She sat on a stepping stool, her elbows resting on her knees. She may have been a senior, about my complexion, with long curly black hair. Her hair had fallen forward to cover her face, so she didn't see me when I walked around the bookshelf. I startled her when I touched her shoulder, and I could see she had been crying. Handing her a tissue, I knelt on the floor next to her.

"I don't want to bother you," I whispered. "But I noticed how troubled you looked in the hallway. I wanted to check on you."

She looked at me with distrust. "I don't remember seeing you around here before."

And I couldn't lie because I would have lost her. "If I tell you who I am, you have to promise not to tell anyone."

She still looked at me with distrust, but she nodded her head.

"I'm looking into the death of your teacher," I said, leaning forward. "My name is Neema."

"Are you a cop?" she asked, pulling back.

I didn't blame her. The relationship between New York's finest and its darker citizens had been contentious for decades. She wouldn't trust me if I claimed to be an officer. "A private investigator," I told her. I even showed her my identification. "I work with my dad." That would, maybe, explain my youthful look.

"But Ms. Stevens just died," she said, still not ready to trust me.

"We were working for her," I said. "But I can't tell you what we were investigating."

She relaxed. "I'm Maria. And if you can't tell me, it doesn't matter. I already know about her family."

My attention sharpened, but I didn't move. "What do you think happened?" I said.

She looked away from me and took a deep breath. "Ms. Stevens didn't tell me a lot. I knew she was adopted, but I know little about her family. She didn't talk to anyone."

I thought about the couple in the picture I had noticed in her home. She had resembled the woman in the photograph. "Was she adopted by a family member?"

The girl nodded. "Her aunt. Ms. Stevens would mention her family in class sometimes. Her mother was killed when she was just a child, and she went to live with one of her mother's sisters."

"Did she ever tell you how her mother died?"

"No, but I've always thought she either killed herself or she was murdered. It was the way Ms. Stevens acted, you know. When people die like that, it's different." She shook her head. "I can't explain it. It's just different."

But I knew what she meant. The grief after a murder or a suicide had a different feel, a different scent. I have always thought the greed of the death demons somehow altered the way the loved ones grieved. Perhaps Maria was sensitive to the spiritual world. Some humans were.

"The other day," Maria started, before her voice faltered. She was silent for a moment before she spoke again. "Ms. Stevens came to school excited a week ago. A member of her family, an uncle maybe, left her an inheritance."

"Did she ever tell you what the inheritance was?"

"I don't think she knew yet. She called out for two days last month. She never told us why, but I think she left town to get whatever her uncle left her."

Now that sounded promising. "Did you guys ever speculate about what it could be?"

"A few of the boys thought she might have gotten money, but I think Ms. Stevens came from money. She didn't get excited about things like that. I've only known Ms. Stevens to get excited over two things: history and a good book." The girl shrugged. "But then I'm just a student. She won't tell me much."

"Did Ms. Stevens have a boyfriend?"

"Neema, I don't know..."

"Look, I won't tell anyone. I know that teachers have close relationships with students sometimes. I'm sure Ms. Stevens did too."

"Ms. Stevens wasn't close to many people," Maria said. "I was one of the few people she spoke to and that was only in the last few months. I think she had a lot going on and needed someone to talk to. Her boyfriend...."

She stopped when the door opened. "Maria," came a loud whisper.

I looked up to see a student standing in the doorway. The bell had just rung, and the hallway filled with students. The girl was the same age as Maria and, I guess, myself. Coming to my feet, I glanced down at Maria before looking at the other girl.

"The cops are here," the girl whispered. "They want to talk to you."

"Okay, now close the door before someone notices you." Maria looked back at me. "His name is Grant," she said, standing. "But I don't know his last name. And he wasn't her boyfriend. I think they had gone on maybe two or three dates." She offered a tremulous smile. "Contrary to what you believe, most teachers keep their private lives private."

"You ever seen him before?" I asked as she walked to the door.

"No, but she got flowers a few days ago. We teased her about them." She opened the door, but glanced back at me. "If I think of anything else, how do I get in touch with you?"

"I'll be in touch," I said, sliding out of the door right behind her.

AS SOON AS I STEPPED out of the book room, I saw the detectives walking at the end of the hallway and immediately turned to the lockers beside me. I felt a little faint as I tried to take in what I had seen. Jasen. Here.

Thirty years since I had seen him, and he was still so damn beautiful. Tucking my head in my chest, I opened the combination lock and buried my face in the locker. He had been only seventeen years old when I left. Even then, his dreams of being a police detective had been a large part of our friendship. Jasen had wanted to fix things I had learned long ago could never be fixed.

He led the detectives down the hallway, and I examined the lock clutched in my hand before I turned around and walked in front of them, in the same direction as they did. I followed the flow of the students into the stairwell. I needed to get into Ms. Stevens' classroom before the detectives went there.

Rushing up two flights of stairs, I made quick work of the lock to her classroom door before walking into the darkened classroom. Her desk was locked, but locked things did not deter me. I went through her desk, noting that she had more personal items in this desk than she did in the one at home.

I pulled out another picture of her and the couple that were her parents. This was another smiling, happy picture, but they looked awkward. Her parents stood next to each other, the man standing with his arm around his wife. Allison stood away from them, her hand touching the elbow of the woman. I put the picture back and rummaged through the drawers on the right.

At the back of a bottom drawer, I found the card for the flowers. Only his first name, Grant, but at least I had the name of the flower shop. I had to hurry if I wanted to find him before the police did.

I looked up when I heard the sudden sound of keys at the door. Dropping to my knees, I peered over the desk and saw the detectives at the door standing behind the assistant principal. I had few choices. There was no ledge beneath the window, and besides, too many people were walking the streets below. All I needed was just one person to think I was trying to jump. I scrambled across the room to the closet and leaped onto the top. I was long, but I made myself fit behind the boxes stored on top of the closet. They came in just as I settled my bag inside a box.

They looked at each other and glanced at Maria before turning toward the door. Right before she turned off the light, she looked back at me, and I knew she came here to distract them. The question was why, but I didn't stay up there trying to figure it out. My hiding place had seemed to shrink, and even though Jasen and his partner had not looked above the closet, they wouldn't overlook the closet when they came back.

I EASED FROM BEHIND the boxes and dropped to the floor. Walking through the spirit world so the cameras wouldn't see me leave the classroom, I hurried through the double doors and into the stairwell. Rushing downstairs, I rushed from the building, wanting to find this Grant before the police did.

Pulling my phone from my bag, I called Raina.

"Sheree is here," she said when she answered the phone.

"Raina, what are you talking about?"

"I told you about her. My sister's granddaughter. Do you ever pay attention Neema? Sheree is my sister's grandchild. Possibly your next partner. I have to pick her up from the airport."

My heart skipped a beat as I thought again of what this meant. I refused to think about replacing Raina. "I need you to find someone for me. A man named Grant Sullivan."

"I'll text you," Raina said, hanging up.

Thirty minutes later, I stood inside a New York Sports Club in Manhattan, watching Grant Sullivan on the treadmill. The photo on my phone had led me to him. I couldn't think of a good reason I was at his gym so I stuck with the pitiful cover story I had given Maria. The treadmills next to him were taken, so I walked over to him and was direct.

"You know Allison Stevens," I said.

He looked at me puzzled, but he didn't stop the treadmill. "Who are you?"

"Maybe we should talk in private," I said.

"Why? Did something happen to Allison?"

"Mr. Sullivan."

He stopped the treadmill. "What happened to Allison?"

"Mr. Sullivan..."

A few glances turned our way as his voice grew louder, "Who are you? And where is Allison?"

"Allison is dead, Mr. Sullivan." I answered after a slight pause. "She was killed last night."

He stepped off the treadmill then, the genuine shock and horror on his face placing him further down my suspect list. Not off though since he could have been a great actor.

"Can we please go somewhere else, Mr. Sullivan? I would like to talk in private."

"Were you her student?"

"No, she hired my dad's private investigation firm. We were looking into an inheritance."

"What happened to her?" he asked. "How was she killed?"

"Mr. Sullivan," I said. "I want to ask a few questions. Can we step out for a moment?"

"Yes." He followed me outside and into the Starbucks a few doors down.

"Are you one of her students?" he asked when we sat down.

I shook my head and pulled the tea closer. "Ms. Stevens hired my dad to do some investigative work for her. I was supposed to meet with her yesterday, but she never showed up."

"Aren't you a little young to be a detective?"

I smiled. "Just think of me like a... Veronica Mars."

He shook his head. "Who is she?"

"You know, television show *Veronica Mars*, high school detective who helped her dad..." At the blank look he continued to give me, I shook my head and leaned forward. "Did you know Allison well?"

He shook his head. "I doubt anyone knew Allison well. She wasn't the warmest person."

"You only went on a few dates...."

He shook his head. "We dated for about a month, and in that time, she never warmed up to me. And it wasn't because she was disinterested."

Even though I had gone to both Allison's home and work, I felt like I couldn't get any insight into her character. This was unusual for me so I understood what he meant. There was something about her that spoke of secrecy. She had distanced herself from her colleagues and seemed to have no close friends. Yet they had talked of her as friendly but disconnected.

I found myself a little more curious about the woman now. Perhaps, she had something to hide, which may have gotten her killed.

"I can't tell you much about Allison, but I can tell you she had a troubled relationship with her parents. It was the way she spoke about them or rarely spoke about them. She told me that some uncle she didn't know left her an inheritance in his will."

"Did she ever tell you what it was?"

"I don't know if she even had the chance to attend the reading of the will. I wasn't able to talk to her about it again." He frowned and shook his head. "I don't understand who would do this to Allison. She kept to herself. She minded her business."

"When was the last time you talked to her or saw her?"

"I hadn't seen her in a week, but we talked maybe two days ago. She rushed me off the phone."

I got one of my feelings and stiffened. "I have to go," I said, grabbing my bag. "If I have questions, I'll contact you." When I stood up, he gave me a blank look. "Hey, let's keep our little talk just between us."

"Yeah, yeah," he said, his hand waving me away.

I left the coffee shop, turning away when I saw Jasen and his partner leaving the gym. He had been the source of that moment of intuition. Hurrying down the street, I turned the first corner and headed down the subway steps. I would circle back home, but I needed to get far enough away from Jasen. I didn't see how I could keep avoiding the man, though, as we continued to investigate the same case.

CHAPTER THREE

I reached home about forty-five minutes later, the aroma of cookies greeting me at the door. That was not a good sign. Raina did her baking when she was hot with anger. Taking a deep breath, I walked into the kitchen to see Raina pulling cookies from the oven while an older woman I had never seen before sat at the breakfast bar.

"I'm afraid to ask," I said, setting my bag on the table. I only glanced at the woman seated on one of our stools, but I sized her up fast. She wasn't as tall as Raina, but she was tall enough. Even though she was seated, I put her at about five feet nine. She was slender but not skinny with smooth skin the color of pecan tan. Her silver and black hair was clipped close to her head, but I could still see the softness of its texture in the way it lay against her head in waves. I wasn't sure what to make of her presence in our kitchen, but from the way she was looking at Raina, Raina and I needed to have a long talk.

Raina grabbed a spatula and slid it beneath a cookie. "Sheree wasn't at the airport when I arrived because she must've thought she had received a free trip to New York. But this is not uncommon. My sister says Sheree has gone off by herself occasionally. A fact she failed to mention before I flew her granddaughter out here." She pointed the spatula at me. "Liz, this is Neema. Neema is my.... partner."

Liz looked a little taken back at Raina's words, but Raina—lost in her anger and her baking—missed her response. Beneath the surprise, I could sense Liz's disapproval and her disappointment. Raina had started on another batch of cookies, made from scratch. Oh yeah, Raina was ticked.

"You're together?" Liz said, her steady voice belying the hint of disappointment in her eyes. I glanced at Raina, and then wished I hadn't. Her eyes widened as she searched for the right words. Raina at a loss was not something I had seen much of during our fifty years ago.

I smiled. "Not like that," I clarified as I went over to the fridge to grab a bottle of water. "As in we work together... on... different projects." I eyed the stool next to Liz but stood at the end of the counter instead, a better vantage point to observe both women. Raina had a little explaining to do. "So where is Sheree?"

Raina looked at Liz who lifted a brow before they turned their attention back to me. "So I called down to Georgia and spoke to my sister. Sheree met a young man on an app." She pointed her spatula at me. "And let me say I don't understand the point of you young people doing this online dating mess. Who meets someone by flipping through pictures on their phone? I mean," she shook her head. "So Sheree and her app boyfriend have been talking for almost a year. He went down to Georgia last month to meet her."

"She met a guy on some app and had him pick her up from the airport?" I shook my head. "I'm a little insulted that you would place me in that category, Raina. I like old-fashioned meet-ups."

"I said the same thing," Raina said. "She went off with a man she didn't know well, if at all. I don't understand these young girls and these dating apps. My sister says the young man only flew down to Georgia for the day. One day and he's trustworthy."

Liz frowned. "Now Raina. Things are a little different now. You said he flew down to Georgia to meet her, and they had been chatting for almost a year."

"That doesn't make it much better, Liz," Raina said.

"Your sister told you that Sheree gave him an ultimatum. If he wanted them to continue talking, they had to meet."

"But she asked him to pick her up from the airport. How does that make any sense?"

I shrugged. "Maybe he surprised her. If he lives in New York, then she would tell him she's heading to the City. I would have done the same thing." I swiped a cookie from the rack. "Let it go, Raina. Sheree will call us when she's ready for a ride. Let her spend time with her friend. Maybe we should take a page from her book." I said.

"Spoken like a true teenager," Raina said, taking out another batch of cookies and setting the pan on the stove. She glanced over at me. "Something you should be mindful of."

Liz smiled as she watched Raina. "Raina's been like this since we came back from the airport. We get to JFK to pick up Sheree, and she wasn't there. Raina asks everyone at the Delta terminal about Sheree." She shook her finger. "One young man even said she was acting a little dazed, compelled.

No, I think the word he used was mesmerized. I remember thinking..."

I stilled, the hand that was reaching for the plate of cookies jerking before I focused my gaze on Liz. She continued to speak, but I had ceased to hear a word she said. To the average person, words like "mesmerize" didn't mean much, but I had been fighting demons for a long time. A person who acted mesmerized may be just that.

I could see Raina from the corner of my eye, her body reacting to the sudden tension. She put the carafe of iced tea back into the refrigerator before turning to face us.

"Did he at least describe the man she left with?" I said, not realizing until Raina looked at me I cut Liz off mid-sentence.

Liz looked at Raina first before she addressed me. "Tall, dark-skinned. Long hair."

I could feel my body temperature rising in recognition, but still I asked, "Did this young man see anything else or even hear anything else? Like maybe a name?"

Liz shook her head. "Only that they were going somewhere in Manhattan. Not too far from the World Trade Center."

"Caesar," Raina barked, the glass slipping from her hand. But I barely heard the glass shattering over the roaring in my head. The iced tea pooled at Raina's feet, who glanced down only for a moment before meeting my gaze. Her face stricken as she realized that she had—in her annoyance—missed several clues. "My sister said his name was Caesar."

The fear in her eyes had to mirror the fear in my own. Time has never allowed me to forget Caesar's execution. His bloated and rotted corpse still visited my dreams sometimes. Whoever had taken Sheree had left a message for me.

"Dammit," Raina said, hitting the counter. "I was so pissed that Sheree wasn't at the airport when I got there that I didn't ask more questions."

"Raina," I snapped. "Punish yourself later. We need to find Sheree now. I have to go change."

I WENT UPSTAIRS, WISHING it were darker outside. The hunting I needed to do would be much easier under the cover of darkness. Exchanging my jeans for a pair of leggings, I pulled on a fitted top. I preferred fitted clothing if I were about to go into battle and didn't want to give away any advantages.

I selected the Dahomean Hwi sword, a blade that my mother had given me many years ago, and the priest had blessed. Married to the king, Dahomean women warriors were to remain untouched until death, but my grandmother had given her life to have my mother, and my mother had sacrificed so much for me. I always wielded this blade with pride. Strapping the machete to my hip, I strapped my bow and arrows across my back. The thin daggers already attached to the outside of my boots had become an everyday accessory, even for trips to the grocery store.

"This guy went down to Georgia about two months ago," Raina said, slinging a set of bow and arrows across her shoulder. "That was before I even bought Sheree's ticket."

"They must have known we were looking at Sheree as a new partner."

"But no one has interfered with your selection of a partner for years, Neema. Why would they start now?"

"One of you needs to explain what you're talking about," Liz said, standing in the center of the living room as Raina and I suited up. "Why does Neema need partners, and what do you mean years? Neema looks about eighteen. And who are they?"

I had forgotten her presence. "You can wait here..." I started.

"Not happening," Liz said. "Raina is strapping arrows and a bow to her back. You have at least two visible weapons, and one is a machete. No way I'm letting you two go without an explanation."

"Liz," Raina said, touching her shoulder. "Let us handle this, and I'll explain things later."

"I was a cop, Raina. I can't just—."

"I'll explain everything to you when we get back," she said, giving Liz a quick kiss on the lips.

"I think you should stay also, Raina," I said filing away that kiss for a later conversation. "Just let me handle this."

"I won't even dignify that with a response."

I huffed in frustration, but Raina could be stubborn. "We're taking the bikes." I said.

"I'm still going."

I shrugged and led the way to the garage. Raina usually stayed at home, but this was her family. She wouldn't stay, and I didn't have time to convince her otherwise. She took one bike and I took the other. We both knew what this meant. A trip back to the old burial grounds.

WHEN WE REACHED DUANE Street, I passed the Monument and had to go back one block. I expected a grand building. Something that announced that over 15,000 Africans were buried in the cemetery that lay beneath Broadway. Instead, I found a gold and brown nondescript building with a federal office atop the museum. Although an Afrocentric image looked out over the sidewalk, it only caught my eye because I knew the African Burial Ground was in the general area. When I left New York thirty years ago, the burial ground had been long forgotten. I had witnessed Lower Manhattan grow over the dead, many of whom I had seen buried. Bringing me back here had been both a clever and cruel move.

By the time I walked through security, I was so angry that I considered drawing an arrow and shooting Sheree's friend on sight.

"I hate what they've done with the place," I said, walking past security with my sword strapped to my back.

"I told you you would hate this... memorial," Raina said, moving with less vigor than she had this morning. I should have told her to stay home—as if she would have listened.

"If the dead could remain unmolested at St. Paul's, then the dead in the burying ground should have been left alone too," I said.

"Yeah, but St. Paul's is where they buried the white folks," Raina said. "They built streets and cities on top of the graves of the black folks."

"And he would make me come here," I muttered.

I walked around the museum deliberately, which was small, with a timeline decorating one wall. The timeline began with the discovery of "human remains" and then traveled to the black citizens of Manhattan who fought to preserve the remains of the dead. Small walnut and cedar coffins with beautiful handmade carvings commissioned from Ghana would be the final resting place of the women, men and children reburied in the old cemetery. I wondered how many I had known, and which boxes held the remains of Caesar, Cuffee and the other slaves who killed that terrifying summer.

Taking a deep breath, I read the timeline, viewed the words from Maya Angelou's "Still I Rise" that flowed from the ceiling, and observed the burial scene of an adult and child captured in wax. The whirring in my head and churning in my heart fought to remind me of the funerals I had witnessed, the day I came back from the dead, and all the days that came afterward. But I refused to get caught in the memories. I didn't have to read the descriptions of the slave days I had lived, but the words seemed to slide past my defenses. Even when I refused to look, I still saw. It had been much easier when New York laid their city on top of the burial ground. Then I could bury my memories too.

When I walked over to the wall of digital graves, my senses sharpened as my body reacted to the nearness of a demon. Sheree's friend stood on the other side of the wall, and I suspected who it was. He would lure me here and remind me that some of these bones belonged to people I knew. People buried with only their approximate age and cause of death. As the sounds of the museum retreated into the background, I thought about destroying this wall of graves. Instead, I unsheathed my sword and opened a space large enough for the two of us to step through the digital wall into the spiritual world.

CHAPTER FOUR

Sheree sat in a chair in the center of an otherwise empty room. The walls surrounding her were the color of flames, reflecting the glow of lamps placed in each corner of the room. Without windows or doors, the room appeared tiny. Sheree's wrists and ankles weren't strapped to the chair, but she couldn't move. Her eyes and mouth were uncovered, but I couldn't decide if that was a point in our favor.

"You should have waited for me," Raina said, drawing her bow.

Sheree nodded her head. "That might have been best."

"But not as fun," a voice said from behind us. I didn't need to turn my head since that voice had become a permanent fixture in my memories. I unsheathed the Hwi, my body shifting sideways as I held the blade before me. The words on the blade glowed with the nearness of the demon.

"Still in that behead first stage, Neema?" he said as he walked behind Sheree's chair. He was magnificent.

"Not for a hundred years now," I answered.

"And I see you still have the blades of Priest."

I looked at the rites of exorcism etched into the blades. The Hwi, along with the sword and the daggers that Priest had made for me were weapons that demons feared, and I understood their fear. The blades made the return to hell a swift and painful process.

I smiled at Baal. "His craftmanship is unparalleled. Even angels knew of him."

Most demons preferred a pure human form when they walked the earth, but Baal liked to let a hint of his demon form shine through. This seemed to add, rather than detract, from his beauty.

He stood before us, close to seven feet tall. Although he wore a tailor-made suit, it couldn't hide his muscular physique. His black skin, smooth and glossy like the Vodou, glistened in the flickering light. Hair the color of flames was piled into a thick bun on top of his head. I watched as the muscles under his suit jacket flexed when he moved. He placed one hand on Sheree's shoulder, his fingernails long, black and pointed. A diamond ring dangled from the nail of one pinky, and I watched it for just a moment before I met those bright green eyes. Baal had always been mesmerizing. I should have remembered that before I brought Raina along.

"I've missed you, Neema," he said, his low voice as dangerous as his eyes.

"Is that why you left me to die that night?"

He waved a hand at me. "That was over seventy years ago. Stop holding onto things." Then he smiled. "And you can't quite die anyhow, can you?"

I sliced the air with my machete as he evaded my blade. One hand grabbed my wrist, and he stood close enough that I could see the flecks of orange in his eyes. My swing had been just as half-hearted as his hold on my wrist. He watched me in amusement, his gaze taking in my face, lingering on my lips to disarm me, but I hid my discomfort. Then he released me and put several feet between us.

"I'm not here as your enemy, Neema."

"But neither are you here as a friend."

He shrugged. "True. I'll just get to the point then. I have a job for you."

"I don't work for demons."

"Even if I help you find the Vodou."

I drew a sharp, painful breath. I couldn't believe anything he said, but if anyone knew how to find the Vodou, a demon prince did.

"What about this girl, Allison?" I said calmly even though I had already shown him how much his words cut me. "Who is she?"

For the first time, Baal didn't look poised. His anger shone through, and I lowered my Hwi in response. Baal wasn't one to show human emotion. He had a problem, and if a demon had a problem, I did too.

"There is a rogue," he said, his words short with anger. "A demon with his own agenda."

I didn't know how to respond to his comment. In almost three hundred years as a demon hunter, I had never witnessed a demon go rogue. None wanted to risk the anger of a prince. Baal was one of the seven princes.

"So, you have a rogue demon," I said. "What does that have to do with me?"

Baal stared at me long enough for me to read his reluctance. It wasn't his idea to involve me. Interesting. "I need you to find the rogue."

"And you couldn't just ask me," I said, looking at Sheree.

"You're unreasonable whenever I request something from you."

"I'll always be unreasonable when a demon desires my soul."

Baal smiled. "How cliché. I want so much more than your soul."

"And if I refuse to help you?"

"You mean will I threaten to kill the girl?" he said, placing a hand against Sheree's neck. "Or will I hurt her family if you don't cooperate? Even turn my sights on Raina?"

Raina jerked, startled, the bow in her hand quivering. "I won't go easy," she said. "And I remember you, demon. You've been banished before."

Baal narrowed his eyes, their glow warning of his anger. "You are not as young as you once were. Don't—."

"Enough," I said. "You got me here? What do you need?"

"For you to do what you do best, hunt and kill a demon."

"We don't work for demons," Raina repeated.

"You can always let this demon run free, but you might not want him loose in the human world."

Raina looked at me, and I shook my head. "What will we get?" Raina asked, her arm shaking until she lowered the bow.

He looked at Sheree. "She needed a little help to fall in love."

"I should have known you were too good to be true," Sheree said.

"You find my demon, and Sheree will think I'm a little less charming."

"You let Sheree go, and I'll consider demon hunting."

He stared at me, quiet long enough to make me squirm if I were uncomfortable with silence. He stepped back and waved a hand at Sheree. Her body slumped forward as if she had been bonded to the chair, and she hopped to her feet, one hand swinging toward Baal. Before she could land her backhanded punch, he slid out of her reach. Baal, like all demons, was quick.

"I suggest you hurry," he said, smiling. "The last time we had a rogue demon, an ark was made, and a flood destroyed the earth."

Baal and the room vanished, leaving us standing outdoors inside the obelisk monument on the Burial Ground. I stood on the top step, my gaze taking in the Adinkra symbols on the memorial wall before I turned to an angry but scared Sheree.

"What the hell was that?" Sheree said, pushing her hair back from her face.

"Now is not the time," Raina said, strapping the bow and arrow to her back. "You should have just stayed at the airport."

"Trust me, I wanted to, but I couldn't help myself."

"Because you didn't want to," Raina told her. "Demons can't make you feel or do something you don't want to do. They only intensify what's already there."

"He still took advantage of me," Sheree said. "When I see him again, I'mma—"

"Do nothing," Raina interrupted. You were lucky that he wanted Neema and not you, Sheree. So why don't you try doing nothing? You don't even know what's going on here."

"And we can explain it when we get home," I said, pointing toward the exit.

WHEN WE REACHED HOME, Sheree kept watching Raina. Raina's face and movements revealed her continuing anger. Although, Sheree burned with questions, Raina refused to even look at the younger woman. I understood her annoyance—while Sheree might have been under the influence of a powerful demon, demons merely took advantage of what was already there. Baal must have spotted a way past Sheree's defenses, which left her vulnerable to him. We didn't need vulnerability.

Raina was both relieved and disappointed to see that Liz was gone. A note on the kitchen counter made her smile, but it didn't lessen her annoyance with Sheree. I left the two women downstairs to hash it out while I went upstairs. Although I desired rest, I needed a moment to think about Jasen.

I took a long, hot shower and wondered how I would keep avoiding this man. It would be foolish of me to hope he didn't remember me. When he was fifteen, Jasen decided we would be together. By the time he was seventeen, all his talk of college and marriage and family were my cue to leave.

But I enjoyed my friendship with Jasen more than I should have. Not since Cuffee or Priest had I allowed a man to become so emotionally intimate with me. Was I involved with anyone? I wouldn't be human if I wasn't. Loving someone, though, had been beyond my capacity for pain. I preferred to leave before I became attached. Then I would allow years to pass again before giving into the desire for human contact that my partner-allies never fulfilled. Jasen awoke dreams in me I denied even existed. As much as I despised this immortal existence, I could either adapt or go insane. Jasen, though, reminded me that as much as I might deny my humanity, I was still very much human.

Dressing in a tank top and pajama pants, I smiled at how some parts of life would always be ordinary and mundane. No one seeing me right now would guess I'd spent much of my life hunting down demons and sending them back to the spiritual world.

Downstairs, Raina made three, thick Cuban sandwiches, poured chips in a bowl and set out the iced tea. Sheree was already halfway through her. Raina had stored Sheree's bags in the spare room downstairs and had seemed to thaw a little towards the younger woman. Having been on the receiving end of Raina's temper, I sympathized with the wary look in Sheree's eyes.

Both women had showered and changed. While Sheree sat at the breakfast bar, making quick work of her meal, Raina leaned against the counter with one ankle crossed over the other. She took a bite out of her sandwich before setting it down next to her. When I entered the kitchen, she looked up at me, but I didn't read her gaze.

"What is this partnership?" Sheree asked before I could sit down. "And why would you need a partner? You seem capable."

I slid onto one of the bar stools and set a plate in front of me. I waited until after I bit my sandwich before answering her. So much of the story I couldn't tell her yet. Not of how I had become entangled with her family after becoming the demon hunter or how I returned to New York to find the first of her ancestors. I couldn't tell her of how I watched her ancestor die right before me nearly two centuries ago. She wasn't ready, and, neither was I. I hated reliving this story every one or two generations. I said, "I couldn't fight the demons alone. Navigating the spiritual realm isn't just about the fighting. I needed—"

"A sidekick," Sheree said.

"We are far from sidekicks," Raina said, her annoyance flaring. She had always hated the term. "Neema can't do what she does without us."

I smiled. "Tracking down demons often takes more work than one person can handle. This is when Raina steps in. She gathers all the information I need to get a job done. She even makes our bows and arrows by hand." I shrugged and smiled at Raina. "What can I say? She's the brains, and I'm the muscle."

"And this is what you want me to do?" Sheree shook her head. "I don't know why ya'll sent for me. I don't plan on getting involved with demons or swords and bows and arrows. Being alive is rather important."

"Nothing has ever happened to Raina," I said.

"But Grandma says Aunt Raina has never had a life because of her work."

"Which is where my sister is mistaken," Raina said, her voice not betraying the impatience I was sure she felt. Raina had never told her sister any details about her life. This included her forty-year commitment to a woman who had just died two years ago. I didn't think Raina's family even knew she was gay. And not because of any feelings of shame. Raina cared little of the others' opinions.

"I don't know if I even believe you're cursed or immortal," Sheree said. "Grandma has never told us anything about demons or Aunt Raina having an immortal friend. In fact, she said she doesn't know much about Neema."

"Your grandmother doesn't know a lot," Raina said. "And I chose not to tell her. Neither did our father."

"And why us? Why our family? Grandma told me that Aunt Raina does the same work that their dad did. Investigative work. You guys private investigators?"

I set aside my plate and took a long sip of my tea. She was convincing herself that there was a reasonable explanation for what occurred in the African Burial Ground. No matter how many times I told this story, it was never easy.

"Did Raina tell you about the supposed slave plot of 1741 in New York City?"

Sheree nodded her head. "Yeah, just now while you were in the shower. So?"

"One man accused of masterminding the plot was a slave named Quaco. When the prosecution's star witness accused him of helping to organize a slave rebellion, he was executed."

"Was he innocent?"

"Back then, it didn't matter. Slaves had no rights. We couldn't even testify at trials except against other blacks. Quaco thought confessing to the slave plot would save his life, but they still killed him. They killed both him and a man named Cuffee."

"But how is this connected to our family?"

"Quaco had a slave wife. A woman who had died in childbirth but left him with a child."

"And that child was our ancestor."

I smiled. "Yes, he was. And his son was the first of my many partners."

"But I don't even understand how you would know you needed a partner."

"I didn't. My mother did."

"And that is enough for one night," Raina said, standing. She had noticed my words slurring. I may have been immortal, but my body needed sleep even more than it had when I was human. "How about I show you our workspace downstairs, Sheree, before we get some rest?"

I piled the dishes onto my tray and waved at Raina to take Sheree downstairs while I took our dishes into the kitchen. I already knew how she would react. Sheree would be skeptical and resistant, but her curiosity would be undeniable. I wasn't sure if I wanted her to be my partner-ally, but she was the only choice Raina and I had.

I WALKED DOWN TO THE basement, stopping at the bottom of the stairs to stand next to Raina. I was a little surprised that Sheree had gone against my assumptions since she seemed drawn to the electronic setup instead of the miniature boxing gym. I pegged as more of a fighter than a computer nerd.

"Something happened that has you a little shaky," Raina said, her eyes on Sheree. "And it wasn't Baal."

"I saw Jasen today," I told her.

Raina glanced over at me before turning back to watch Sheree on the computer. "Why did you see Jasen?"

"He's the police detective investigating this case, Raina. And I don't know how I'll keep avoiding him."

"Maybe you shouldn't."

"And how do I explain this?" I looked down at my body, throwing my hands up. "How do I explain that I haven't aged a day? I've never had to before except to one of you."

"I don't know, Neema. But you won't be able to keep avoiding him so you may not have a choice."

"He thought you were my mother. Maybe if you talk—"

"Neema," she interrupted. "You shouldn't do this with an audience. The boy used to love you. He wrote letters to you for five years after you left. You better think about what you're planning to say because eventually, you'll see him again."

And I knew she was right. Even if I didn't want to admit it. I had to find this rogue demon, and to do that, I needed to know who killed Allison Stevens. And if that meant seeing Jasen again, I'd better figure out what the hell I would tell him. And soon.

CHAPTER FIVE

Allison's family lived off the Grand Army Plaza Circle in Prospect Heights, Brooklyn. I had paid little attention to the apartments near the plaza or anywhere else in Brooklyn when I settled on Bedford Stuyvesant years ago. Driving down Eastern Parkway, I noted the busy street as pedestrians traveled to and from the Brooklyn Museum and the Botanical Garden on the left side. The Circle, located across from the main library, was surrounded by four lanes of traffic. I moved to the furthest lane as I rounded the circle and slowed down to locate her parents' condominium. After driving around twice, I parked a block from their building on Plaza Street West. The condominiums spoke of a wealth that didn't surprise me.

I stepped out of the car and smoothed down my black camisole and black tapered, dress slacks. Grief was crushing, but I had learned to manage my sensitivity. I slid into a fitted black and mauve jacket, the single button fastened in the front. My clothing had been carefully chosen for comfort

As I slipped into the spiritual world to bypass the doorman, I could feel demons throughout the building shivering with anticipation. My passage through the gateway was so swift I didn't have time to look for their exact location, but I stepped cautiously into the elevator. Demons were just as conscious of my existence as I was of theirs. I huddled into the corner of the elevator next to the panel as a young couple, dressed in black, spoke to the doorman before entering the elevator with me. The woman smiled as she settled against the back of the elevator, her blond hair falling in wisps around her face from the loose bun atop her head. Her eyes were wet with unshed tears, and she clutched the man standing next to her. He patted her hand but stared straight ahead.

When I followed the couple out of the elevator, the woman faced me. "Are you here to see Allison's family?" she said.

I nodded my head. "I'm a former student of Ms. Stevens."

"We're heading to her parents' apartment. You can walk with us if you like."

I TRAILED BEHIND THEM, studying the hallway. We were on the twelfth floor with only two elevators on one end and the emergency stairs at the other. I glanced through a window, but the ground was too far down for an easy escape. I wouldn't die, but the fall would make a mess until I recovered. I noted both exits before I stepped into an apartment filled with an assortment of friends and family; Allison had known a diverse group of people.

My gaze sought Allison's mother, seated in the living room on a divan. She was flanked by two women, one her age and the other about Allison's age. The two older women had the same toffee-colored hair as Allison, but while one woman bore the same blue eyes, heart-shaped face and olive skin as Allison, the other woman's thin, pale face and honey colored eyes highlighted by her pixie cut. The two women were close in age although the thinner woman had the sheen of illness. She gripped Allison's mother's hands, the occasional spasm of her hands barely detectable, but I missed little.

The younger woman was a pale, red-head, who despite her difference in coloring, bore an uncanny resemblance to Allison. She sat on the other side of Allison's mother, just enough distance between the two of them for me to notice. A demon stood behind the two women, her eyes closed as she savored their grief. A smile played across her lips, and I was struck by her beauty. She was snowy white, with raven-black hair piled in curls on top of her head. A few locks had fallen against her cheeks, the disarray adding to her beauty. She was shorter than most demons, but wrath demons often were. One woman was overcome with rage, but I couldn't tell which one. It did not mean well for this family if one of the seven deadly sins had come to their home. It meant either that others were here or more would follow. I didn't like that death demons and one of the Sin Demons had attached themselves to this family.

This demon had delicate features, her slender frame rocking as her skin flushed with the taste of their anger. Her smooth nippleless breasts showed through the white gossamer fabric of her gown as it fluttered around her. It was not my first time seeing a demon feed, but I had only seen one demon feed so sensuously—Baal. I plastered a smile on my face before I glided over to the divan to greet Allison's mother. The demon's eyes snapped open at the sound of my voice, and she stared at me with a growing alarm.

"I'm sorry for your loss," I said to Allison's mother, sliding one of my hands into one of hers and leaning forward to kiss her on the cheek. "I graduated last year, but Ms. Stevens was one of my favorite teachers at..." I drew a blank on the name of the school so I let my voice trail off as if I were choking back tears. As much as I hated to intrude on their grief, figuring out what had happened to Allison took precedence.

"Thank you," her mother said, squeezing my hand.

I stepped back and smiled at the two women before gliding over to a tray of drinks, my eyes still on the demon who watched me. Lifting a glass, I walked the room, smiling at a few folks and speaking to others. The room had less than fifteen people inside, with most standing at the edge of the grief emanating from the center of the room.

I followed the gaze of the wrath demon when she glanced at a man who had settled into a corner of the room. The demon that disengaged himself from the man startled me. He had been so closely attached that he covered the man like a film on a projector screen. When he flickered into view, he watched me as the female wrath demon had, his black eyes filled with both fear and anger. Like her, he was short and snowy white but his black hair lay against his back in a neat plait.

He wore the same thin, white fabric as she did, his smock and pants fluttering as he moved away from me and closer to the female demon. While I had left my exorcism blade in the car, I still had the smaller daggers strapped to my forearms. Perhaps they both knew my style because they moved to the far side of the room, their black eyes boring holes into me as I moved away from them.

I WANDERED OVER TO the man who had settled in a corner of the room, oblivious to how close he had come to being emotionally possessed. His gaze was blank as he stared at his untouched glass of brandy. He also had a similar coloring to Allison, another one of her relatives. I stood next to him, one thigh touching the table as I waited for him to look up at me.

"I'm Neema," I said, when he acknowledged my presence. "I was Ms. Stevens' student."

He attempted a smile, but it only touched one corner of his mouth before fading. "We've heard from a lot of those," He nodded toward the chair nearest to him. "Sit down. This will be a long day." He took a long sip from the glass, and I realized this was not his first. He held his liquor well, but his movements were the slow and deliberate movements of a drunk man.

"You know Allison was my niece," he said. "Ruth," he nodded toward the divan. "Esther and I are siblings. At least from Father's second wife."

"And who is Esther?"

"Allison's mother. She was the eldest."

I must have given him a puzzled look because he continued his explanation after another long drink of his brandy. He set the bottle on the table next to a silver flask.

"Ruth took Allison in after Esther killed herself."

I looked at him, his matter-of-fact tone taking me back.

He shrugged. "Do you expect tears, perhaps? Why should I cry because of Esther's selfishness? Just because she's dead doesn't mean I'm not entitled to my anger." This time he uncapped the flask and took a drink. The smell of alcohol was strong, but he seemed unfazed. "Allison was twelve when her mother committed suicide. Cruel don't you think considering the girl's father had just died the year before?" The intensity of his anger explained why the wrath demon was drawn to him. His rage was potent.

"May I ask you a question?"

"You're what? Eighteen? Nineteen?"

I smiled. "Eighteen." His skeptical look didn't surprise me. I had often been told that I was mature for my age.

"Then you're old enough," he said, studying me. He didn't say for what, and I refused to ask for clarification.

"Allison changed a lot after college," he said. "She was always an outgoing girl in high school with plenty of friends and a busy social life. She went away to college, and when she came back, she wasn't the same. Helen and I would talk about how much Allison had changed, but Ruth didn't like to admit it." He looked over at the women on the couch, but the look wasn't a kind one. "Helen is my wife. She's seated next to Ruth."

I didn't bother to look since I knew who he referred to. "You think something happened while Allison was in college?"

"Could have," he said, finishing the brandy. "But she can't tell us now, can she?" He watched me so I schooled my expression. I didn't know if his comment was a sign of his drunkenness or if he wanted to shock me. Why he would want to shock me, I didn't know.

"I'm not sure how you want me to respond."

"I'm the youngest of my siblings," he continued. "About ten years younger than Esther and Ruth. That would put me near your age."

Since he was at least several years over fifty, I doubted he was anywhere near my age. "Honestly," I said. "I'm unsure of where...."

He held up a hand. "I've always had a thing for tall, buxom girls like you."

I wasn't sure how or why this conversation had taken such an inappropriate turn, but he wasn't the first man his age who liked my youth but sensed my maturity. It made for the most uncomfortable moments. Even in times like this one. "Sir...." I began.

"Please call me Peter."

"Ms. Stevens said an uncle left her an inheritance in his will." I ignored him and got to the point. "Do you think that might be connected to her death?"

"You aren't her student, are you?" His gaze had sharpened, and I realized that he had wanted me to feel uncomfortable. My guise as a student had not fooled him at all. And he may have been drunk, but he was still sharp.

I looked at him, and then put a hand over his. "The young lady sitting next to your wife, is she Allison's sister? Cousin?"

"Does that matter?"

"Just curious. How well did she get along with Allison?"

He slid his hand from beneath mine and moved back. "None of us would hurt Allison."

"Not even for an inheritance?"

The look he gave me wasn't friendly. He glanced at the divan and I noticed that his wife had looked back at us before she turned away. The female wrath demon had drifted back over to the women and sat so close to Helen that I couldn't tear my gaze away. She rubbed her face against Helen's cheek, one hand caressing the woman's chest and stomach. The demon watched me before her eyes drifted shut, and she sank partway into Helen's body.

I jerked my attention back to Peter, but he was looking over my shoulder.

"Dad, is this one of Allison's students?" The red-head now stood right behind me, her eyes watchful and distrusting.

Peter looked at me, but didn't give me away. "Yes, sweetheart. I'm sorry. What was your name again?"

"Neema."

"Cindy, Neema was just telling me how much Allison inspired her." He stood up and grabbed his empty glass. "It's time for another brandy," he said, pressing the glass into Cindy's hand. She glared at both of us before she turned and left.

"Meet me at Prospect Park near the band shell tonight at about 10. I can speak then," he said, before he walked away from me with careful but sure steps. I didn't trust him. At all. But I needed to talk to him. The sooner I could find out what this inheritance was and determine its irrelevance or even relevance, the more I could focus on why the death demons had gathered around Allison.

CHAPTER SIX

I waited for a beat, making sure that the demons were preoccupied with their feeding before I walked out of the room. Heading down the hallway, I slipped into the bathroom first. I flushed the toilet and turned on the faucet sink. Waited for a minute or two, I went back into the hallway to search for the bedroom that had once been Allison's. Her room was the second door I opened. I glanced around before slipping inside.

Allison's move toward minimalism had taken place after she left her parents' home. Remnants of her childhood filled this room. Cheerleading, ice skating, and gymnastics trophies; medals and certificates for a variety of subject areas; stuffed animals placed on a bold, fuchsia and black checkered comforter. A high school mascot jacket draped across the chair in front of the desk as if Allison would enter the room at any moment.

The room was spotless, and a framed picture of Allison perched on one corner of the desk. Seeing her open, genuine smile in her high school graduation picture made me realize just how different she had looked in the pictures I saw at her apartment. Something had made Allison more withdrawn over the years, which might have led to her death. The change had been significant enough for her Uncle Peter to notice.

I squatted down and combed through the desk drawers. Everything was arranged as if a sixteen-year-old Allison would walk through the door. It was a little creepy. Her aunt Ruth had left the room alone once Allison went off to college. Pausing, I looked around the room again.

Stuffed animals organized in front of the pillows; most were new; but a few were well-loved. Bookshelf with her trophies on the top shelf and a few books stacked on the bottom two shelves. A photo album face down on the bottom shelf. Desk bare save for an empty organizer and a desk lamp. A single composition notebook, with a flower cover, lay on the table. I looked back at the high school jacket and realized that this room looked staged. Dusted, spotless, comforter smoothed against the bed—as if Allison would walk through at any minute with a book bag bouncing against her hip. I had walked into a shrine.

Going over to the bookshelf, I pulled out the photo album and flipped through the pictures. That she had a photo album when most people her age kept their photos digital was intriguing. A few of the pictures were of family, but a lot were friends from high school. All the pictures had been taken before she left for college. The last picture was of Allison and a gentleman old enough to be her grandfather. I removed the picture from the album and flipped it over. 'Uncle Joseph and me' was scrawled across the back of a picture taken during a visit to Mississippi. I took out my cell and snapped a picture before placing it back in the album and replacing the album on the shelf.

I went back to the desk and searched the bottom drawer. As I dug in the back of the drawer, I could hear raised voices outside. I slid the drawer closed and removed my heels so I could move silently. I cracked the bedroom door from a crouched position and peered straight into the living room.

My heart thundered when I saw Jasen standing just a few feet away, his partner behind him. Allison's uncle Peter stood in front of them, his voice rising in anger. He still didn't appear drunk, but Jasen had never been an idiot. He would know he was dealing with a drunk man.

I eased the door closed again and hurried to Allison's closet. Bits of their argument traveled to the back of the house, and I knew Jasen was trying to convince an offended Peter that intruding on the family's grief was necessary if they wanted him to find Allison's killer. The more time passed, the harder the investigation would become. I could slip into the spiritual world to slip by Jasen, but I had already used the gateway one time too many. The demons would notice me soon, and I didn't want one to hitch a ride back. I had to be fast.

Sliding the closet open, I searched through the shoes until I found some used sneakers. They were a half size too small, but I would make this work. I slid my black heels to the back of the closet, tucking them next to another pair of black heels. The closet was so big and stuffed full of so many clothes and shoes that no one would notice my things. The tank top and tapered slacks I wore allowed for fast movement, but the dress jacket did not. I hid the jacket in the closet and pulled out a black zipper hoodie that was too snug. Few women stood as tall as my nearly six-feet frame, but Allison had been almost as tall as I was. We differed, however, in build. Whereas I had a solid, muscular build, she had been model thin. I kept adjusting the hoodie around my breasts, annoyed at its tight fit.

Giving up, I threw the hoodie into the back of the closet and looked for another. The one I found this time must have belonged to a boy. Curious but in a hurry, I tossed the hoodie on, its loose fit covering my face if I bowed my head right. I padded back to the door and peeked outside only to see both detectives turning toward me led by Cindy, Allison's red-headed cousin.

I COULDN'T CHANCE RETURNING to the room, so I slid out of the door and into the spirit world. The demon that had led me to Allison's death stood there waiting for me; the soulcatcher in his hands aimed at my chest. Around us, the apartment shimmered, a dull, paler version of the place I had just left. Entering the gateway between worlds was like sliding into a dull gray and dusty brown version of either the human realm or the spiritual realm. Sometimes I could feel this place trying to draw life from me, so I tried to avoid using the gateway. If I stayed too long, I would be weaker, and I needed all my strength to stay ahead of Jasen.

"I knew you'd come back," he said, his voice filled with satisfaction. He no longer looked like either the blond haired Southern boy I had chased to New York, nor the dark-haired, grunge-looking youth I had sent back to the demon-world. His yellow-tinged skin was like those of the death demons and he had the same tall, lanky build. His clean-shaven head, showed his fall in rank. He stood amongst the least of the demons and from the look in his eyes, he blamed me.

"I don't have time for this," I responded, my eyes on the soulcatcher. The material it released was like a spider web, difficult to break. This demon wasn't the first nor would he be the last to use the soulcatcher on me. I could break the net, but there would be hell to pay while I did it.

"What do they call you?" I asked, trying to hide my urgency. I couldn't linger here or there would be a ripple seen by everyone in the room.

"It would be foolish to reveal my name to you."

"Even here," I said, glancing around. "I am the Demon Hunter. Would you like to test me?"

He hesitated, but my reputation proved greater than his need to hold onto his name. "Alastor," he whispered, the hand holding the soulcatcher trembling.

I smiled at him, moving so quick his hands still gripped the soulcatcher even though it was now in my hands. "Leave now, and I will pretend this never happened."

"I need to get back to the human realm."

"Sorry," I said, "I don't think you'd enjoy an attempt to possess me. And I don't have time to fight you." I fell back just as he pulled out another soulcatcher, the web brushing my heel before it whizzed past my feet. The pain was immediate and excruciating, but I didn't have time to dwell on it. Turning midair, I leapt through the gateway and back into the human realm, slamming into the front door. A woman screamed when I landed on all fours, my shoulder hitting the door so hard that I wanted to scream too.

I HAD THE FRONT DOOR unlatched before either detective could recover from my sudden appearance. The Sin demons had moved far away from the front door the moment the gateway had opened. I didn't spare them a glance as I leapt through the doorway and slammed the door shut behind me.

I raced down the hallway and headed for the emergency exit at the end of the hall. I could hear Jasen and his partner burst through the apartment door behind me, their footsteps pounding to the rhythm of my racing heart. I couldn't let Jasen catch up with me; that would be a disaster. But the webbing from the soulcatcher slowed me down. I couldn't chance speeding up since that would only speed up the poison. While the weapon didn't work the same on me as it did on other humans, it would weaken me for days if I didn't take care of it as soon as possible.

I rushed down the stairs as fast as I could, but they were right behind me. At forty-seven, Jasen was still fit and kept pace with his younger partner, both men speeding down the steps only a flight or two behind me.

I didn't stop even when I burst through the emergency door and into the bright sunlight. The heat of the day made the hoodie warmer, and even though I looked ridiculous, I couldn't take it off. Instead of heading toward my car and chancing a dangerous car chase, I had to lose them in a public place. I would double back for my car.

I ran across the plaza and headed for the Brooklyn Botanic Garden. Enough people were walking about that

I could blend in with the crowd. Slowing to a brisk walk, I passed through the open gates and joined a group of teenagers walking into the gardens. At one time in my life, these gardens had been familiar. Some things had changed a lot since they were first built in the early 1900's, but it had been a place of refuge for me each time I had returned to New York. It would be again.

I rushed down the steps and across the walking paths so I could circle around to the exit on Washington Street. I pulled the hoodie as far down as I could even though people kept turning to look at me. The day was too warm for a hoodie, but I didn't want Jasen to see my face.

When I passed the visitor center near the Japanese gardens, I saw Jasen's partner standing at the gate. If he turned to look at me, he would notice my hoodie amid the t-shirts and shorts. The Whisperer demon standing behind him noticed me though and smiled before she pressed her lips against his ear and whispered. I didn't need to hear to know she meant trouble for me.

Then I heard a shout behind me, Jasen's voice like a cool breeze "Kenny! There he is!" He shouted so near I couldn't even hesitate.

I sprinted toward the Japanese Hill and Pond Garden, and both detectives raced after me, our movements unfolding in my mind like a series of still photographs. As I hurried past the pavilion and across the bridge, I almost knocked a child into the pond. His screams cut off as I caught him and tossed him back onto the bridge, never breaking stride. Jasen and his partner fumbled behind me, trying to avoid the people walking around the pond. A few yelps and an irate tirade let me know they failed to avoid everyone.

Swerving to the left, I headed toward the Celebrity Path. If I could circle back around to the Washington Street exit, then I could head back up Eastern Parkway, get my car and leave. But Jasen chose just that moment to stumble onto the path in front of me, his gun raised and ready. He must have come around another way, their plan to flank me. I came to a halt on the path, my hands out as I turned my head, still trying to hide my face. I also needed to prepare for Kenneth who was behind me. I took a small step backward, limping as I contemplated flight.

"Don't move again, kid," Jasen said, his voice deeper and more commanding than it had been thirty years ago. This was a man used to being obeyed. "Who are you?"

I stayed silent, unsure if my voice would betray me. It had been thirty years yes, but Jasen had always paid close attention to everything about me. I could hope but not be sure he had forgotten the sound of my voice.

"Don't piss me off, kid. Who the hell are you?"

I didn't see a way out of this, and I couldn't risk stepping through the gateway, not with an angry demon waiting there to capture me and the silken web from the soulcatcher creeping up my damn leg. I didn't have too many choices for getting out of this situation without getting shot. Sighing, I raised my hand to take off my hood when I saw Kenny from the corner of my eye.

He stood behind me, his gun pointed at my head. Head shots hurt like hell and if I could avoid one, I needed to. I could see the whisperer demon still standing next to him, her eyes on me as she whispered in his ear. Her long reddish-brown hair had wrapped around them both as her hold on him tightened. When he took a step closer, he drew Jasen's attention.

I watched as a few visitors rounded the corners only to back up when they saw two men with their guns pointed at me.

"I got this man," Jasen said right before Kenny pulled the trigger.

I heard the bullet in the chamber first, my senses sharpening for the hunt. I turned to the side, the bullet whizzing by my face before it headed toward a nearby tree. Twisting to the left, I grabbed Kenneth's wrist with both hands, driving the gun straight into the air. Another shot went off before I plucked the gun from his grip. Tossing the gun aside, I wrapped one arm around his neck, using his body as a shield.

My other hand gripped a dagger and plunged it into the demon's chest. She was still smiling when flames spread from the blade and her body burned. As the flames spread, she had no chance to scream before she turned to ash. She would be angry when she woke up in hell. And there would be plenty of demons to share in her anger.

"Put the knife down," Jasen ordered.

Kenny, who was my height, leaned against me. I was the only reason he didn't sink to the ground since she had drained a great deal of strength from him. But I struggled to stand myself, my right leg numb almost to my hip as the poison burrowed deeper. Holding up the hand with the dagger, I placed the dagger into a back pocket.

"What the hell was that man?" Jasen said. "I told you I had it."

"I don't know," Kenny said. "I must've lost it for a moment."

"Let him go," Jasen said.

He was leaving me no choice. I had to speak. Damn. "Put your gun down first," I said, trying to drop my voice several octaves.

He still blinked and lowered his gun. "You're a girl," he said. He tried to get a look at my body, but Kenny was a good shield. My face buried in his neck as I continued to hide from Jasen.

"Back off," I growled, so focused on Jasen that Kenneth surprised me when he snatched off my hood. I stepped back, letting him drop to the ground.

Terrified, I met Jasen's eyes. He had stumbled away from me, shock and disbelief plastered across his face. I imagined that I could see his thoughts flashing by us like he had spoken.

"Dinah," he breathed.

And I shook my head. I had gone back to the name my mother had given me. "Neema," I told him. "And I can explain."

And just like that his face switched from shock and disbelief to rage. "Damn right you will." He said, grabbing my wrist and dragging me out of the gardens.

CHAPTER SEVEN

New York City

June 1741

When I came to, I pulled myself up on shaky legs. The sun shone on my skin, but there was a light breeze lessening the heat. I looked down at my blood-splattered dress and groped at my throat. I remembered getting shot but, except for the blood, I didn't seem to have a wound on my throat.

Someone had taken my body from the clearing and laid me in the shade of trees. Me, and from the look of the bodies lying near me, a few others. Looking up, I realized that a man stood behind a tree and watched me. It took a moment, but I remembered him. In fact, I remembered when his wife had asked my mother for help to prepare his body for burial.

The dead man watched me, his eyes expressionless, his lips a tight line. I stared back as I drew in a breath, my hand still clamped against my throat. I wanted him to speak, to explain how he could stand there in the burying ground even though his wife had buried him a year ago. I wanted to ask him questions, but he stared at me. His body so still I grew afraid. After a while he gave me a sharp nod, his face still blank as he moved along.

I realized that I had just seen my first apparition, and I remembered all the stories Mama had told me. Apparitions showed themselves only to certain people. My mother had been one who could sometimes see them, but I never had. And I didn't want to now.

Then I figured that maybe I could see the dead man because I was dead too, which meant that I had become an apparition. Only that could explain the smooth skin where the men had shot me. I studied the back of my hands, wondering why I could feel the heat from the bright sun on my skin. Being a ghost didn't seem much different from being alive; at least I didn't feel different. Touching my arms, I felt solid, but from the stories my mother had told me, apparitions no longer had a human form. Maybe Mama had been just a little wrong about this though.

With my attention no longer focused on the apparition, I looked around the burying ground. Three bodies lay on the ground beside me, and a burial shroud covered them to prepare for burial. I had knocked aside the shroud placed over me.

With the executions happening so swiftly, Mr. Delaplaine the cabinetmaker could not keep up with the number dead. For now, the bodies lay in a shaded part of the burying ground to protect them from nature. Once Mr. Delaplaine completed the coffins, the bodies would be washed and prepared for burial. Now, the stench overpowered. I didn't understand the nature of an apparition, but my sense of smell still worked in the same way it had when I was alive.

I pulled back each shroud, shuddering when I peered into the distorted faces of slaves; two of whom I knew. I didn't see the body of Cuffee and prayed that this meant he might still be alive. Huddled under the shade, I waited for the cover of darkness. I had heard of my mother being able to see ghosts, so maybe others could see me too. I had never heard of a human injuring a ghost, but my entire world had just changed. I wasn't sure what was possible anymore.

AFTER SUNSET, I VENTURED out of the burying ground. I had grown spooked by the sounds of night, re-membering the Vodou who had terrified me a few days ago. A pair of folded breeches lay next to a dead man for his bur-ial. Apologizing to him, I exchanged my petticoat for his breeches. I wasn't sure if a ghost even needed to change her clothing, but I found the petticoats to be cumbersome. I might be dead, but I still thought like the living.

I slid the breeches on the wrong way at first, never having paid attention to how men wore their breeches. Peeling them off again, I turned them so that the ties faced the back and struggled to close the pants. They were a little snug, but more comfortable than my petticoats.

With thoughts of the Vodou burning inside me, I tucked my discarded skirts under the shroud of one of the dead women. Moving was easier, and I walked through the Com-mons. I didn't want someone else with a gift of seeing to alert others to a ghost in their midst. I didn't know how one got rid of ghosts, but none of the stories I heard growing up made it sound painless.

Rather than taking the usual route from the Commons down Broadway, I cut across the North Ward and then down to the East Ward. Though many of the horse and carriages didn't travel in the evening, there were a few people in the streets. I felt foolish ducking and hiding from people who couldn't see me, but it was habit. My mind hadn't gotten the message yet about my death. I was growing used to the idea, but my first instinct was to hide.

When I rounded the last farm on the border of the East Ward and the Docks, I saw a creature I had never seen before, a creature so monstrous that I blinked again and again to clear my vision. I ducked behind the house and sat on my haunches. But the couple walking down the middle of the lane drew my attention. Against my desires, I came from behind the house.

My eyes wide, I crouched there at the edge of the lane as if no laws forbade slaves to be out after dark. A woman and a man walked toward me, but they were in their own private world. Her ice-blue skirts belled around her and brushed his ankle as her hand rested in the crook of his arm. She was lovely with her golden hair piled atop her head in ringlets. The color of her hair matched the skin of the monster standing beside her. I snapped my mouth shut and averted my eyes when the creature looked at me.

I could feel his gaze crawling across my skin as he walked behind her, his face buried in her neck. His bronze hair was pulled high at the crown of his head and flowed in streams around the two of them. As she laughed, he ran his tongue across her neck as if he could taste her joy. He wore only a pair of black breeches and black suspenders. His naked chest gleamed in the moonlight as he rubbed against the woman's back. She walked on, her and her companion unaware while my heart beat against my chest. I kept my eyes down, afraid to look up because I didn't want the creature to notice me. No, something warned me of the danger if he did.

After they passed, I still hesitated to move, but I had to continue or risk capture. Careful not to look back even though I felt compelled to look at the creature again, I hurried away from them. Maybe, because I had died, I could see things I had never seen before. Maybe that creature, like me, was also a ghost but a different ghost.

Ducking to avoid the night watch and weaving through the busy streets of the Docks, I soon reached my master's home and the kitchen where my mother and I slept.

My mother sat on her cot, her hands folded in front of her while Miss Cecilia, the master's wife, stood before her.

"Hanna has to return soon, Sarah," Miss Cecilia said.

I started when I realized that she meant me. Only they called me Hanna. My mother called me Neema, and I had always thought of myself as Neema. She refused their name for me and before the master's family, she would only address me as Child.

"And if she's gone for good?"

"Then you will not like how Thomas responds. Please bring her home, Sarah."

"I will do what I can," my mother responded, her tone ending the conversation. Even as a child, I had never understood my mother's hold over this family. Miss Cecilia hesitated for a moment before she left the kitchen and headed back to the house.

Taking a deep breath, I wondered how to enter the house. It felt as if a lifetime had passed.

"I know you're there, Neema," my mother's rich lilt drifted through the window. "Come inside."

I wasn't surprised that she had felt my presence. I moved around the side of the small house and entered the kitchen. My mother sat on her cot, her legs folded beneath her body. She sat tall, her body rigid as her hands rested on her knees. When my mother struck this pose, I knew she was about to act on one of her prophecies.

"There is something different about you," she said, looking up at me when I entered the room.

I smoothed my hands over the breeches that still felt a little awkward, but she shook her head. "I don't refer to your breeches." She studied me, her gaze sweeping from my bare feet to the tangled mess of my hair. "And I told you to wait for me in the burying ground, Neema. Why did you come here?"

"I got shot, Mama," I said, falling to my knees before her. "These men, they shot me and then this woman came and I died and I saw this nightmarish creature and now I'm here and I don't know what's happening." My hands shook as tears threatened to fall, but I couldn't let them. Mama would call my tears wasteful since they wouldn't change a thing.

"Neema," Mama snapped, her hands pulling at my shirt as she searched for a wound. "What do you mean someone shot you?"

I tilted my head back and placed a hand against my throat. "I was shot Mama. Right here. And I died. I know I died, but I woke up somehow. And now I.... I'm a ghost."

She touched my face with the back of one hand, her eyes studying me so I felt as if she could see everything that had happened over the last few days. And maybe she could.

"You aren't dead, Neema," she said, her voice low but intense. "I don't know what happened to you in that burial ground, *but you aren't dead*."

"But Mama, they shot me and...."

"Did something happen before the men came to the burial ground?"

"A woman came to see me, and.... and she looked.... unnatural. Like something was wrong about her. Like...."

"What did she say to you?"

I didn't want to answer her. I still felt the sting of being blamed for Cuffee's death since I blamed myself too. "She blamed me for the lost of some priestess, a hunter and another person. What did she mean Mama? She told me I would live until she gets them back and then those men shot me."

She rose before I finished speaking. Her deep brown skin glowing in the candle light. My mother, when she needed to protect me, shifted into fighting mode. In these moments, I could see the Dahomey warrior that her mother had been. I had my height and build from my mother, but I didn't have her forbidding presence.

She put up her cot and pulled out items from the little hidey hole she had made in one corner of the kitchen. When her sack was full, she pulled out a long, wide knife I had never seen before.

"What do you need with that knife?"

"This," she said, slipping the knife into a strap at her side, "is a machete like those the Mino carried, the women who fought for the Dahomey." The fierce look on her face was fearsome. "And I may need it to keep us safe."

She grabbed my wrist then and led me out of the door as if she thought I might flee. I wanted to.

"You must take me to the place where you saw her," Momma said as she strode through the streets. She did little to avoid the night watch men, but the streets were empty. Her hand gripped my wrist as she pulled me behind her. "We have to return to the burying ground."

"Must we go in the dark?" I whispered.

She stopped and pulled me behind a row of houses, her eyes boring into mine as her low voice hit me like sharp jabs. "This is not a time for fear, Neema," she said. "We need to know what she did to you."

"Perhaps it would be wiser for us to leave this be."

"Perhaps," she said. "But we won't."

She pivoted on her heel and continued pulling me behind her. If we were caught, we would be punished but my mother marched through the city. The further we moved from the Docks, the more my heart thundered with fear. Manhattan's Northern lands were a lot less populated than her southern tip. I had gone to the burying ground to hide, but I feared what populated the woods. I hid my fear, however, or Mama would lose patience with me.

"Who was she?" I whispered, but my mother's voice drifted through the night air.

"The Vodou," she said, filled with a recognition and knowledge that frightened me. My mother knew who this woman was, and the grim look on her face meant nothing good.

WHEN WE REACHED THE burying ground, Mama found a small clearing shielded by a circle of trees. I huddled beneath one tree like a coward as I watched Mama. I found myself both impressed and intimidated by her efficient movements.

"What happened to Cuffee?" I asked. "The Vodou said he was dead because of me."

Mama paused in her preparations, the smells from the pot she stirred making me drowsy. "He and Quaco were burned at the stake the same night you left."

I closed my eyes against the pain even though I had already known Cuffee was lost. Even if I had been praying his life be spared, he was dead the moment they arrested him and accused him of conspiring to start a slave rebellion.

"The Hughson's trial starts tomorrow," she continued, her hand stirring the pot again. She set the spoon aside and removed the pot from the small fire she had made. Standing up, she dug a small hole in the approximate spot where the Vodou had appeared. At least as approximate as I remembered.

She poured the contents of the pot into the hole and I expected them to bubble or even boil, but the liquid mix glowed in the moonlight. Then my mother spoke in a language that was nothing like the English we spoke. I could hear the cadence of her native tongue though. When I was young, she had sung sometimes in the language of home. I had never learned the words, but I recognized the sound.

Mama stepped back, her stance wide and firm. She looked formidable. The thin purple and black cotton robe she wore hugged her tall frame. The skirt split in the center like breeches, but they were loose. She stared at the liquid, and I did the same.

I sat up as a form rose from the hole that Mama dug, arms outstretched as if climbing through a gateway. Her hair was still braided in a silver and black rope down her back. Black liquid ran down her body like sand, spilling to her feet until it spread across the ground. She was taller than Mama by almost half a foot, and I didn't bother hiding my fear since neither woman looked my way.

"WHY HAVE YOU SENT FOR me," the Vodou said, her voice low and deep but filling the night air, her stance threatening.

My mother, though, stood proud and strong. "What have you done to my child?"

"Reminded her that a loose tongue is a sin."

"And her punishment?"

I had eased around the circle until I stood behind my mother. This gave me a clear view of the Vodou's face. Her smile, tight with anger, was chilling.

She was just as frightening as she had been the other night, her ebony skin glistening in the moonlight. Her features were sharper than I remembered, almost feline. Her black eyes traveled from me to my mother, only a green ring around her pupil offering relief from the blackness of her eyes and skin. I noticed her hands for the first time. The flesh and nail seemed as one, nails so long she could have slashed my mother's face without moving from her spot.

She wore only a strip of cloth across her breast that knotted behind her neck. It was the same jade green of her eyes and matched the loin cloth that covered her pubis. I could see the taut buttocks flowing into her long, powerful legs. I had never seen a woman dressed as she, and I was both shocked and fascinated. I stared at her, almost startled when she spoke again.

"Did she not tell you?" the Vodou said, gazing at me. "She will live until the priestess, the hunter, and the discerner walk again."

My mother gasped, falling back a step. "But that could be for centuries. *This because of a loose tongue*? The punishment far exceeds her crime."

"You more than any know how destructive words can be Priestess." The Vodou said.

Mama pulled the machete from her side, one hand drawn back to bring the blade across her body. The Vodou only smiled, but Mama didn't lower her blade. "You have no right to punish her."

"I am the Vodou!" She said. "No human will warn me."

"Immortality is not to be granted lightly."

The Vodou looked at me and tilted her head. "But is she immortal, Priestess?" She waved her fingers in the air, drawing a symbol I didn't recognize, but my mother did.

Mama brought down the blade, but the Vodou caught her wrist. Then Mama brought up the elbow of the other arm so fast that the Vodou's head snapped back before she could move. She caught Mama around the waist in a tight hug, and Mama struggled against her grip.

My eyes darted around in fear as a castled appeared above us, and water beat against the sand as people moved around. I knew this could not be real, but it felt as real as the woods that had just surrounded us. Blacks, chained together, were prodded toward a dungeon by other black men with weapons. A few of the women cried and moaned as they shuffled forward, their bodies thin with hunger. A ship bobbed in the distance, white men walking around as the ship's crew prepared for their African cargo. Mama had told me enough about her capture, captivity and march to the Gold Coast, so I recognized the place where we stood. She had told me, but nothing in her words could have prepared me for the misery I saw on these black faces.

"You play tricks with me," Mama said, the remembered pain in her voice a reminder of her vulnerabilities.

"Why do you say that, Priestess? This place is not a trick. It is there," the Vodou pointed at Mama's head. "All over your memories. Tell your daughter what this place is."

One arm freed, Mama pushed against the Vodou who didn't budge. Just as the black concoction had opened a door into her world, it also held her trapped within its boundaries. She couldn't move from the circle that bound her.

Mama moved back, the machete at her side. "Why have you brought me to Mina?" Mama said.

"You almost died here at Mina." The Vodou's voice dropped to a whisper. "Did you think a loose tongue was but a small thing here.... at Mina? What happened to the one who betrayed you? How did you punish her for her loose tongue? Or perhaps you should see the dungeons again to help you remember." She lifted her hand.

This time Mama caught her wrist, her face so close to the Vodou that the two women drew the same breath. "I have seen enough," Mama said. "I will never go down to those dungeons again. Even in this way."

The Vodou smiled with satisfaction. "No, I didn't think you would." She pulled back from Mama, her arm easily falling from Mama's loose grip. "At least the punishment I bestowed on your child is more merciful than the one you granted in the dungeons of Mina."

The fight in Mama faded, and perhaps that was why the Vodou had taken her back to the Gold Coast. Mama had few weaknesses, but her time in Mina, her time on the slave ship burned in her memories.

We were back in the woods where the fire had died down. I wished that I could erase the image of the place Mama had called Mina, but as she told me the stories of her voyage to America, her voice had always struggled to hide the pain.

"Your child cost us," the Vodou said. "She cost me."

"Not on purpose. Take back your curse."

"Should I show her the same mercy you showed the woman who betrayed you?"

Mama drew in a sharp breath. "Neema has no part in your quarrel."

"I didn't mean for Cuffee to die," I said, tears threatening to fall. "I didn't mean for any of this to happen."

The Vodou looked at me with such intense hatred I stepped back. "I waited a millennium for the one called *Qua-*

co," she said. "And with just a few words to an ignorant servant girl, you cost him his life."

"I...."

"Enough! You will live until I get back what you cost me."

"Take back your curse, Vodou. You are forbidden to grant anyone immortality."

"She may not be immortal, Priestess, so perhaps you should focus on how to keep her safe." She focused on me then. "Tell your mother about the creature you saw on the way home from the burial ground, Neema," she said before she vanished.

Mama turned and grabbed my arms with both hands. Her grip was tight as she shook me. "What did you leave out, Neema?"

"I told you. I saw this creature, this thing that looked human but wasn't. He was yellow with golden hair."

Her grip on me grew even tighter while her eyes widened. "And did he see you?"

"He was...." I couldn't think of the right word.

"Feeding," Mama said. She moved back. "You saw a demon. But did he see you?"

I shook my head. "No, he didn't see me. Why Mama? What.... What did she do?"

"God help us. She gave you something worse than immortality, Neema. No human can kill you, but a demon can. They can kill your flesh, but trap your soul. And when they find out you can see them...." She paused, a look of fear on her face I had never seen. "I don't know how to keep you safe."

"Mama...."

When tears came to her eyes, I realized just how much trouble I was in. "When they find out—not if Neema, because they will find out—when they find out you can see them, they will hunt you. And I don't know how to keep them from taking you."

I stared at her wide-eyed, scared. For the first time in my eighteen years, my mother didn't know what to do. It would do no good to ask *where* they would take me. And I was sure I didn't want to hear her response.

CHAPTER EIGHT

I sat on the bench as Jasen paced back and forth, the thunderous look on his face battling with a look of disbelief. I tried not to favor my leg, but it was more difficult to ignore the pain.

He had dragged me over to McNair Park across from the Washington Avenue exit of the Botanic Garden. A few people glanced at us with curiosity until he flashed his badge, and they returned to minding their own business. One man, though, waited until I gave him a little nod and a smile. Just when I thought Brooklynites jaded beyond measure, one would surprise me.

With my first, full view of Jasen, I could see that aging had gone overboard with kindness. He had filled out from the scrawny kid he used to be. A little shorter than me at 5' 10", he was fit. I could see it in his forearms and his black slacks. He had foregone the jacket from the other day, but sported a business casual look that showed respect for the family wake we had just left.

The goatee flattered his chocolate skin and bald head, and if I ever forgot that he was now thirty years older than me, the salt and pepper of his beard and the maturity in his face would remind me. Staring at him, I understood why I had fallen for him back then. I also remembered why I had left him.

"You aren't Dinah," Jasen said again. "You must be her daughter."

I didn't bother to respond since I had already answered him several times. I could have lied, but I wanted to be honest. Besides, lying required too much work, and I wasn't interested in having to keep a story straight. It had been so long since I had made the mistake of allowing someone other than one of my partners discover my immortality. By now I should be a master at caution.

"Jasen, I can't sit here while you...."

"Oh, you damn well will sit there until I figure out what the hell is going on here."

"If you would just sit down, I can explain."

"You don't have to explain. Just tell me where Dinah is."

"There is no Dinah. There's just me, Neema. The same girl you met thirty years ago."

He stopped pacing and looked at me, shaking his head. "You say that as if it makes sense when it makes no sense at all. You must be Dinah's daughter."

"If you would stop being so stubborn, I can explain...."

"Tell me where we first met. If you're who you say you are, tell me where we first met. Who was there? What..."

"In Harlem."

Jasen stilled then.

"That was back when you wanted to be a rapper. Run DMC had just come out with 'It's Like That.' You were coming out of Sylvia's and nearly knocked me over."

"You mean you knocked me over," he said, in response, as he had said so many times before when I told this story.

As soon as the words passed his lips, he stared at me in shock, moving until he sank onto the bench next to me. "You aren't possible," he said, his elbows planted on his knees as he leaned forward. "Who are you? Why.... how can you look the same? How do I know Dinah didn't just tell you this story?"

"I'm immortal," I said, my eyes never leaving his face.

"No such thing."

"Neither is still being eighteen after thirty years, but here we are. And we have to get past this if you want to solve this case."

"And how are you connected to this, Di.... Neema?

"Believe me, you're not ready for that, either."

"People don't live forever," Jasen said.

"I do." I stood up and put out my hand. "You got a card?"

Jasen looked up at me, his face troubled, confused. He handed me a card, and I programmed his number into my phone before I wrote my name, address and cell phone on the back. When I handed it back to him, his hand trembled as his fingers brushed mine. "Is this why you left without a word?" he said, his voice hoarse.

"As hard as it is for you to believe me, Jasen, it's even more difficult to explain."

He stared at me, his eyes studying my face as if he could commit every feature to memory. He had done the same when we were two teenagers falling in love. Well, he had been a teenager. I had been a two hundred-and forty-year-old demon hunter.

"Call me tonight, Jasen." I said, touching his shoulder. "We can talk more then."

He still sat on the bench when I reached the corner. When I walked into the house, I closed the front door behind me and leaned against it for just a moment. To right my world before I took care of my leg. I closed my eyes and took a deep breath. It wasn't as if I were still a love-struck teenager. I had put Jasen behind me many years ago and, besides, he was forty-seven years old. Even if I lived for another hundred years, he would never be for me again. He was about to retire and even though he hadn't been wearing a ring, I had noticed the paler skin on his left hand from the imprint of a wedding band.

Besides, what I had felt for Jasen had changed a long time ago, which didn't lessen the shock of seeing him and talking to him again. Once I found this demon, I would have to leave New York, but this time I would have to stay away until.... I ignored what that thought did.

"Guess immortality isn't easy on the heart."

Opening my eyes, I saw Sheree standing in the doorway to the sitting room, scrutinizing me. I had yet to be alone with her since she had settled in because I didn't want to deal with what her presence meant for me and Raina.

"I don't know what you're talking about," I said, pushing away from the door. My tone wasn't friendly, and her stance became defensive. I wasn't doing a good job of making her feel welcomed.

She pushed forward anyway. "I recognize the signs," she said. "I guess in this you're just as human as the rest of us."

"Is there something you want?"

She looked at me with annoyance before she closed her eyes. When she spoke again, however, she sounded patient. "Aunt Raina wants you," she said.

"Tell Raina I'll be right down, but I want to change first," I walked past her and headed toward the stairs, but some small movement caught my eye and made me look back.

"I know why you're upset," she said, shrugging. "I get it. You and Raina have been together for fifty years. She... she told me what that was like for her. For you."

"Sheree—" I said.

"I get it, Neema," she said. "And I don't even know if I want this. I mean a demon kidnapped me." She waved a hand toward me. "And you're immortal. None of this makes any sense. You don't have to worry about me taking Aunt Raina's place because I don't even know if that's what I want to do."

She left me in the foyer, feeling small as she headed back downstairs. I had been distant since we took her from Baal, but it wasn't her fault that Raina was aging. Limping upstairs, I headed to my room to inject the antidote to the soulcatcher. The pain as the antidote ran through me would be an excellent reminder of why I needed to avoid the demon world.

"AUNT RAINA ASKED ME to look at Allison's friend, Grant," Sheree said, turning away from the computer as I entered the basement. "I searched the Internet and looked at social media to get you any useful information." She acted as if our earlier conversation hadn't taken place.

"And did you find out anything?"

"Yes. Social media makes people's lives a lot more accessible."

Sheree turned back to the computer, her face glowing in a way it hadn't yesterday. She didn't fit my image of a computer geek. At all. A discreet brown hair piece with blond highlight replaced the shoulder length purple-tinted curly locks from yesterday. The wavy mass draped over one shoulder in a plait. I touched my short, curly natural, always a little self-conscious when I saw the many looks that a single black woman could achieve. Although I loved my hair, sometimes I was girly enough to want a different look. But while fighting with long hair might look sexy, it was dangerous as hell.

Sheree's pecan tan tone was lighter than her aunt's, but she had the same full figure as Raina. Her makeup wasn't as colorful as yesterday, but it was just as flawless.

Her nails clicked across the keys as she worked. "Before Grant was dating your girl Allison, he dated this other chick who claims he was abusive."

"She put that on her Facebook page?" I said, sitting next to her. The girl on the computer screen had coloring like Allison.

"Not in those words, but it's easy to figure out. Just look at her page. She's got a picture of a physically abused woman and wrote—"

"My ex sure knows how to hit on a woman," Raina said, as she slid on her reading glasses. "At least she's creative."

"And consistent," Sheree said, pulling up pages that showed similar comments decorating her wall. "Most people label their Facebook page private or at least filter their friends, but this girl allows anyone to be her friend."

"I'm surprised Grant hasn't requested Facebook remove the page."

"It wouldn't matter if he did. Facebook pages are notoriously impossible to have removed. Even if someone opens an account under your name, you can't just request to have the page taken down and expect it to be that simple."

"Either way, if Grant hits on women, outing him on Facebook isn't a motive for murder," Raina said.

Sheree shrugged. "Maybe not for rational people." She pulled up the photo album then and showed us pictures of the same young woman, dated a year ago, bruised and battered.

"This doesn't prove that Grant beat her," I said, studying the pictures. "A great makeup artist can do wonders."

"I didn't find arrest records for him, but money and connections can make any of this go away."

"There were too many demons at Allison's home for this to be domestic violence. For a beating like this, there may have been one, maybe two demons at the most. If at all. Some people are just this sadistic."

"But it won't hurt to go see her and make sure that Allison's boyfriend wasn't abusive," Raina said.

I looked back at Raina and then at Sheree. "Fine. You get me this girl's address, and I'll pay her a visit tomorrow." I moved back from the table. "Right now, I have to prepare for a rendezvous at Prospect Park."

I ARRIVED AT THE PARK just before ten. The park was still open so even though there weren't many people around,

I would have preferred an empty park for our meeting. I didn't like meeting Allison's uncle in such a public place, but I could understand his caution. He didn't know me.

I had opted for the daggers tucked in the straps at my hips. I disliked close combat, but the daggers were much more discreet when there were people nearby. Priest, the same man who forged my sword, had prayed over my daggers and sealed them with holy water long ago. I left the Hwi and the sword and bow and arrows behind and hoped I wouldn't need a weapon at all.

I parked on Flatbush Avenue and entered through the Children's Corner by the Carousel. Few people visited any of the parks this late at night, particularly women alone, so I didn't pass many visitors. I took the quicker route through the East Wood Arch so I could meet Allison's uncle by the boathouse.

As much as I liked Prospect Park's arches, I thought they were a little eerie after sunset when there was still a soft light on either side of them at dusk while the tunnel itself was pitch black. As enhanced as my vision had become, it couldn't create light. I liked having a bright light in any place I entered, especially once I had learned about the things that lurked in the dark. I often wondered what humans would think if they could see what walked amongst them every day. For the first eighteen years of my life I hadn't known.

I pulled the handheld work light out of the holster strapped to my waist. I looked like I was wearing a tool belt, but I preferred having my hands free as much as possible. The work light, less than a foot long and about two inches in diameter did a beautiful job of lighting those dark places.

It could also deliver a powerful blow if I found myself in a tough spot that involved a human rather than a demon.

I felt better once I lit the arch and ensured that no demons lurked in its shadows. Hurrying forward, I took a path to the left toward the boathouse. I had a clear view once I rounded the bend, but I didn't see Peter standing either on the side or in front of the boathouse. The sense of foreboding that traveled through me felt strong enough to be a premonition. Not surprising since I was meeting Allison's uncle in the park late at night, a perfect time for something to go wrong.

I peeked through the gate covering the windows, but I couldn't see anything in the dark. Walking along the front of the boathouse, I hurried to the other side. The wrongness grew stronger, and I stood still and waited. When I tuned out all the distractions of the human world, I could feel demons more strongly. And I sensed at least two nearby, the stench of their feeding so powerful that I gagged. They usually stayed far away from me, disappearing before I could get near enough to sense their presence, but these two were bold.

I left the boathouse and headed toward the Cleft Ridge Arch. Demons loved dark places, and I knew I would find them there. The Arch wasn't far from the boathouse so I arrived there in a matter of seconds. Two young men stood over the body of a woman who lay unconscious on her side. With her body turned away from me, I couldn't see her face. One boy held onto her purse while the other peered inside.

Such a stupid cliché but one was black and one was Latino. That alone made me want to beat the hell out of them. They were both dressed in jeans, a t-shirt, and baseball caps.

They were so engrossed in whatever they had found in her purse that neither heard my entrance until I tapped on my work light.

I should have known. I could see the demons shining inside them like they had passed through an MRI that detected demons instead of bones and organs. The demons were low level, stronger than the whisperers but weaker than the shapeshifter demons that walked in human form. Of the three, I disliked these demons the most, the hijackers who possessed humans.

"You boys looking for something," I said, startling them. I swung my light, hitting both on the upper arm near their shoulders before they could move.

The one holding the purse dropped it. "Mind your fucking business, bitch," he growled, taking a step toward me.

"Mind your language." I said, punching him against his lips.

His friend reached a hand toward me, but I jabbed his leg hard enough with my stick to drive him to the ground. Somersaulting behind him, I wrapped my hands in his locks before he could move. My blade rested against his throat as I yanked back his head. He didn't flinch nor bleed, but the demon inside him moved away from the blade, her body now partly outside of his. I could see her muted brown skin and short, slicked back dark brown hair.

Complete possessions were confusing and chaotic. Explaining to the victim a demon hijacked them proved difficult unless someone in their family was a believer. The demons could make the possessed perform actions against their will. While the relentless whispering in the ear of humans could wreak havoc and the stronger demons who took on human form could fool even believers, it was the hitch-hikers, the hijackers, who left the greatest damage. How to explain to the hijacked that he cheated or stole or, even sometimes, killed? That part never got easier with time.

"Leave him," I said to the other boy who held a hand to his bleeding lips.

"You are no priest, demon hunter," the demon said, "Who are you to perform an exorcism?" I got a better glimpse of the boys now. The demons had latched onto them fast and strong, but I could see the boys near the surface, ter-rified. The possession had been so swift they must have been aware when the demons took over. That worried me more than if they had been unaware.

I pressed the flat of my blade against the boy's neck until I nicked him. The demon screamed, her body seizing before she jerked. Her body fought against itself, trying to stay in-side even as the blade burned. The boy spasmed against me, and I struggled to hold on.

The demon flew out of the boy and landed against the opposite wall of the tunnel. I stepped back and let the boy drop as I withdrew my other blade and threw it toward her. She howled as the blade skewered her hand to the wall, her hate-filled eyes promising retribution.

"I taste Priest on that blade," the demon spat.

I smiled. "His faith could move mountains. Now why don't you leave the boys alone?"

"We didn't come for them anyway," she said.

I fell back as the other boy lunged at me, reluctant to hurt him when I knew a demon rested inside. Stepping aside,

I used his momentum to push him toward the other wall, his head hitting with a loud crunch. Stumbling, he clutched his forehead, disoriented. I reached for him with both hands, but the demon leaped free before I could use my dagger.

"You can't stay," I said, throwing my other blade.

The demon that had just freed himself ducked, but I wasn't aiming for him. My blade pierced the female demon's chest, and a look of surprise flashed across her face. Her body glowed like embers as her insides burned. The howl of anger was nothing I hadn't heard before, but the sound was still creepy. When the glow consumed her, her ashes swirled once before the earth swallowed them. Now there would be yet another demon sitting in hell, plotting revenge.

"Why did you come for me?"

The demon looked back at my daggers protruding from the wall and then looked at me. "Not you," he said, looking at the woman still unconscious at our feet.

His eyes flicked to the left, but I moved first, tackling him before he could run. Rolling to my feet, I grabbed both of my daggers, but he had rolled to the side. One blade missed him, but the other sliced his arm. His brown skin bubbled black where the blade cut him. He tried to move from me again, but I knocked him back on his back. This time my blades didn't miss.

Both boys looked at me, wide-eyed and fearful. But there was little I could do. They would be arrested without knowing why. I went over to the woman who had yet to regain consciousness and made sure she still had a pulse. She bled at the temple and the color had seeped from her skin. The red hair gave her away, but I still needed to see her face. Turning her onto her back, I sat back on my haunches and shook my head. What the hell was Allison's cousin, Cindy, doing at Prospect Park? Whatever the answer, I was sure her presence wasn't a coincidence.

CHAPTER NINE

I rose early after a fitful sleep, still thinking about those boys at Prospect Park. In the beginning, before the police became more organized, I had let my fair share of the recently possessed off with a warning and a prayer. Now I often bore the added guilt of having to report culprits I knew weren't acting on their own. I picked up my phone and dialed Jasen's number before I ended the call. Jeez, I was like a schoolgirl. Tossing the phone on the bed, I headed for a quick shower before I left for the hospital.

Before the ambulance arrived last night, a quick look through the woman's purse hadn't told me much, and I still didn't understand why she had shown up instead of her father. She had still been unconscious when the ambulance left so I had to wait until morning. When I dressed and went downstairs, Sheree sat in the kitchen eating a bowl of cereal.

"You're up early," I said, grabbing the orange juice from the fridge.

"Early morning phone call," Sheree said, every hair in place even at this hour. She wore a satin nightgown and a robe with matching slippers. It was discreet and not meant for me. When Sheree saw me glance at her, she smiled.

"This was before I found out Baal was a demon." She shrugged. "I was gonna let him—"

"I don't even want to know," I said, lifting my hands. Laughing, I grabbed the keys to the bike. "When Raina gets up...."

"What do you mean, when Aunt Raina gets up? She didn't come back home last night."

Shocked, I banged my hip on the table as I spun back to look at Sheree. "What are you talking about?"

Sheree's eyebrows moved suggestively as she watched my face. "She left right after you did. Said she needed to go see a friend and she would be back."

"And you didn't find out where she went? Or even let me know she hadn't come home."

"With the way she was looking and smelling, I didn't think she was coming back. Besides, Aunt Raina is an adult."

"I know but—"

"But you're overprotective. One thing I've realized in the short time I've been here, Neema, is that Aunt Raina can take care of herself. She knows how to stay safe, and Liz doesn't seem dangerous." Sheree stood up and placed her bowl in the sink. "She's learned a lot from you. She'll be okay without you."

I could only watch as she left the kitchen because I knew she was right. Raina would be okay without me. And that was the problem, wasn't it? I didn't want her to be. She was the closest thing to a family I had. Sometimes, when I remembered how alone I was, the yearning for my mother and that tight-knit, albeit slave community, overwhelmed me. I had been the only one of my mother's three children to live past childbirth. She never told me how she lost those babies, but I had always wondered. I had been glad I didn't have to watch my family members die generation after generation. But I also resented not having a family, and I resented the thought of Raina leaving me to have a life of her own.

As I left the house, I forced myself to focus on the task at hand. I had a killer to find and thinking about this situation with Raina would not help me solve this case.

JASEN AND HIS PARTNER were in the hospital waiting room speaking with Allison's mother when I arrived. Jasen didn't acknowledge me, but his partner gave me a puzzled look. Kenneth hadn't seen me since he tried to shoot me in the gardens so I was sure he had questions regarding my presence. I headed toward the other side of the room until Ruth, Allison's mother, called me back.

"Neema right?" she said, her voice strong but worried.

I stopped in my tracks and turned back to face her. Even though I had seen her a few days ago at the wake, I didn't like when people remembered me. It was less complicated for me if I went unnoticed. When I turned back to them, they were all staring at me.

"Hello again, Mrs. Stevens...."

She shook her head, "Mrs. Lasko, Ruth." She gripped a tissue she used to swipe at her eyes. "Stevens was Allison's last name, her dad's last name. I.... Did you know Allison was my niece? I adopted her after my sister, Esther, died. Cindy says she saw you talking to Peter at the house the day of the wake."

I glanced at Jasen who looked at me. I wasn't sure how to interpret his expression, but I could sense his distance. He wasn't ready to accept what I had told him the other day. I couldn't let that concern me now though. I had much greater worries since demons had been sent to the park to stop me. Demons, in the beginning, had thought me a joke. Those had attacked me when they realized that I could see them. Some had threatened anyone in my life once they realized that attacking me head on was not smart. After decades of proving my strength, they had grown wary of me. It had taken longer to make them fear me.

Their boldness in attacking Cindy and risking my attention worried me. In the years since I had become a demon hunter, I had made so many enemies, and no enemy was more dangerous than a demon.

"Peter told me he had plans to see you last night," Ruth said, her hands clutching the tissue as she glanced at me. "He wanted me to know just in case anything happened. I.... I don't know why he thought something bad would happen, but I guess it did. You didn't see him last night, did you?" She sounded so hopeful I didn't want to disappoint her, but I had no choice.

I shook my head. "I didn't see Peter last night. I also didn't get the chance to talk to Cindy. She was unconscious out when I found her."

"I.... I don't understand what's happening. First, Allison and then Cindy." Ruth shook her head. "I don't know what to say to Helen. I told her I would stay here with Cindy while she checked in on Peter."

"Mrs. Lasko," a nurse peeked her head in the waiting room. "Cindy's awake."

Ruth gasped, one hand covering her heart as she whispered a prayer. I smiled as she turned and followed the nurse down the hallway. Moving to follow, I stopped short when Jasen lifted an arm to block me. He glanced at Kenneth who continued with Ruth while Jasen spoke with me.

"You have no business here, Di.... Neema."

"Well, that's where I have to disagree with you, Jasen. I'm right where I need to be. I need you to move."

"This is a police matter."

"It's a lot bigger than that."

Kenneth came back into the hallway and glanced at me before he grabbed Jasen by the arm and pulled him to the side. I didn't need to stand by them to know what had happened. Cindy had asked for me, and I didn't blame her. Jasen didn't look happy when they walked back over; in fact, he looked downright pissed. I couldn't help being a little kid about it and smiling.

"The young woman, Cindy, wants to see you."

"Ladies first," I said, spinning on my heel to lead the way down the hallway.

CINDY RAISED HER BED just enough so she could look at the people crowded in her hospital room. Ruth sat next to the bed and held one of Cindy's hands between both of hers. I walked over to the bed, relieved not to see any demons milling about the room. Demons seemed to have a thing for this family. I studied Cindy for a moment, and even though I saw no demons attached to her, I could see traces of the demons that had attacked her last night. I slid a small cross under her pillow as I leaned forward to press my cheek against hers.

"Thanks for helping last night," she said. "Aunt Ruth told me you interrupted a mugging. I was unconscious when you found me."

I nodded my head, but she didn't see me since her eyes drifted shut for a moment.

"Cindy is exhausted," Ruth said, moving to stand, but Cindy slid her hand free to wave her fingers at her.

"No, Aunt Ruth," she opened her eyes. "I need to talk to Neema. Dad planned to see her."

"I didn't see your dad, Cindy. If he showed up at the park, I didn't see him at the boathouse."

"I asked him not to go. Told him I would go in his place, but dad is stubborn. I don't.... I don't know where he is. Mom went to see if she could track him down."

"Do you remember what happened?" Kenneth, Jasen's partner, asked.

Cindy's eyes drifted shut again before she looked at us. "I was coming to the boathouse to see you when two boys trapped me in that.... that tunnel. It was.... it was scary." Her voice dropped just a little. "Something was off about them. I don't know how to describe it."

But I did. I had seen this so many times over the years. Humans who sensed the demon presence inside of another human being. Possessions were just shy of normal. They weren't the spinning and twisting of movies about the demon-possessed. Demons tried to pass unnoticed, so they preferred to pretend at being human. Until their true nature took over and the human body they possessed got caught up in mischief. That was when the demon became more notice-able.

"Dad said you asked about Allison's inheritance."

"What was it?" I asked moving closer.

Cindy smiled. "Nothing that would get her killed, if that's what you're thinking."

"Just some old photos," Ruth said.

"Not to Allison, Aunt Ruth. Allison loved old photos and old postcards. She would rather get tangible history than money. Uncle Joseph sent her an old box of photos and postcards. Maybe from the early 1900's to about the middle. She was excited about getting them, you know. Allison was that kind of person."

"But not everyone understood about her passion."

"Obsession is more like it," Cindy smiled. "That's why she studied history in college."

"And that's what your father wanted to talk about?"

"Dad didn't want you to chase an inheritance that didn't matter. Allison brought the box by the house three nights ago—"

"The night before she died," Jasen said.

Cindy frowned. "Yeah, I guess. Dad figured that if you could see the pictures for yourself, you could focus on something more important. He was concerned about—"

"Cindy!"

"Aunt Ruth." Cindy closed her eyes again and swallowed with difficulty. Ruth put a glass of water to her lips before she spoke again. "Go see Grant."

"Grant has nothing to do with this, Cindy," Ruth said.

"Aunt Ruth has always had a soft spot for Grant, but Dad didn't trust him. Go see Grant." Cindy's body drooped with exhaustion. "Let me rest, but...." She grabbed my hand. "Promise me you'll come back." Her voice slurred as she fought to stay awake. "Dad wanted me to tell you..." She fell asleep mid-sentence. Understandable though since the girl had been unconscious since this morning.

"Helen should be back later," Ruth said, smoothing hair away from Cindy's face before she smiled up at us. "I'm sure she'll find Peter. Why don't you come back tomorrow? Both Helen and Peter should be here by then."

I left the room before the nurse could shoo us out. I was sure that Jasen and Kenneth would head straight to Grant's place, so I would go see the ex-girlfriend first.

KENNETH GRABBED MY arm as soon as we stepped outside the hospital, and I let him. I would never convince Jasen to work with me if I fought against either of them.

"I don't know who the hell you think you are or how Jasen knows you, but if you get in our way, I'll throw your ass in jail."

I stared at Jasen and waited for him to say something to either me or Kenneth.

"You're not the police, Neema."

"Nor do I want to be," I said, shrugging. "You stay out of my way, and I'll stay out of yours."

Kenneth took out his handcuffs, but Jasen put out a hand to stop him. "I don't want to see you at Grant's house, Neema."

I smiled. "You won't. But why don't you call me later. Even better, you should come by. I'm sure that Raina would love to see you."

He gave me a sharp look before nodding his head. "Okay, Neema. I'll talk to you later."

"And bring Kenneth," I said as they turned to walk away from me.

I hadn't seen demons near Cindy, but I had seen the trace of one on Kenneth. I would have to make sure no demons got that close to me or anyone I knew.

CHAPTER TEN

Grant's ex-girlfriend lived in Queens, an area I didn't know like Brooklyn. As much as I liked the pseudo-suburban feel of Queens, I couldn't seem to stay away from Brooklyn's rough around the edges ambiance. Whenever I returned to New York City after several decades away, I always ended right back in Brooklyn.

I parked on the street just a few doors down from her house, hoping that talking to this girl would take me closer to finding Allison's killer. I waited for a few minutes before I got out of the car and headed toward her house. I tried the upstairs apartment first. After a good two minutes, a partial face peered at me through a cracked doorway, the chain giving her a false sense of security. I could get inside her apartment within seconds, but I desired her cooperation.

"Carmen," I said, my gaze sweeping up and down the street.

"Who's asking?"

"My name is Neema. I wanted to ask you about Grant Sullivan."

"I got the message the last time one of you came," she said, her voice angry. "Now leave me alone."

I grunted as the door bounced off my hand, but I could still see a sliver of her face through the crack. "I wasn't sent here by Grant. I wanted to ask you questions about him."

"What questions?"

"His girlfriend was murdered a few days ago."

She pushed the door closed before I heard the chain slide, and the door opened all the way. "Did he kill someone?"

"Would it surprise you if I said yes," I said as I walked past her and into the apartment.

"Grant never struck me as a killer, but then, I would have never believed him capable of a lot of the things he does."

She closed the door and led me toward the living room. "I was about to have some iced tea. Are you interested in a glass?"

"Sure," I said, smiling as she left the room. I glanced around, but there were no pictures on the walls of the living room. Sitting down on the couch, I rifled through the magazines fanned on the coffee table, but nothing in this room revealed much about her character. I found it interesting that she had no paintings or photographs.

"What message did you get?" I said as she came in with two glasses of lemonade. She set one glass on a coaster in front of me and then sat down in the opposite chair.

"Grant has warned me before about the statements I make on social media." She lifted her glass and took a long sip, her hand shaking. "His warnings were abstract threats until a month ago."

"When he started dating Allison?"

"He sent two of his *friends* to my job. They were waiting for me in the parking garage."

"Tell me about your relationship with Grant."

"I met him at an exhibit in Manhattan. That was back when I worked in a museum, conducting tours. He was in one of my groups." She grimaced. "I thought it was cute. He told me he joined the group so he could meet me. He had topped by the museum on his lunch break."

"You doubted him later?"

"I doubt everything about Grant. He lies."

"When did things go bad between the two of you?"

Carmen smiled. "He always made his little comments. Grant's a snob, you know. My mother was from a wealthy family in Venezuela and came here on a student visa. When she got pregnant, she thought my father would marry her, but he didn't. He was a WASP who wanted another WASP. You can imagine what it was like for my gently bred mother working odd jobs, cleaning. Americans think all Latinos are illegal immigrants, so they treat us all the same."

"Was Grant like that?"

"I think sometimes his misconceptions got the best of him. He was okay for the first three months, but then he became a little mean. That snotty mean."

I nodded my head. "Like a Mean Girl."

Carmen's laugh was half-hearted. "He thought he could say whatever he wanted, and I would take it. I didn't."

"You broke up with him?"

"And he didn't like it."

She leaned forward and slid open a compartment beneath the coffee table. Reaching inside, she pulled out a stack of pictures and placed them on the table in front of me.

I looked at each picture. They were of her face first, one eye swollen and the side of her face a deep purple. The bruises also decorated her body, one above her breast, another across her ribcage. They continued down her back and even across her thighs. The anger and hatred on her body jumped off the page.

"I thought he would kill me," Carmen whispered. "When he knocked me to the ground, he kept kicking me. I begged him to stop, and I don't beg for anything."

"I don't understand why he isn't locked up."

"He had an alibi, and it came down to my word against his." She shrugged. "He can buy people. Something I can't do."

"But you put it on Facebook."

Carmen gathered the pictures and pulled them toward her. "I never thought I'd ever fear anyone as much as I fear Grant. He convinces you he's this wonderful person, you know. You believe he's everything he appears to be, until he reveals these little cracks in the image."

"The last woman he dated was a schoolteacher, Allison Stevens."

Carmen nodded her head. "I went to see her, to warn her about Grant."

"When was this, and how did she react?"

"I saw her maybe a week or two ago, and she seemed distracted. I wondered if she was even into Grant. She seemed distant from our conversation."

"Unless she didn't believe you."

"Or she didn't care. I remember thinking how much that would have ticked Grant off. He believed he deserved a woman's undivided attention."

"Which brings me back to the question I asked you in the beginning. Would it surprise you if I told you that Grant killed Allison?"

Carmen looked at me for a moment before she answered. "I didn't think Grant capable of beating me until he did. So yeah, I believe he's capable of just about anything."

THE RIDE TO GRANT'S house was long and silent. I kept thinking of the pictures of Carmen, and I wanted to give him an ass whooping myself. There was something cowardly about men beating on women, and a little demon too. I saw no demons around Grant when I spoke with him at the coffee shop, but that didn't mean he was untouched. I drove over to the gentrified portion of Williamsburg, an area where the brownstones were expensive, and the neighborhood was less African American. Grant lived in a beautiful three family building with an unmarked police SUV parked in front of it. Annoyed, I drove to the end of the street and parked at the corner. How long did it take to ask a few questions? I had been at Carmen's house long enough for Jasen and Kenneth to interrogate Grant and leave.

After about five minutes, they walked out of the brownstone, but then Grant did too. Jasen and Kenneth headed to their vehicle while Grant turned up the block toward me. I had to switch to a non-existent Plan B. Watching in the review mirror, I saw Jasen and Kenneth climb into the car, and I slid down in the seat until I couldn't see anything over the windshield. Maybe talking to Grant away from his house would be a better choice.

I pulled out my cell phone and dialed Sheree.

"I'm not at the house," Sheree said when she answered the phone.

"Do you think you could locate Grant for me?"

"I can try when I get back to the house."

"And how long might that take?"

"Maybe another hour. Raina asked me to run an errand with her."

"I'll call back," I said and ended the call. I glanced at the screen and noted three minutes had passed. Long enough for Jasen and Kenneth to leave. Sliding back up in my seat, I turned the key in the ignition. A sharp knock on the window startled me, and I looked up to see Jasen staring at me with a grim look.

Groaning, I shook my head and would have pulled off if he hadn't been standing so close to my car. Besides, Kenneth had pulled their SUV up close to the back of my car. I'd risk hitting him if I tried to maneuver around them. I rolled the windows of my vehicle down and turned the car back off.

"You didn't think I'd make a note of your car when we left the hospital?" he said, the annoyance in his voice clear.

"I didn't give it much thought."

"And you came to see Grant even after I asked you to stay out of this."

"I thought you'd be gone when I got here."

"You get in our way Neema, and I *will* arrest you."

"And I promise you I won't stay in jail."

The look he gave me was so parental that I was reaching for him in anger before I caught myself. I pulled back just as quick, noting that Jasen had reached for his gun.

"I'm not one of your children, Jasen," I said. "I may look young, but I'm not. You would be wise to remember that."

"Has it come down to you threatening me?"

I sighed. "Never that. My preference would be that you and I work together. We can cover much more ground that way."

"You're not a police officer, Neema."

"I was one at several points in my life. That has to count."

His impatience showed, and he glanced down the street for a moment. I could see the annoyance in the set of his jaw. "Why don't you tell me what you got from Grant?" I said.

"I can't discuss that with you."

I shook my head and cranked up the car. "When you decide you want to compare notes, please call me. But now I have to go."

"If you obstruct—"

"I won't. Now if you'll excuse me."

He gave me a long look before he stepped back and motioned Kenneth to back up. Kenneth glared at me, inching back so I knew it was deliberate. I waved at them before I pulled off.

As I rounded the corner, I noted that Jasen and Kenneth were following me, so I drove to the nearest gas station.

They stopped, so I got gas even though I was almost at a full tank. I pretended not to watch them as they sat in their car and watched me. Waiting for them to pull off, I stood in front of the gas tank a little longer than necessary. Removing the pump from my car and sliding it back into place, I sighed when they pulled off. They took long enough.

THIS TIME I PARKED several blocks from Grant's house, far enough so that Kenneth and Jasen would have to take plenty of streets to find my vehicle. I hurried down each block, the scabbard of my sword bouncing against my back with each step. I wasn't sure if demons were near Grant but I wanted the weapon which caused the greatest damage. When I reached his brownstone, I considered breaking and entering first before I rang the bell. I scanned the street, watching for the SUV. Ringing the bell again, I had taken out a lock pick when he came on the speaker.

"Who is this?"

"Neema," I stood in front of the video. "I met you a few days ago when I spoke to you about Allison."

There was a short pause before he responded. "Yeah, I remember you. What do you want?" He didn't sound as friendly as he had the other day.

"I have a few more questions I wanted to ask you, if you don't mind. Questions about Allison."

This time his pause was long enough to worry me. I thought I would have to break in, but he buzzed me up. Sliding through the door, I closed it as I saw Kenneth and Jasen passed on the cross street. They would have to drive around the block to come up the one-way street. I hoped they would drive by Grant's house and not try to come inside.

I climbed up the stairs, not wanting his neighbors to notice me. When I reached the top of the stairs, the door stood open.

"Hello," I said, stepping inside the apartment.

"Come on back," Grant said, stepping into the foyer. He looked comfortable in a t-shirt, sweat pants and bare feet. His blond hair was wet and tousled as if he had just gotten out of the shower. I could understand why his boy next door good looks drew women. He made you want to trust him.

I closed the door behind me and walked deeper into the apartment, following him into the kitchen. I almost drew my sword when the demon attached to the ceiling like a damn salamander hissed at me. He dropped to the ground and slid away from me, his eyes filled with hatred.

He was tall for a wrath demon, his white skin contrasting with his short black pants. The drawstring on his pants was loose so his pants drooped below his waist. I kept one eye on him and the other on Grant who had turned to face me with a bottle of water in his hand.

"The police were here today," he said, "and I already spoke to them. I'm not interested in talking to you."

"You let me in so you must want to talk about something."

"I got a call about a visit you made today."

"What visit?"

He smiled. "A mutual friend of ours." He took a long sip from his bottle, watching me. "Please, don't act like you don't know what I mean. That's just a waste of our time."

"You have someone *watching* her?"

"I have someone keeping me informed. And that's not cheap."

"So you allowing me up here had nothing to do with Allison?"

"In a way. I don't want you to think I killed Allison. And you seem to be moving in that direction."

"The only direction I'm moving in is the truth." I watched as the demon moved closer to him. He hid his anger well, but the demon could sense it. The demon had stopped looking at me and stared at Grant. I waited for him to lick his lips, but he spared me a look at his fork-like tongue.

Grant set his bottle aside and crossed his feet at the ankle. He leaned against the counter so you might have thought we were having a friendly conversation. But the smile on his face didn't reach his eyes.

"So, did you kill her?" I said when it was clear he would only stare at me.

"You didn't ask me that question when you met me the other day."

"I didn't know you beat on women then."

He shook his head like I had just said the most foolish statement. "Is that what Carmen said? That I beat on women?" Then his smile dropped, and he grew serious. "I guess I'll talk to Carmen again."

By now the demon had drawn so near to Grant that his face was buried in Grant's hair. He sniffed, inhaling as if Grant smelled like apple pies. I should have just chopped off both of their heads right then. But I left the humans, unless unavoidable, to others.

"I don't think you want to bother Carmen again."

"And what are you going to do about it?" he said, pushing off the counter.

I stood there as he walked toward me, stalked me like a creep in a movie. I was several inches taller than him, but he was one of those men. He thought his gender made him stronger than a mere woman. As the demon draped over him like a sheet, he smiled even as he grabbed my throat.

I clamped onto his wrist and squeezed until his hand loosened from my throat. He stared in shock when I turned his wrist to spin him around, his arm twisted behind his back. He lifted on his tiptoes to escape the pain, but I showed no mercy. The demon had moved away from him as soon as I grabbed Grant. This time I spoke to the demon.

"I command you to leave."

"I would rather stay," the demon growled at me.

"I would enjoy that too," I responded. "I have the sword of Priest. The Exorcism."

He flew to the other side of the kitchen, giving Grant a last disappointed look before he melted into the wall.

I walked into the living room, using Grant's arm to push him along. "You're crazy," he said, struggling against me, but that only caused more pain. I shoved him onto the couch and withdrew my blade. His gaze widened as he took in the sword, but I would never harm him. The sword was only a warning.

"You're fucking crazy," he said, again, the tremor in his voice making his words shaky.

I placed my blade against his neck. "So why don't we try this again. You tell me what you know about Allison. You stay away from Carmen. And I don't bother you again."

"I'll call the police."

"And then I'll come back and have another talk with you. I don't think you'll find my talk as peaceful as the ones you have with Carmen." I stepped back from him and sheathed my blade. "Now if you behave—"

He was up before I could finish my statement and charged at me. I hit him hard enough in the chest with my forearm that he lifted off his feet as he flew back into the couch. The couch rocked, but it didn't fall back. He held both hands against his chest, wheezing, but he would be fine. Bruised maybe and in pain, but I had only hit him hard enough to gain his attention.

I waited until his breathing calmed down and then sat on the coffee table in front of him. "Was Allison still seeing you before she died, Grant?"

He watched me like he wanted to rise again, but I placed a firm hand on his knee. "Don't make this any more difficult than it needs to be. I don't want to hurt you. Not badly at least."

"After Carmen went to see her," he said. "Allison didn't want to see me anymore. I called, left messages, even sent her flowers two weeks ago at her job but she refused to see me."

"So, you went by her house."

He only gazed at me, reluctant to answer, but I smiled. "Guys like you always drop by unannounced, Grant. You can't seem to take no for an answer. Tell me about the night you went by her house."

He sat up then, his face resigned, and the arrogance gone. He rubbed his chest and shook his head. "You hit hard for a woman."

"You go down soft for a man."

He grimaced before speaking, "I went by Allison's about six days ago. Right before she died. I had called and text her but she wasn't answering so I dropped by."

"Did you notice anyone else stalking her besides you?"

"Checking in on someone I'm dating is not stalking. Anyway, when I dropped by, Allison had just returned from Mississippi. She had flown there to pick up her inheritance from a great uncle."

"Do you know what the inheritance was?"

"Old photographs and postcards. She had them spread out on her floor, studying them. I had interrupted her."

"Is that what she told you? That you were interrupting her."

"Yes, but that was Allison. When she got lost in history, it was impossible to capture her attention."

"Did you notice anything else?"

"Besides those photos, no. She was home alone, and she wouldn't let me inside."

"Do you blame her? You beat Carmen."

"I didn't—"

I held a finger up and shook my head. "Don't waste your breath. I've been around long enough. So, she wouldn't let you in, and that was that."

"Told me she had to get back to those stupid pictures. Asked me not to come back."

"And did you listen to her request?"

"I had no other choice. She was dead two days later."

"Unless you killed her."

"I didn't kill her. I already told you that."

I stood up, hands on my hips as I stared down at him. I had already threatened him and even though pulling out my sword would still be effective, I didn't want to keep repeating myself.

He looked up at me, still leaning sideways on his hip, propped up on one elbow. "I can tell you this much, Allison was spooked that night."

I shook my head, puzzled. "But you said she had a bunch of pictures and postcards. How would that matter?"

"To you and me they might be a bunch of pictures but for Allison, if she was up late studying those pictures and postcards, they were important."

"I didn't see pictures lying around when I went to her apartment." He gave me a questioning look, but he didn't respond. "So where do you think these photos might be?"

"I didn't get the chance to know Allison well. Her obsession with history, American history was obvious. She was up front about her interest, but she was close-mouthed on everything else."

"If I find out you sent me on a wild goose—"

"I can't guarantee it's important, I'm just telling you how important it was to Allison."

I stepped back, knowing he had no more information. "Don't make me come back, Grant. And I *will* check on Carmen if I need to."

He shook his head. "Believe me, I don't want to see you again. Ever."

WHEN I ARRIVED HOME, Sheree tapped away at the computer while Raina practiced some intricate moves we learned from a Brazilian capoeira master years ago. Raina had liked the concept of avoiding a fight more so than fighting. She was and always had been a beautiful sight to behold when she moved. I, less inclined to dance around and perform rather intricate gymnastics steps, preferred good old-fashioned boxing although I was skillful with my martial arts. Had to be when those I fought didn't need guns

"You were out this morning when I left," I said, unable to keep the annoyance from my voice.

She unfolded her frame to its full height and damn near glided over. She was tall and even at seventy, still had her muscular build. I think that's what had drawn us to each other. Though I was taller than Raina by a few inches, we were both built in ways that men often found intimidating. She hadn't minded since she had realized at a young age that men didn't catch her interest.

"I had a date last evening," she said. "Not that it's any of your business, Neema."

I tried to hide my flinch, not wanting to acknowledge what I had seen with Liz the other day. Raina moving on meant that Raina was *moving on*. "I—I'm glad you—"

"No, you aren't," she leaned forward and kissed me on the cheek. "I have been with you for fifty years now, Neema. I know you. But you'll get used to the idea. You always do."

She smiled before she headed toward the stairs. "I am about to shower and change and get ready for an early dinner date. You kids have fun."

I shook my head at her retreating back then glanced over at Sheree. "I retraced Allison's steps," Sheree said, her body but not her face or her glance shifting toward me, "hoping that might give us a clue to why she was killed."

"And what did you find?" I said, walking over to the desk and peering over Sheree's shoulder.

"She had just come back from Mississippi a week before she was killed."

"Same thing Grant said. She went down to Mississippi to get her inheritance from an uncle."

"She checked in the same number of bags on her return trip so it wasn't tangible."

"No, it was tangible. Her uncle left her a box of old photographs."

"Old photographs," Sheree said, glancing at me. "From an uncle down in Mississippi. That should be interesting."

"A great-uncle," I said, my mind churning with so many thoughts I wanted to both stand up and sit down. I moved as my body attempted to do both. "Maybe I should find out what Allison inherited."

I wanted to kick myself for dismissing those photographs earlier. They had been significant enough for Allison to take a few days off work to fly down to Mississippi to retrieve them. And maybe Allison hadn't been the only person who thought so.

CHAPTER ELEVEN

When I returned to the hospital the next morning, as soon as visiting hours allowed, Cindy was being tended to by the nurse, so I sat in the waiting room with her mother.

"Did you find Peter?" I asked after we sat for a moment in silence.

Helen waited until the silence had grown awkward before she answered me. "Peter likes to deal with any problem from the inside of a bar. He's home sleeping it off." She frowned. "Although that isn't quite your business, is it?"

"I wish it were that simple," I said, leaning back. "There's a killer..."

"And how is that your concern? The police can find Allison's killer. They don't need your help."

I took a deep breath and focused on keeping my impatience in check. "We seem to have gotten off on the wrong foot."

"No, we did not. I remember you from Allison's wake. Peter was taken with you. He's always had a taste for exotic women."

"Is that a euphemism for..."

Helen smiled. "I'm explaining what Peter likes. I'm sure that his plan to meet you at the park last night was not just about Allison."

"Well, I assure you my only plan involved information on Allison."

She studied me before she spoke. "Peter thinks Grant was involved in Allison's death, but I don't believe that."

"Not his character?"

Helen smiled. "A man like Grant raised me, Ms..."

"Neema," I said. I had grown out of the habit of explaining my name. "I only use the one." I shed my surname when I shed slavery. When I needed a last name, Dahomey worked.

"Men like Grant are bullies. They threaten, they hurt, they even torture. They don't kill though because they enjoy pain and fear punishment. When you grow up under men like Grant, you learn to recognize them no matter how much they try to hide."

"Did you warn Allison about him?"

"Allison was never one to listen. We disagree on too many things much too often."

"Your daughter is ready now," the nurse said, poking her head in the waiting room.

Helen gave me a slight nod, and I followed her into Cindy's room. Cindy looked better than she had yesterday, her body propped at an angle so she could scan the room. A fresh bandage was on her head, and I figured that they would release her soon.

"How are you feeling?" Helen said, sitting on the bed next to Cindy. She gripped one of the younger woman's hands in hers, the only visible sign she was distraught. "The doctor says you should be able to leave tomorrow."

She smiled. "There's no need to worry, Mom. I haven't lost consciousness again. Everything is fine."

"It's good to see you again," I said, stepping closer to the bed. "I hope it's okay I returned so early."

"No, no, no. Anything to catch Allison's killer, right?"

"It keeps coming back to this inheritance," I said. "I went to see Grant yesterday. He said he dropped by Allison's about a week ago and she was obsessing over the pictures she had gotten from her uncle."

"Great-uncle," Helen said, "Uncle Joseph. Joseph was their mother's brother, the last sibling still alive. He moved his family down South in the fifties and never looked back."

"Did you see what he gave her?"

Cindy shrugged. "I couldn't see why Allison made such a big deal out of it. Uncle Joseph gave her a bunch of old photos. Dad didn't even know the people in the photos. That's why we figured that they didn't matter. There wasn't much there except pictures of strangers."

"The pictures don't matter," Helen said again, her gaze intense as she studied me. "There doesn't seem to be a motive for Allison's murder and that worries me. A motive might at least lead the police to a suspect."

Cindy reached for my hand and pressed a piece of paper against my palm. "There's no harm in looking at them though. Mom has never liked Allison's tendency to ask invasive questions. She sometimes forgot that we weren't all sources for a history paper. Her inheritance was just one more opportunity to be inquisitive."

"It wasn't that I didn't like Allison's need to ask questions," Helen said. "She couldn't seem to turn the research questions off. And I'm hoping that she didn't ask the wrong person the wrong question."

"Which is why we have to find out who did this to her, mom," Cindy said, sighing as she rested her head against the pillow. "Dad checked out the private investigation business that Neema has with her dad, and they seem to be good. There's no harm in her seeing what she can find."

I shouldn't have been surprised that they had checked out my cover story. Wasn't that why Raina had developed a good one? But still. I didn't like that they had investigated me. It seemed to belie their lack of concern toward the photos.

I curled my fist around the paper in my hand and wondered what Allison had discovered.

I SAT IN THE CENTER of the floor, photographs spread before me as I struggled to find meaning in them. I had gone to the address that Cindy had given me and gotten the pictures from her roommate. Allison had entrusted Cindy with the photographs, and Cindy had stored them in a small photo box in her room. I could understand why Allison would have found the photographs intriguing. As a history buff, she loved the memories, the legacies captured in these photos. The Mississippi of the 1950's and 1960's was divided in two. That division was on display in these photographs, and my anger rose at the reminder of a difficult, heart-breaking time in my life.

"You should take a break," Sheree said, standing on the mat next to me. When I looked up, she handed me a coaster and a glass of iced tea. We had fallen into an awkward truce over the last couple of days, and these little peace offerings seemed to be part of her character. I mouthed a thank you and placed the glass on the mat next to me as I moved a few photos around.

"You've been studying these photos for over an hour," she said, kneeling beside me. "Maybe you should take a break and then look at the pictures with fresh eyes."

I know I'm overlooking something. Everything keeps coming back to this inheritance, these photographs, but there's nothing important."

"Tell me what you see?" Sheree said, settling on the mat next to me. She pulled a picture closer to her and peered at it.

"How about you tell me?" I said, sitting back. "Maybe the fresh pair of eyes I need are yours. Raina told me that photography was a hobby of yours."

Sheree smiled and set the picture back down. "Whoever took these pictures was an amateur too, but you can tell that he loved the camera. The camera man was Allison's uncle, Joseph, right?"

I nodded as she moved closer to the other photos, her gaze sharp and focused. Raina said Sheree had a good job in computers before she took a leave and joined us. She studied computer engineering in college, but had a real knack for coding and a few geeky things I knew little about. Her colorful weaves, lengthy nails and all-around country flavor didn't equal geek, but what did I know. I hoped that she would of-fer greater insight into the photographs.

"Where were these pictures taken?" she asked.

"Mostly in Mississippi," I said, turning my attention back to the pictures. I hadn't realized how much she resembled Raina in the way she carried herself. I could see why Raina thought Sheree would be the perfect companion for me. She would bring me into the twenty-first century.

"These photos are amazing," Sheree said, holding up a few of them. Each picture was in a protective sleeve, con-tributing to their pristine condition. "They span several decades." She squinted. "You can see the Colored and Whites Only signs in the background."

I stood up suddenly. I had noted the same signs, and the anger threatened to spill over. Every day, I struggled against the anger that always lurked beneath my memories. Segrega-tion had reflected the code and laws of slavery if not the act, and I tried to avoid any reminder of slavery. Not because I wanted to deny what had happened, but because none of my anger or resentment or frustration could change any part of it.

"Neema," Sheree called after me as I bounded up the stairs. My heels tapped the floor as I strode toward the back-yard and shoved the door hard enough it closed on its own. While the signs had brought my resentment back to the sur-face, I was frustrated because I couldn't unravel the mystery of the pictures. I walked the short length of the backyard and stopped just shy of kissing the wooden fence.

I WANTED TO FIND ALLISON'S killer, *and* I needed to find that rogue demon. Both tasks grew tougher by the minute.

"You've got to get a hold of your emotions, Neema," Raina said from behind me. The heat from the afternoon sun presented a nice contrast to the slight breeze. I turned to face her, struck by her timeless and flawless beauty. Her face glowed, and I knew it was because of a woman I had no reason to resent but resented like hell, anyway.

Her almost wrinkle-free skin looked taut and young, its nut-brown color glistening with health. Her silver hair, cropped close to her scalp, offered a sharp contrast to the brown of her skin. If I could age, I always told Raina, I wanted to age like her. She looked as if she should have been featured in Essence's tribute to black women who aged gracefully. Her love for bold and rich colors was clear in every piece of clothing she wore. Today, a rust-colored gown flowed from her shoulders to her ankles. Not for the first or last time did I wish I possessed her looks.

She smiled at me. "I know that look on your face."

"I'm admiring your beauty."

"There is a blessing in immortality, Neema."

"A point I have disagreed with these last two centuries."

Raina nodded her head, but we had disagreed over this point often. I knew she would never understand how I felt. "Sheree says you're frustrated."

"I know that these pictures have something to do with Allison's death, but I can't connect the two." I shook my head, hands clutching at my hips. "What could be in these pictures, Raina, that got her killed."

"You told me her uncle lived in Mississippi."

"Yeah. He moved down to Mississippi in the 1950's."

"He must have been in Mississippi when you and Dad went down there."

I gave her a sharp look, my mind spinning as I ran through the pictures again in my head. "And you wanted to go down to Mississippi that summer."

"1964," Raina said, "but Dad thought it was too dangerous."

"It had become a breeding ground for demons." I ran a hand over my face. "Especially after Chaney, Goodman and Schwerner were killed."

Before I finished the last sentence, I ran back into the house and down the stairs, Raina close on my heels. When I stood in front of the photos spread out on the basement floor, I wanted to kick myself for not noticing the obvious.

"You know what's missing here," I said, staring at the photographs I had arranged in chronological order.

Raina stood close beside me, staring down at the photos. "This isn't the Mississippi that I remember."

"Allison's uncle was an amateur photographer who took pictures of the Colored signs. And look at some of these buildings."

"From the 'wrong' side of the tracks."

"Colored signs but few black people. There were battles happening down in Mississippi in the 60's, but not one of these pictures speaks to those battles. And how could he not have a single picture of Freedom Summer?"

"So where are the pictures?"

I shook my head. "She didn't give the pictures to her cousin so she must have felt that wasn't the safest place."

"So where do you think they might be?"

I wasn't sure, but I had a good idea of where to start.

STANDING OUTSIDE OF Maria's apartment, I waited next to my car. She hadn't reached home yet, but she had seemed to expect my phone call. She lived in a beautiful, renovated three-family house in Stuyvesant Heights. If the inside was as well-kept as the outside then Maria's home would be impressive. I found myself even more interested in her background.

Glancing at the time on my phone, I grew impatient as I waited. I felt so sure about Maria's connection that I wanted to confront her. As much as I wanted to find Allison's killer, there was a significant part of me that wanted to put distance between Jasen and me. Although I hadn't wanted him to know I was still alive. I hadn't expected him to ignore my existence when he found out. I wanted to speak to him, to explain something for which no explanation many any sense.

When I saw Maria walking up the street toward me, I set thoughts of Jasen aside and moved forward to greet her.

"I was wondering when you would show up," she said, offering me a friendly smile. "Why don't we head upstairs and I can tell you what I know?"

"You know why I'm here?"

"I told you, I was wondering what took you so long." She bounded up the steps, shifting her bag to her left shoulder as she searched for her keys. I followed her up the stairs, a little puzzled about her response to my visit. I had sensed there was a mystery surrounding Maria, and I was correct.

I followed her up a flight of stairs to a second-floor apartment. When I stepped inside, my senses went into overdrive. The furniture in the apartment was sparse, two plush cranberry-colored chairs sat on either side of a huge area rug, black splashes of color suggested paint splatter. The rug almost all black had the impress of a wine glass with a cranberry stain covering part of the rug. I enjoyed the sparsity of the living room, but with no television or computer in sight, I was curious about her bedroom. And I wondered how a teenage girl lived in this apartment alone, and where did she get the money to afford this place?

"I know you have a lot of questions," Maria said, "but I want to answer your questions about Allison first."

"You misled me."

"No, I didn't. Allison entrusted me with her photos, and I needed to know more about you before I shared them with you. You weren't truthful about your father, were you?"

I chose not to answer and walked deeper into the apartment. The door to the bedroom was cracked, but I could see the corner of a neatly made bed. When I looked back at Maria, she watched me with a slight smile on her face.

"I keep the pictures in my room," she said, setting her bag on the floor before she pushed open the door to her bedroom. The room housed a bed and a Chester, no mirror, no other furniture. I leaned against the doorway and watched as Maria pulled out the bottom dresser. She got down on her belly and reached a hand toward the back of the drawer. When she stood, she handed me a big yellow envelope.

"Allison gave me these last Saturday."

"The day before she died."

Maria nodded. "So, I figured they might have been important. But I didn't want to hand them over to her family or to the police." She cocked her head sideways. "But you're different. You see things that most people don't see."

"That's not always a good thing."

"But it's not bad either."

"Have you looked at these?" I said, opening the envelope and peering inside.

The look on her face was grim as she shook her head no. I slid the pictures onto the bed and felt a little weak in the knees at the images peering up at me. Reaching a hand toward the bed, I sat down, my eyes glued to the photographs.

"My God," Maria said, shaking her head. "No wonder Allison was spooked."

"I bet no one has ever seen these photographs," I muttered, looking at Maria. "They would be in a museum somewhere." I looked at my hands. "I need gloves," I said, impatient as Maria rushed into the kitchen.

I pulled on the gloves and touched the photos with shaky hands. The 60's had been a volatile time in the South, and I had spent most of that time as angered as I had been at the close of the Civil War. My life had been filled with shades of anger.

I flipped through a handful of rare postcards that featured lynchings. The existence of these postcards always amazed me. They spoke of an America that many preferred not to acknowledge. I, however, could never forget. But the photographs held my attention. Some photographs I recog-

nized from Freedom Summer back in 1964. I wasn't surprised to see the photographs of James Chaney, Andrew
Goodman, and Michael Schwerner. Their murders had
rocked the nation and shocked the international community. The picture was taken before their murders, before the
spotlight shone on Mississippi. Their picture didn't fascinate
me, though, as much as the picture of a young man with a
bright pink circle drawn around his face. This, I knew in my
heart, had been the photograph that so captured Allison's attention regarding the past, and I removed my gloves.

CHAPTER TWELVE

New York City
July 1741

Since most of the homes in Manhattan housed only one to two slaves, my mother decided that I would be much safer in the swamps of Harlem. I disagreed, but I didn't dare tell her so. She sent me up there that night to hide from the anger of the Constables. Caesar and Price had been hanged on the gallows. Cuffee and Quaco were burnt at the stake. John Hughson and his wife were hanged last night, and they even hanged the white woman pregnant with Caesar's baby. Just a week ago, even though there had been cries of hysteria and protests against the mass arrest of slaves, the Constables had arrested the Catholic priest John Ury. The panic hadn't died down enough, and I had grown anxious. I was tired of hiding away from civilization.

I'm not sure what possessed me to go against Mama's wishes. I had never done such a thing before I died because I had died that day in the woods. I discarded the skirts that Mama had left for me and put back on the breeches I had worn the day I woke up in the burial ground. I pulled on the cap and a shirt that disguised my curves. I aimed to go into the city tonight even though Mama considered it much too dangerous.

The makeshift cabin sat deep in the woods, and I was sure I wasn't the first slave who had hidden within its walls. It was secluded enough that only the brave and determined could find it, and that was only if they knew where it lay. I wasn't sure if I could find my way back to the Dock Ward tonight, but I had noticed several nights ago that my sight seemed sharper than it used to be. I could see at night like it was daylight. If this was a side effect of my curse, I had yet to determine my feelings toward the change. I remembered stories of the witch trials in Salem. I wanted no one to accuse me of witchcraft.

Closing the cabin door, I walked along the narrow path to the edge of the swamp, my mother's dagger clutched in both hands. She had tried to teach me to fight the few times she came to Harlem, but I was a slow learner. I held the dagger before me, my feet sure and steady as I walked along the swamps toward the streets of Manhattan.

The sounds of night spooked me, but I shook off the terror. If I could survive the last few months of hysteria that captured New York City then I could handle animal sounds.

When I reached Hughson's Tavern, the darkness reminded me of all we had lost. Visions of Cuffee smiling at me came swift and hard, causing me to stumble. Hughson's Tavern only turned dark after the last man went home. To see it dark now meant John Hughson and his wife would never return. Word was that the Judge spared their daughter Sarah the gallows, but I wondered if she would return to this place. They stood accused of fencing illegal goods, but we all knew they were executed because of the supposed slave uprising.

Glancing around, I looked over the empty streets before I lifted the bar over the door and slid inside. The West Ward, even with its proximity to the North River, was not as populated as other parts of the city. I was less likely to cross paths with other people, but I was still cautious.

Closing the door behind me, I took a deep breath before turning around to face my memories.

"I've heard of you," a voice said out of the dark, and I jumped. A hand drifted to my chest as I tried to still my thundering heart.

When I stepped deeper into the room, I could see a man seated at the same table that Cuffee and I had always claimed. Even seated, his height was commanding. He would stand several inches over me which wasn't common. He was also new to these parts because he could have never blended in. His skin was the smooth unnatural black of the woman who had cursed me, and he shared the same bright green eyes. His hair, though, was a reddish gold that fell over one shoulder in a long, thick braid. It had the woolly look of the African slaves, but it was straight instead of curly. The end of the braid rested against his thigh. Although, he wore the loose-fitted clothing of the slaves, the way he sat was not like an enslaved man. In fact, it was easy to see he had never known slavery.

He stood with grace, and I tried not to stare at him. He was compelling, but his smile terrified me.

"Who are you?" I said, nervous as he moved away from me. I didn't find his move in the opposite direction comforting.

His gaze held mine just a little too long, and I squirmed in response to the silence. He enjoyed my discomfort, his tongue darting out as if he could taste it. I struggled not to react to the sight of his tongue, the slit in the center making it resemble a pitchfork. Clutching the door behind me, I fumbled at the bar, but I couldn't move it from my poor vantage point.

"The question I am most interested in is, who are you?"

"Neema." I said.

"Yes, but why you?" He tilted his head to study me. "Why did the Vodou choose you?"

"I don't .... What do you mean?"

He stood over me before I finished my question. He was much too close, his hand resting against my throat. "I know that you've seen us," he whispered. "And I can't allow someone like you to live."

My eyes widened as I stared into his bright gaze. Mama had said only a demon could kill me so this man before me must be a demon. I wasn't sure what a demon was, but it couldn't mean anything good.

He stroked my cheek. "The Vodou knew I'd come for you."

"And so did I," a voice said from behind him.

His grip on me loosened as he stepped back. "This does not concern you."

"*She* concerns me."

The demon stepped further away, and I glimpsed the man who stood behind him. He was not as tall as the demon, but he was built just as strong. His brown skin resembled that of the natives, and his straight black hair was parted down the center and gathered into two braids. He wore a silver breastplate over a shirt and breeches as if he were about to enter war. The hilt of a sword showed next to his hip. I took a sharp breath as the room seemed to brighten slowly at his presence. Impossible but he glowed, a soft light licking at the shadows until the demon and I stood in its dim cast.

"This has nothing to do with you, Rafael," the demon growled, his anger so intense that I could feel its heat on my skin.

The man Rafael stared at the demon, his voice devoid of emotion."You should leave now Baal," he said, the threat in his voice so clear I trembled.

"If it's not me, another will come for her when they discover that she can see us."

"Perhaps, but that will not be today, and it will not be you."

Baal stared back at me with such hatred in his eyes I knew I had a dangerous enemy. Now I understood the deep trouble the Vodou had made for me. She gave me a gift laced with the cruelest of curses; she had ensured that I would spend the rest of my life hunted by demons.

Baal inclined his head toward me. "The next time I come for you, I will not fail."

I slumped against the door when he vanished, so afraid that there was no place for my fear. I couldn't catch my breath as Rafael watched me without sympathy. Doubled over, wheezing, I saw dark spots like my world were about to black out. I clutched at the wall, refusing to fall to my knees before this stranger. I didn't know who he was, if he were a danger and I didn't want to fall at his feet.

When I reclaimed my breathing, I adjusted to full height, knowing we would meet each other eye to eye.

"Your immortality is blasphemous," he said, "no human should be immortal."

"I don't want demons to take."

He paused, gazed at me, studied me before moving closer. When I tried to take a step back, he stopped moving. "A demon wanted to take your soul." he said, "but you are not for demons."

"I don't understand."

"You will," This time, when he moved toward me, he did not stop. He placed a firm hand on my shoulders and held me in a tight grip I dared not break. I stared at him as he laid the palm of his hand against my forehead.

"We need earthly soldiers," he said.

"I am not a soldier."

"You will be."

"I can't fight."

"You either learn, Neema or they *will* kill you. The Vodou left you vulnerable for that purpose. It's a fitting revenge: immortality with a catch. But you will not die by the hands of a demon. You will be what they come to fear."

"But *I*'m afraid."

"Not as afraid as they will be." He stepped back from me, and I felt the loss of his warmth. The glow surrounding him emanated a soft heat I hadn't noticed. "The slaves in the South have found refuge in a fort built by the Spaniards. Go to Ft. Mose where you will find a former slave known as Priest. He will help you."

"I don't understand why *you're* helping me. Aren't you a demon?"

"Go see the Priest, Neema. He will know you are coming."

"But.... but what *are* you?"

He smiled. "Most call us angels."

Even after he vanished, I stood there in shock. I didn't understand what I had just seen or experienced, but since I should have been a corpse, this promised to be the first of many strange experiences.

I SAT ON THE FLOOR between Mama's legs, my head resting on her lap as she drew a comb through my hair. She carved the comb herself out of wood, and its smooth glide lulled me to sleep. She had been angry when I first appeared on her door step, demanding that I return to Harlem. Only when I told her about the demon Baal did she relent and allow me refuge. Her touch on my hair was light as she crafted a plan. Quick and nimble, her hands made two neat braids, one on each side of my head.

"I will have to send for Jacob," she said. "He should be able to get you down to South Carolina."

"I'd rather stay,"

"This is not a choice, Neema. You must go. You're no longer safe here."

"Then come with me Momma. We—"

"They think you're dead, Neema. But they will come after me."

I turned to face her then, her hands drifting away from my finished braid. When I looked up at her, I could see her sorrow and her determination. She was preparing to send me away.

"Momma, you know Jacob has no patience for me."

"But he will keep you safe."

She rose, her movements so like mine I wondered, not for the first time, what I had inherited from my father. She withdrew a knapsack and packed it with food.

"I won't go, Mama."

"Even if you don't know what angels are, Neema, I do. I need you to go get Jacob and bring him back here." I opened my mouth to express other doubts, but Mama shook her head. "Enough Neema. Go get Jacob. You leave tonight."

Jacob lived and worked in the Dock Ward. He was almost a head shorter than me with a lean but strong build. He was son to one of the few women that my mother had counted a friend. Even though his mother had passed several years ago, he and my mother still had a close relationship. Jacob was skilled at working the land, so it would just be a matter of time before he left Manhattan. Mama had only asked that he warn her when he goes. Though they had a familial relationship, Jacob had little patience for me, so I dreaded seeking him out at the docks. He considered me useless and did not bother to hide the fact. Mama had trusted him with the news of my survival since she needed him to take me to Harlem.

He was lifting one of those heavy barrels onto the docks when I wandered into view. Since it was dark out, few people were down at the docks. Jacob, though, always worked whatever hours he saw fit. He was as untamed as they come. When he saw me walking toward him, his lips twitched in distaste before he ignored me.

"You already know Mama sent me," I began.

"I don't have time for you, Neema," he said, pulling a barrel off the boat as if it didn't weigh a hundred pounds. I grabbed his wrist and held on even though he could have shaken loose. He released the barrel and stepped back so he could face me.

"Mama sent me," I said, again. "I need to take you to her now."

"I'm working, Neema."

"Now, Jacob," my voice was firm, filled with something new, some bit of strength I had never had. His head tilted as he gazed at me, surprise flickering in his eyes.

"Master William—"

"They will not notice long enough for us to leave if we leave now."

He walked off abruptly, headed toward my master's house, and I ran a short way to catch up with him. We walked in silence and with purpose, which marked our movements for the rest of the evening.

Mama packed us some food, but Jacob's hunting skills and my basic understanding of plants would have to suffice. The journey to Ft. Mose would be long and arduous, and we couldn't take much with us. We would have to avoid the white men and Indians that lay between us and the Spanish fort. Though not all would be hostile, we couldn't trust anyone but ourselves, not even the slaves we would encounter.

Mama handed me her machete with a solemness that would always remind me of its importance. A machete, though, wouldn't make me any more of a survivor, any more of a fighter. I could only pray that whatever waited for me at Ft. Mose was enough to save me.

Even though there was a sense of urgency, Mama gripped my hands for so long they throbbed with pain.

"I can't promise you I will see you again, Neema," Mama said, "but you must get to Ft. Mose no matter what. And I will try my best to meet you there one day."

"Mama...."

"We have to go now," Jacob said. "Before Master William looks for me."

I still clutched my mother's hand, sensing that the moment I let go, I would never see her again. Though another woman and man owned me, my mother had always clarified that I was her child. I didn't know how I would survive without her.

She grabbed my face between her hands and held me steady so I couldn't break her intense gaze. Her serious expression brought a finality to this moment. "The years ahead will not be easy, Neema, but you cannot let that stop you. And the Vodou will be angry that her curse failed, so be careful."

"Mama..."

"We must go now," Jacob said, tugging on the sleeve of my shirt.

Mama had always protected me, shielding me from the worst of slavery. I didn't know how I would survive without her watching over me. I gripped her hand, forcing Jacob to tug me from her grasp before I walked away. I glanced back only once, my mother's hands on her womb and her heart the only clue that my leaving devastated her. Her face as always was both majestic and impassive, and one I would never see again.

CHAPTER THIRTEEN

I awoke to the crackling of branches, my heart thundering as I thought I was back in the burial ground again. Looking around, I saw Jacob seated before a fire. I had fallen asleep as he went hunting for our dinner. We had been traveling in the forest for so long now I had wondered if I would ever be clean again.

"You hungry?" he asked, watching me. He had grown more watchful of me after we left Brooklyn. Questions hovered in the air between us. Shock. Maybe even fear. He had been careful not to touch me, reminding me with his silences and distance of just how wrong everything had gone in Brooklyn.

I jerked my head forward, wary of him too. His reaction had scared me and shown me the danger posed by my inability to die.

"We get to Ft. Mose," I said, not for the first time, "and you can be on your way."

He frowned. "That won't help me to unsee, to forget."

"Well. That's gonna have to do for now Jacob because I can't take back what happened in Brooklyn."

We were silent while he stoked the fire, and I sat huddled in the blanket Mama had packed. We had run out of food long ago in our journey, and now we survived on what we could find in the forest. Jacob, with an uncanny sense of direction, led us straight to Ft Mose. I had felt its call when I.... woke up in Brooklyn. Even though I didn't know the man, Priest was like a call toward freedom, like the angel pointing me toward Priest and Ft. Mose had created a strange bond.

"We aren't far from the Stono River," Jacob said, his voice low.

"I don't.... I'm not sure what you mean."

He tried to hide his disgust. "It's only been two years since the slaves down here fought their masters."

"You mean the rebellion."

"A man fighting for his freedom can *never* be a rebellion."

I refused to rise to any of Jacob's baits. He had wanted to cross words with me since we left Manhattan, but he was the least of my worries.

"I don't want to wait here long," he said. "We rest just for a moment more before we move on because the trouble has not faded. South Carolina is as dangerous for us as New York."

I thought of my aching feet but dared not complain. Jacob would only see my complaints as another sign of weakness, further proof I was undeserving of either his grace or my mother's faith. I rubbed my feet and watched him. He had grown used to my stares even as they annoyed him.

I stilled as I saw him stiffen with alertness, two fingers going to his lips. He put out the fire with dirt before he reached for the dagger at his side. He had taken it off a dead man in Brooklyn without a thought. Now, he held the dagger as he beckoned me toward him. We walked as one through the woods, my steps placed in his. Although he had heard the crackling of branches underfoot at the careful tread of men, I had heard their breathing and now sensed their intentions. Somehow these men knew of our presence and had come here for us.

"Let me lead," I whispered. "I know..."

"I will never follow you," he said, his hatred of me never so clear as it was in that moment. Jacob had always thought me useless, and he couldn't seem to let go of that image. Two months of running and surviving together had not changed his view of me.

"It's foolish of you to ignore me Jacob. I can help."

"Quiet," he said, pausing. His grip on my wrist tugged me down so we met eye to eye. I had already proved to be stronger than I once was, but challenging Jacob was too much trouble. We only had to make it to Ft. Mose. I had to hold on to that thought.

"We keep moving."

"Niggers don't roam free in South Carolina," a voice said behind us.

We turned as time slowed to a crawl, and every sound around us was magnified. Leaves rustled in the light breeze, and shadows danced around us in the sunset. I could hear the chomping of a deer, the trickle of a nearby stream, and the controlled breathing of the man standing beside me.

Two white men stood watching us, but only one had the long barrel of a gun pointed at Jacob's face. Having been shot in the burial ground, I did not want to be shot again so I watched them both. The one with the gun watched Jacob, but the other one, the more dangerous one, watched me.

They both wore breeches and shirtsleeves, but their shirtsleeves were rolled to their elbows like working men. The thickness of their physiques and the streaks on their shirts showed that these men, like the South Carolina slaves, worked the land.

The dark haired one who watched me had a keen handsome face that the women of New York would have swooned over. His dark brows scrunched together with thoughts I preferred not to know, and he rested one hand on a young black boy standing behind him.

I didn't want to look away, didn't want to look at the boy, but I had to see again the face that had betrayed us. This was the boy that Jacob had ordered me not to help. A few miles back, a few days ago. He had reminded me we couldn't trust Negro or white, slave or free. He had demanded that I leave the boy alone, and I had. Until Jacob turned his back. I had gone to help a child, a slave boy of about nine-years-old because I had thought Jacob foolish in his fears.

I looked at the boy who only smiled, his eyes filled with cunning. He turned his head to look at Jacob, and only then did I see the demon. Because the demon inside him still stared straight at me. I could see its red skin just below the surface of the boy's. The demon's eyes were just an impression, but I could see its eyes. That was enough to terrify me.

The demon stretched, readjusted itself, and settled deeper into the boy's body. When the boy looked back at me, I could see that the demon had taken full control.

"If you are the one the Vodou cursed," it said, "we have nothing to fear."

I didn't know what to say since I knew it was correct. I was no one to fear. "Only time will tell," I said, wanting to sound fearless but sounding timid instead.

"We saw this boy a few miles back," Jacob said, one arm in front of my waist as if to shield me. "I warned you not to help him."

"But she did," the boy said, stepping forward. The demon inside him no longer hid, and I was sure that even Jacob could see the difference now.

"I did not know what you were," I snapped.

"You are new to our world. How could you have known?"

Jacob tried to shift in front of me, but I stayed him with my hand.

"I swore to protect you," he said.

"Not in this, Jacob."

"No, not in this Jacob," the boy hissed as the dark-haired man now aimed his long barrel at Jacob. "I am unsure of what will happen if these men take aim at you but him...." The boy tilted his head toward Jacob. "He will not survive. So perhaps you will simplify this dilemma by following us."

I looked at the two men who had spread out on either side of us and jerked at the sight of the demons flowing over their bodies like water.

Skin the white of fresh, fallen snow with raven-black hair, these two demons glared at me with rage as they whispered in the ears of the men. I didn't understand what made them different from the demon housed inside the little boy. Although the pale demons had fused with the men, they weren't like the other. No, the demon inside the boy was the one to fear.

"We will go with you," I said.

"We can't let them take us, Neema."

"If we don't, you will die in these woods tonight, Jacob. And I can't allow that to happen."

"She's wise, Jacob," the boy said. "You should listen to her."

"And you betray your own."

The boy shook his head. "Humans always see so little. Who, do you think, are my own?"

We walked only a few miles before we reached our destination, a large plantation common in the southern colonies. We stood beside the back porch as one man went inside.

"What did you do?" Jacob whispered, glaring at me. Although the other man could most likely hear us, Jacob didn't seem to care.

"You left to hunt," I said. "So, I circled back to help the boy."

"Even after I warned you."

"How was I to know he was a demon?"

"Did you learn nothing in Brooklyn?"

"He seemed so young...."

"There are no children in slavery, Neema," Jacob said, "They take even that from us."

"I will never believe that," I said, as the door opened and a man stepped onto the porch. He bore a resemblance to both men who had captured us so I realized the other two men were brothers. White-skinned demons swirled around his legs, a tangle of limbs as they rubbed their bodies along his torso. Their long, forked tongues darted out to touch his cheeks, and their eyes closed. They inhaled him as if he were a delicious meal. Twice as many demons whispered in his ear making me wonder if his sin was greater. They halted when he looked at me, their black eyes studying me.

"We don't like runaways here in South Carolina," the man said.

Jacob shook his head. "We ain't..."

The man held up his hand. "Don't bother lying. I can always recognize the stench of slavery. Just have to figure out the best course of action."

"We can always kill him," one of the younger men said. It didn't matter which one since the idea was troublesome either way. "We can find another use for her." The dark-haired one had spoken, and his nostrils flared as he looked at me. I recognized that look, and my hands clenched in response. No white man had taken me in slavery, and none ever would.

The demons separated themselves from the older man and flowed down the steps toward me. The world faded in color: less green, less brown, less alive as they surrounded me.

I stood still as one touched my hair, and another sniffed my skin. They had a savage beauty with their bright glowing smooth white skin and black as night hair. The strips of cloth that covered their loins seemed to be more about me seeing them than modesty. Two of them had strips of cloth wrapped around their chests. A couple were female although I couldn't tell the difference.

"So, you are the one," a demon whispered, its gravelly voice filled with curiosity.

"She doesn't look like anything to fear," another said.

The men, including Jacob, became so still they seemed frozen. I almost touched Jacob, but didn't want to draw more attention to myself. The surrounding land had turned gray as if covered in the ash from a fire. I knew this land, drained of all vibrancy and life, belonged to the demons. They were more alive in its grayness.

"Not yet," the boy said, coming from behind the two young white men and standing closer to the porch. "But she will be if we allow her to live."

"What is this place?" I whispered, looking about in fear. "Am I.... am I in the place the priests call hell?"

The boy laughed. "What they say is true. You are unprepared for us."

I looked away from him to hide my fear, but I could see that even the other demons had sensed fear in me.

Color seeped back into the world, and Jacob jerked beside me. Jacob was shackled while I had thought the world had frozen around me. The older man had gone back inside the house. The younger men prodded us with the tip of the long barrels until we stood outside a windowless, wooden building. The building was close enough to the main house that anyone could look out of the windows on the east side and watch its doors. It was far enough away, though, that they could watch without guilt. While the building didn't have the bars of the New York cells, it was still a cell. I had never been caged in one.

"Jacob," I said, reaching out to touch his arm, but he pulled away from me.

"They putting us in the stockade til morning," Jacob said. "Til they decide what to do with us."

"Jacob, please...."

He shook his head. "I have nothing to say to you," he said. "Keep your distance and your words."

We were shackled to the walls at opposite sides, and he was stripped down to his breeches. Blood clotted from the blows he had taken in the face as they shackled us to the wall. I too was stripped of my breeches and shirt. I may have felt less shame if I wore my shift, but the shift had been uncomfortable beneath the men's clothing. Instead, I had bound my breast with strips of cloth and wrapped cloth over my genitals like a baby. No woman would allow herself to be exposed in such a way, and the dark-haired young man had taken great joy in stripping my body. I shuddered again at the thought of how he had brushed against my breasts and touched my most private of areas while he removed my shirt and breeches. He had lingered long over my breeches until his brother called for his attention. I still sat with my legs curled to my chest as I thought of his invasive touch.

"Jacob, please," I tried again, but he sat with his back to me. They had folded our clothes within sight but not within reach. My mother's machete and Jacob's blade sat on top, and I hated them even more for that.

"I would rather not look at you," he said. "Each time I warned you, and each time you failed to listen. You did not listen in Brooklyn. You did not listen here. I told you to leave the boy alone."

"I thought he was a child."

"In Brooklyn, I told you to stay out of sight."

"I thought that slave would die."

"Be a savior once we part ways. Not while I stand beside you."

"Jacob...."

My voice faltered when the door opened, and one brother stepped inside. He was the one who had been staring at me since they found us in the woods. He smiled when he noted my gaze and stepped deeper inside, making room for his brother and the little black boy.

"You said morning," Jacob said.

"No, Father said morning." He looked at me. "You're not like these other women. They're small, weak. You look strong."

I lifted my head. "You will regret touching me."

His laugh was exaggerated as he looked at his brother. "You hear that. She thinks I fear her."

"Maybe we should wait until morning, Thomas. Father won't like...."

"Father won't mind. He never does." He walked over to Jacob and knelt before him. "What's she like?" he said. "Is she skilled?"

Jacob smiled. "You'll never know."

I jumped when the barrel of the gun came down so hard on Jacob's face I could hear his cheek crack. Pulling at the shackles, I tried to reach him, afraid to scream. "You don't have to hurt him," I said.

"I know," Thomas said as more demons filled the small space. While the white demons increased in number, two demons with yellow-gold skin had sidled next to Jacob. They all glowed, and I could see them feed, a thin mist traveling from the white men to them.

"He's just a boy," I said to the red demon inside the little boy slave.

Though the boy watched Jacob, the demon turned to look at me. "You should listen to Jacob," he said. "There are no children in slavery."

"But I can still see the boy inside. He calls me."

"Kill them now," the demon said.

I focused on the boy, seeking the glimmer of light I had sensed when I first helped him. "His name is Samuel," I said, sitting straighter. "Samuel, come forth."

The demon looked at me in alarm before it screeched in anger. "Kill them now," he screamed and the other demons whispered louder.

Demons slithered along the floor and walls, some gliding around the bodies of the white men like snakes. I tugged at the shackles, but they held fast. Jacob faced me now, his eyes widening as he sensed the demons but couldn't see them.

Thomas shifted his focus toward Jacob, the blade that Jacob had carried gripped in his hand.

"He's only human," I said, so close to pleading. "Please spare his life. He knows nothing of your world."

"Death," one of the yellow-gold demons hissed, "tastes so sweet."

Thomas lunged toward Jacob, and I had no time to react before he plunged the blade into his chest. Screaming, I yanked at the shackles, wishing I could snatch away the demon who whispered in Thomas's ear. The chain pulled from the wall bringing me to my feet as one end wrapped around the neck of a demon. The other demons froze and turned to stare at me as the chain glowed like fire. My only thought was to send this creature back to wherever it had come from. When I scooped up my mother's machete, I could feel the heat of her power. She had used whatever magic, whatever knowledge she had of the spiritual world and poured it into this blade. The machete sliced into the demon, setting its insides aflame until it burst into burning ash.

Thomas looked down at the knife in his hands in horror then threw it away when he took in Jacob's limp body, struggling to breathe. I stared at demon after demon, shackles dangling from my wrist, one hand gripping the machete while the other looped a chain. My hair, loosened from its braid, formed a halo around my head, and I felt stronger than I ever had. For the first time, I felt not just what the Vodou had done but whatever Rafael had done to vanquish my mark of death.

"There is no need for anger," a demon said, but I wasn't angry. I was hunting.

Tossing the chain, I reeled in demon after demon, moving with a swiftness that reminded me of my more than human status. I wasn't neat or graceful, but I was powerful and swift. I plunged my blade again and again until every demon had vanished, and the only one left standing was inside the boy. The look it gave me held a little fear. Its arrogance had disappeared as soon as it realized that the curse the Vodou put on me had changed. I was no longer the easy prey of demons.

Thomas crouched next to Jacob, turning his hands. "I've never killed a man before," he said. "I don't understand what happened."

"We couldn't have made him do it," the boy said, "not unless it was there. We only feed desire; we feed...."

"I only care about the boy," I said, "leave him be."

"You won't kill him."

"If I have to."

The boy shook his head. "You won't kill him. That's not in your nature."

"I can't let you keep him."

"I enjoy this boy. And I plan to enjoy him for a time." He smiled. "Unless you know how to take this body from me."

I stayed silent, but my silence said enough. He shook his head. "You know so little. Perhaps in our journeys, dearest Neema, we will cross paths again." And with that, he walked out of the stockade. I couldn't stop him since he was right. I didn't know how to rid the boy of this demon, and I couldn't kill him.

Turning to Jacob, I knelt beside him, but he could not be saved. His eyes drifted open at my touch, but he closed them again and turned his head away from me.

"Jacob," I said, "don't turn away from me. I need you to know how sorry...."

'Go to the fort, Neema," he mumbled.

"Jacob."

"Go, Neema." Blood had dribbled onto his lips, and his face paled with death. "Go," he said, again. "You will never get the forgiveness you seek from me." I turned to Thomas and his brother. Neither man moved as I walked out of the stockades with the shackles dangling from my wrist, the machete gripped in my right hand, and another dose of guilt.

BY THE TIME I REACHED Ft. Mose, I had become re-signed to my loss of humanity. The shirtsleeves and breeches I had stolen soon after leaving the plantation in South Carolina were crusted with dirt and other debris. My machete still, no matter how many times I wiped it, bore the blood of both animals and humans. It had also sliced through demons, each time seeming to sacrifice a little magic that my mother had sealed in its lines. I almost fainted when I found the fort. Slaves from South Carolina to Florida had talked of this sanctuary, a refuge for slaves that welcomed all fugitives. I had not been the only fleeing slave seeking sanctuary in Ft. Mose. I had joined none though, and none had joined me. After losing Jacob, I had thought it best to travel alone.

Tucking the machete into the waistband of my breeches, I approached the walls of the city. Caution had been a hard, fast lesson for me. I was not the same Neema who had left New York City months ago. Not even a child would receive help from me.

I struggled to understand the place that stood before me now. In the woods of South Carolina, I had heard of the Spanish fort, the place where slaves could go to find refuge. Before me, however, stood a crumbled wall made of nothing more than dirt and stakes. A building that might have been a watchtower was torn to the ground. The fort may have been filled with homes once, but everything had been destroyed by human hands. My hands dropped to my sides as a sense of loss swept through me. I had been guided by the thought of finding Priest and making sense of the last few months of my life.

"The English destroyed the fort after the trouble in South Carolina," a voice said behind me.

I spun around, arm bent in front of my face, machete in the air as I prepared to defend myself once again.

A woman, beautiful with coppery brown skin, stood before me. Her black hair flowed to her waist, and she wore a simple dress that fell to her knees.

"You are Indian," I said.

"That's what the Europeans call us. Yes." She smiled. "They took and renamed. Many of my people are gone now." She waved her arms. "We filled this land before the white man came and gave us his sickness. Now we are so few that soon we will be no more."

"Are you Iroquois?"

"They call us the Timucua."

"And do you know what happened to the people who once lived in this fort?"

"They returned to St. Augustine to the Spanish priests."

"All of them?"

She tilted her head as she studied my face. I struggled to hide my exhaustion. I could not allow any weakness to slip past my defenses. "Do you seek someone in particular?"

I wouldn't lose much by telling her my purpose. "I search for a man known as Priest."

Her body changed imperceptibly but my senses had grown keener these past few months. "How do you know of the Priest?"

""I know little of the Priest except that he can help me."

The woman watched me, taking in the breeches and the shirt stiff with dirt and blood. I had washed but washing helped little when I only faced another attack. "Priest might not want to see you."

"I have traveled from New York," I said, "I will try."

She tilted her head. "I can't allow you to see where we must go."

"I would never tell..."

"And I will make sure you won't. The Priest has trusted few with his secrets. I am one of the few. The rest stand beside him."

The thought of being blindfolded or vulnerable in the hands of someone else unnerved me. I had learned firm lessons of trust on my travels like not to trust anyone except myself.

"You can remain here, distrusting me," she said. "Or you can allow me to take you to Priest."

I had no other choice but to follow her. I nodded my head once then took a deep breath when she dropped a bag over my head. My hands itched to toss the bag away, but if I didn't do this her way, I would never see Priest. Her fingers slid against mine, warm and gentle to the touch, as she tugged me forward.

I followed her voice and responded to her movements, but more than that, I could feel the pull of Priest. With every step we took, I drew closer to him.

———

I BLINKED AGAINST THE setting sun as she drew the bag off my head. We had walked for a good distance before

entering the woods and the deeper we walked, the more uncomfortable I grew. We were far from civilization, far from
any of the Florida settlements. When I stepped into an unsteady raft, I realized just how well this fugitive camp was
hidden. We had already walked for a day, and our travels
weren't over. I looked back the way we had come, but I saw
nothing but trees—no path to follow, no clearings. I was...
unnerved by that sight.

The Timucuan woman rowed us a short distance to the
opposite bank of the pond, but a little further down from
where we had emerged from the woods. "These waters," she
said, "have deep crevices, so it isn't safe to cross by foot."

"They hid well."

"They must. For any fugitive to survive, they must find
places with natural defenses against the slave catchers. Few
would venture this far."

She landed the raft on the bank and then dragged it into
a copse only a few feet away. From where we stood, there was
nothing to see, but I followed her despite my mounting distrust. We walked until nightfall, and when night fell, I saw
that the fugitives had built themselves a village—a town that
stood but not out in the open.

A boy of about seventeen climbed a few feet down from
a makeshift tower nestled in a tree. He must have seen us
coming in the distance and now faced us with his arms
crossed before him and a musket tucked in the crook of his
elbow. A light-skinned mulatto with green eyes and sandy
brown hair, he looked white but was of African descent. He
wore breeches and a shirt with jagged cut sleeves. A bow
dangled in one hand while he studied us. Only a year older

than him, I understood the maturity in his eyes. Jacob had been right. There were no children in slavery, at least not after our fifth or sixth year. He may have been only seventeen, but he studied us with the focus of an older man.

"Why do you bring this girl to us?" He said to the Indian woman, but his gaze stayed on me.

"She asked to see Priest."

"And do you intend to bring all those who ask for Priest?"

She smiled. "You have grown up much since the last time I saw you, Timothy. Are you a guard?"

He didn't answer her. "This is my home. Not everyone is welcome into our home."

"Let the girl in, Timothy," a voice said behind him.

A woman, a darker version of the boy, stepped through the wall of mud, sticks and spears that surrounded their haven. The place looked like a smaller version of what I had just seen at Ft. Mose. The woman had her bow strung, an arrow cocked and pointed at me. Her words may have said let me in but her stance didn't. Unlike the boy, she wouldn't hesitate to shoot me.

"Let her in," she said again, "But we will watch her."

The Indian woman smiled. "You've taught your son well, Lily."

"We live in a dangerous world," Lily moved, and the boy stepped aside, allowing us to walk before him.

"What is this place?" I asked as the Indian woman pulled aside shrubbery to reveal a handful of buildings built from the trees that had once marked this area. The buildings were of various sizes, simple but sturdy.

"Not all slaves seek refuge in the white man's cities," she said. "We cannot trust the British, and the Spaniards only accept us when we take on their gods. Some of us want peace and freedom without conditions. When the English attacked Ft. Mose, most of the fugitives went to St. Augustine, but we came here."

They spent years creating this space. We entered a common area, a tavern large enough to house every member of this small village. They had created a community. A few people moved about the room, talking and laughing. I had never, not in eighteen years, seen so many blacks gathered in one place without a beating or some other punishment happening in the background. Manhattan had never witnessed a gathering of slaves greater than three. I stopped and stared in awe because I had never seen a more beautiful scene.

"You can't go to Priest like this." Lily said, glancing at me.

I looked at the back of my hand, cringing inside at the sight of caked-on dirt. I hadn't grown immune to the dirtiness, but I had come to terms with my inability to stay clean while traveling.

"We will only go see Priest once you have washed." Lily studied me from foot to head before stating what she had made obvious with her measured looks. "You are filthy, and you smell worse. You do not want to meet Priest in your present state."

She then glanced at my machete. "Priest is also a blacksmith," she said. "Perhaps he can forge additional weapons for your journey home."

"Staying was never in my plan." I began, but she already walked ahead of me.

"Lily has always been protective," the Timucuan said.

Lily led the way around the crude bar and out of a doorway in the back of the building. "Shortcut," she said, torches lighting the path as we took the short walkway. She entered another building, and I realized that we had entered a public bathhouse. A woman folded towels as we entered a room filled with steam. "Who should say has come for Priest?" Lily said as I looked around the room.

"Lily, let the girl save her words for Priest."

"No," I said. "Let her protect her Priest. I am called Neema," I moved deeper into the room, peeling away the shirtsleeves and breeches that had stiffened with dirt. I so yearned to be clean until I cared little that the women stood in the room with me.

The cloth I had used to bind my breast was just as filthy as the cloth covering my most private of parts. I had not bathed in so long I had forgotten what it meant to be clean. Unbraiding my hair, I could only think about sliding in the water and scrubbing away the horror of these last months. I dipped a toe in the steaming water before I sank into the bath. I removed my bindings only after I had submerged myself in the water. Dropping them next to the tub, I settled into the water, so pleased to be bathing I almost cried.

The Timucuan woman looked at me and smiled before she set the towels and a bar of soap next to the tub.

"I will find Priest," Lily said, leaving the room with the sound of laughter in her voice.

"Priest may have taken second to a bath," the other woman said, closing the door behind her.

I could still see over the top and under the bottom of the door since it was more a gate than a door but I cared little. My every thought centered on my bath. Even my skin tingled with thoughts of cleanliness.

Closing my eyes, I rested my head against the side of the tub. My sleep had been troubled since leaving Brooklyn, but had grown even more troubled after Jacob's death in South Carolina. The demons had come for me in full force after I left the plantation in South Carolina, and I had grown weary under their relentless attacks. Weary but unable to sleep. The horrors of the last few months danced behind my eyes each time I slumbered. Perhaps a month ago, I had given up on peaceful sleep, yet now I felt as if I could rest. Finding Priest—perhaps because the angel had sent me to him, perhaps because I was at the end of my journey—represented a haven for me. This explained why I fell asleep as I lay in the tub.

As soon as my eyes closed, though, a noise startled me awake. I reached for my machete and opened my eyes. A man sat across from me, his forearms resting on his knees with my machete in his hands. He turned the blade, studying it before he looked at me.

Even seated, I could see he was a big man. Not only would he be tall, but he was wide, thick, strong arms and legs of power. He was darker than my walnut brown complexion. Like me, he didn't bear the lightness of the favored slaves or the darkness of the slaves who spent their days under the sun. His head was clean-shaven, but his face had the shadow of a beard.

His eyes, a lighter brown, were startling against the deep brown of his skin and his broad nose and full lips created a symmetrical beauty that seemed almost at odds on such a large man.

"I am called Priest," he said, his voice a deep rumble. The room filled with him, his body, his voice, his presence.

I did not fear him, but I was wary. "I was told to come to Ft. Mose. To find you. But the fort had been destroyed."

"Who sent you to the fort?"

I had yet to tell anyone of the new world I could see since no one else seemed aware of the demons. "The water is cooling. And it isn't proper for you to be in here with me."

He studied my face without interest. "I do not live by silly customs. Tell me who sent you."

"You will not understand."

"Who sent you?"

"Priest...."

"I will not ask again."

The command in his voice moved even me to obedience. "An angel named Rafael."

He sat back then, my answer not at all what he had expected. He set my machete aside. "Angels do not exist," he said, but he didn't sound convinced or convincing.

I picked up the soap and rubbed my skin. "You know of that world," I said. "I hear it in your voice. You know of both angels and demons."

"I know that neither exists."

"If you know of the angel Rafael, then you know of the demon Baal."

He started before he could stop himself, his lips tightening as he made a decision. When he looked at me, I was afraid to hear him acknowledge that he knew of them too.

"I have never seen either one," he said. "But I have seen them in dreams...."

"Not dreams," I said, pausing in my bath. "That's not how my mother describes it. You've seen them with the second sight."

"And I've seen you," he said. "Are you the Demon Hunter?"

Hearing his question jolted me. Even in my journey from South Carolina to Florida, I had refused to call myself a demon hunter.

"Lily will bring you to my home when you are done," he said before he stood and left the room.

I STOOD IN THE DOORWAY of the Priest's room so exhausted that I struggled to stand. Lily brought me a dress I refused to wear. I couldn't protect myself without the right clothing, so I settled for a pair of breeches from Timothy and a shirt where he had cut the sleeves. I preferred not to have all that fabric covering my arms. With my skin squeaky clean and my hair brushed and braided, I felt like the woman my mother had raised, the woman that Cuffee had loved. Even when I dressed like a man.

Priest sat in a beautiful, wooden chair carved to accommodate his long muscular frame. Though he sat still, face expressionless, I could sense trouble beneath the surface. I didn't want to delve into my ability to know this man since I did not like the connection between us.

"You say you saw an angel," he said, looking up at me from the wooden carving taking shape beneath his hands.

I moved to the bed before I spoke, too tired to remain standing. It was as if the last few months had decided, at that moment, to take their toll on me.

"How do I know you saw an angel?" he said.

"You don't and neither do I. I only know he called himself Rafael and sent me to Ft. Mose in search of Priest. Aren't you the Priest that I seek?"

"You're only a girl," he said, shaking his head. "You cannot be this demon hunter."

"I agree," I said, giving into the need to lie down on his bed. This was why the white women and men lie in bed until late morning. I would have too if I had known such softness and comfort existed. Closing my eyes, I rubbed my face against a blanket so soft that I made sounds that should have shamed me. I promised myself only a moment of this new luxury, but I couldn't seem to open my eyes. Although I wanted to converse with him more, I gave in to the desire to rest.

A small sound woke me next, my hand latching on an arm close to my head.

"This is why no one would come near you," the Indian woman said. "You are dangerous even when you sleep."

I looked around, but she and I were in the room alone. She shook her arm free of my grasp and stood full height above me.

"You slept for three days, like the dead," she said, pointing toward my arm. "We couldn't wake you, but you still protected yourself against any perceived threat. You fight even as you sleep, and every wound we nursed healed. How is this possible?"

I looked down at smooth skin where I had worn deep cuts right before I found Ft. Mose. That had been my last fight. I swung my legs out of bed, feeling stronger than I had in months. Sleep had been what my body needed to renew itself. Another lesson in immortality.

"Priest wants you to learn to fight."

"I don't...."

"He says he had a vision, and the vision told him you are strong but have much to learn. He says he was told to make you a warrior."

I looked up at her then. I had defeated all who threatened me once I left New York but at great cost. Being both strong and immortal mattered little if I only had the two. I needed greater skills. "So, he will teach me...."

She smiled. "No, I will teach you. Priest wants you to learn the arts of the Eastern world."

"What is this eastern world?"

"A far away place. What the Chinese do is like dancing."

"And how have you learned this... fighting dance?"

She smiled, but her smile only reminded me of how little I knew about her. "There aren't too many places in this world I have not been," she said.

I didn't know what to make of her words as I washed in the hip bath left near the bed. She turned her back to give me privacy but didn't leave the room.

"Why have you not told me what name to call you?" I asked as I followed her out of the Priest's room.

She gave me a measured look as if she wanted to see if I was worthy. Her smile was slow, filled with both warmth and amusement. "You, dear Neema, may call me Dagon."

CHAPTER FOURTEEN

New York City
Present Day

My heart thundered for the entire ride home, my gaze turning to the box of pictures next to me. I didn't want to think about that summer over fifty years ago. I had been one of the bright, idealistic college students traveling down to Mississippi to help black citizens register to vote, but unlike them, I had been hunting demons. The demon wars of the 1960's had brought out the worst in humanity, and that time had taken a toll on me.

The pictures in that box were a reminder of that time.

I swerved the car into the driveway of the townhouse and grabbed the box before heading up the stairs. Before I could turn my key in the lock, Raina greeted me at the door, her eyes filled with messages.

"Your detective friend is here for a visit," she said by way of greeting. "He says it isn't official, but his tone sounds pretty official."

"Did you two get the chance to catch up?" I said, handing her the box of pictures. "Look at these for me, will you?"

"Of course," she said, smiling. "He didn't seem too pleased about the reunion."

I smoothed down my shirt before nodding my head at her. The thought of seeing Jasen again made me nervous.

When I walked into the sitting room, he stood at the window overlooking the street, one hand resting in his pocket. The room was one we didn't use often, too formal for my taste and too colorless for Raina's. She called it our room for unwanted guests. Beautifully decorated with a plump brown leather sofa and a leather wingback chair with a matching ottoman, there was nothing homey about this room. Jasen must have rubbed Raina the wrong way for her to install him in this room. Alone.

I had expected to see his partner Kenneth but was glad I didn't. This visit was less formal than I expected.

"What did you do to Grant?"

"I have no idea...."

"He's terrified. Refuses to speak to us. I know it was you." He turned away from the window and walked towards me, his movements threatening. "You went back even after I warned you away."

I walked deeper into the room, keeping the sofa between us. "Why? Did he say I did something to him?"

"You already know he didn't. If he did, this visit would be official. You can't interfere with our investigation, Neema."

"You could always work with me."

He shook his head as he watched me. "I've been careful to stay away from you."

"Whatever was between us...."

He smiled. "That isn't it. This isn't about old feelings Neema. You.... you can't exist."

"I thought we already cleared that up."

"It's not that simple."

"It is simple, Jasen. Either we work together or I'll always be one step ahead of you."

He looked away from me then, and I studied his face. I hadn't allowed myself to do that yet and now a little nostalgia and a little regret crept in. Leaving our friendship had taken a toll on me too.

"All roads keep leading to dead ends," he said.

"Grant had nothing to do with Allison's death."

"How do you know?"

"I just do."

"So, what leads to Allison's death?"

I wanted Jasen to work with me. But I didn't want to work with him. "What did you find out about her inheritance?"

"The one left by her great-uncle." He shrugged. "Just some old photographs. The cousin said Allison liked to collect old photographs, postcards, drawings."

"Did you think it's worth pursuing?"

"And waste precious time?" He shook his head. "We're looking at Grant for this one."

"Maybe you shouldn't ignore the old photo—"

"I appreciate your help, Neema, but I have to do real police work, not chase ghosts."

I smiled. "How long you think I've been living Jasen? You don't think maybe I'm just as skilled at this as you are?"

"I don't want to know how long you've been living which is why I didn't and won't ask."

"If you don't want to work with me, don't want to ask questions, why did you come here tonight?"

"You disappeared one night when I was seventeen, and I always wondered what happened to you. I always thought maybe I had pushed too hard and—" He stopped and shook his head. "I promised myself that I wouldn't talk about this. I thought I was ready to see you but...."

"This is new for me too Jasen. When I leave, I'm gone for good, but I had to come back to New York. I never meant for you to see me."

"I'm visiting Allison's aunt in the morning," he said. "I'd like you to come with me."

I looked at him puzzled. Why would he want me anywhere near his case? I didn't want to ask questions just yet though. I'd rather tag along than be cut out. "If this is official...."

"She asked for you," he said. "Said she won't talk to us unless you come along. I'd love to know why."

"So, would I." I said, tilting my head.

My curiosity was still piqued long after I showed Jasen to the door and shut out his inquisitive looks. He may not have wanted to ask questions, but the questions simmered beneath the surface. I was glad to see him go though. I wanted to get back to the photographs itching for my attention.

RAINA, AS ENTERPRISING as she was, had taped most of the photographs to the basement wall, her face focused as she concentrated on each picture. I couldn't quite read her face, but I could always sense when Raina was upset.

She didn't like to remember Freedom Summer, and I didn't blame her. I hadn't wanted her to go down to Mississippi, but she had been an inquisitive nineteen-year-old college student. I couldn't do a thing to stop her and after we came back to New York, I had spent many days wishing I had been a lot more insistent.

"Look how young and idealistic they look," she said, staring into the green, blue and brown eyes of the almost all white college students who had traveled down to Mississippi. "We were all so foolish back then."

"Not foolish," I said. "Hopeful."

"I think Allison's great-uncle took most of these pictures. He must have been right there in the thick of things, but I don't remember him."

"Did you go through the pictures we have?"

"Not yet," she shook her head, but her gaze remained on the photos on the wall. "I can't seem to move from this spot. We were planning to change the world."

"And we have, Raina. We've battled many a demon who came to wreak havoc on earth. Especially down in Mississippi."

She pointed a trembling finger toward two marked photographs. "We need a clear view of his face. Liz says she's good at photo enhancement."

"Liz that you've told me so little about. I haven't seen her since the day Sheree arrived."

Raina glanced at me and smiled. "Liz plans to stop in tonight. I had Sheree email her a copy of the photos. She should have answers when she comes."

"How kind of her," I said.

Raina smiled. "I have always been inspirational."

I only nodded my head as I turned my focus to the pictures taped to my wall. Raina wasn't the only one who had difficulty facing that summer.

Freedom Summer

BY 1961, I HAD GROWN weary of the demon war. Battles had broken out across the nation but not like those in Georgia, Louisiana, Alabama, Mississippi—all the states that led the South in the murder of its Black citizens. I had only been about a century old during the Demon War of the 1860's, and even though a century may seem experienced enough to conquer demons, I had sometimes been outmatched. Retreat had often been a viable option, particularly after integration failed. Yet, as horrific as the turn of the century had been, the demon war a hundred years later almost destroyed me.

I was not at the best place in my life that summer. Earl Ray, my partner at the time and Raina's father, had his own struggles and had become more of a burden than a help. He had come back from World War II filled with an anger and resentment that grew to dangerous proportions by the time Emmett Till was murdered. The strength required to fight demons was a strength Ray just didn't have anymore. Even though I needed him in Mississippi, I took a green, idealistic Raina instead.

I had liked the enthusiasm of those college students, but their optimism was foolish. CORE and SNCC made Mississippi the ground zero of their voting rights campaign, but Mississippi had a low number of black voters for a reason. The danger and viciousness that citizens faced in trying to register only rivaled the poll taxes and literacy tests. College students may have believed they could change Mississippi, but the black and white citizens had been far outnumbered by the feeding demons. The hatred permeating the South had been like an aphrodisiac, calling demons up from hell in droves. I hadn't wanted to go down to Mississippi, hadn't wanted to walk into a war where the other side outnumbered me, but I had no other choice. One didn't just say no to angels, not without consequences.

Now, as I stood before the pictures taken by Allison's uncle, I remembered the insanity of that voting campaign. It took more than registering voters to change the minds of people, and even when the minds appeared to change, the heart was a more dangerous foe. History would not be kind to those who so violently opposed change.

"Do you ever think about James?"

I turned to look at her, recognizing the sorrow in her voice. "How could I not? He showed us the ins and outs of Meridian."

"I never told you I met with him alone when we went back down to Mississippi that summer. A few nights before he died."

"The night the demons tried to kill Ms. Hamer. I told you to stay at the house." I shook my head. "I didn't even know you had left."

"I meant to tell you, but then James and those two white boys—Andrew and Michael—went missing. I felt.... guilty."

"Men like Chaney can't be thwarted when they have a mission. He believed in the cause, believed in freedom, in voting. You wouldn't have been able to stop him."

"But I should have tried harder, Neema. Here was James, this twenty-one-year-old kid, talking about the dangers of registering. What kind of world did we live in where people died trying to vote?"

"You realize that the world is much clearer and the decisions easier to make through the perspective of a seventy-year-old, right?"

"I was mature at nineteen."

"But everything looked different in Mississippi."

"Don't forget how New York City was back in the 60's. They didn't embrace us."

"Things were still different down in Mississippi, Raina. James was from Meridian. He knew what those people were capable of."

"But he didn't think they'd kill him. He *never* thought they'd kill those white boys."

"None of us did," I said, shaking my head.

"Hate to intrude," Sheree said, poking her head partway down the stairs. "But Raina's lady friend is here. Do you want me to show her downstairs?"

I looked at Raina and frowned. "Sure, why not? Our secret lair no longer feels like a secret."

"Behave, Neema. I like her."

And I watched Raina as she went to the base of the stairs to meet her lady friend. Liz was, maybe five years younger than Raina. Her skin was dusky and her hazel eyes swept the room. Like Raina, she was thin, but her tailor-made suit was all business to Raina's more artistic style. Her features were keen with light makeup and salt and pepper hair clipped close to her head. She resembled an aging Lena Horne, which meant she was stunning.

I could imagine the sight she and Raina made: two gorgeous black women interested in each other.

"Neema," Raina said, a gleam in her eye. "I don't think I got the chance to tell you that Liz was a former captain for the NYPD."

I couldn't hide my surprise. "No, Raina. You failed to mention that fact," I inclined my head toward Liz. "I would have never pegged you for a police officer."

"Many people don't," Liz said, "which made me one hell of a detective."

Raina smiled. "Liz called in some favors for us."

"Which wasn't easy," Liz said, glancing at the wall of photographs beside us. She walked closer to them, her sharp gaze revealing her law enforcement background in a way her appearance hadn't. "Are these from Freedom Summer?"

"How could you know?" Raina said. "You were, what, thirteen?"

"But I wanted to go down to Mississippi. The picture you sent me was from Freedom Summer too, Raina." Liz pulled a file out of the bag on her shoulder. "It took a little digging, but I think I found the boy in your picture."

I GAZED AT THE FOLDER in Liz's hand, frozen at the thought of learning more about the boy in the photograph.

"His name was Chet Joseph," Liz said, handing me a picture of a smiling boy of about seventeen, younger than he had been in the picture taken during Freedom Summer.

Liz opened the folder and flipped through the papers. "He was reported missing back in 1964, but there were few clues regarding his disappearance. In an interview, his mother revealed that he wanted to be a part of the Mississippi Summer Project." She handed me the affidavit of his mother's statement. "She didn't want him to go down to Mississippi though."

"Mississippi was dangerous back then," Raina said. "No parent would have wanted their child down in Mississippi. Especially those of us from the North who didn't quite get the nuances of Southern society."

"He attended Queens College."

"Like Andrew Goodman."

"The Mississippi Summer Project recruited up here in the North," I said, reaching a hand out for the folder. Liz was reluctant, but she handed me the folder.

"You know you shouldn't even have that file," she said.

I nodded my head, distracted by the contents in the folder.

"I got this information under one condition," Liz said.

I looked up at her. "I won't tell anyone I have this information."

"That isn't it," Liz said, shaking her head. "My nephew had to get this information for me, but I had to promise you would fill him in."

"And let me guess. Your nephew is Jasen."

Raina looked a little guilty because she had known all along that she was dating Jasen's aunt. The look I gave her was not friendly.

"In fact," Raina said, slowly. "Jasen is coming by here in the morning to pick you up."

"So he knows."

"Only that you think you have information about his case," Liz said. "He doesn't know about this boy."

"Or that you're heading to Jersey," Raina said.

I wasn't feeling any kindness toward Raina at this point. "I'm not interested in taking a day trip to Jersey."

"Well, you'd better," Raina said. "Jasen is coming by in the morning so you can fill him in on a new lead. That's how you got that folder. When he gets here, you need to convince him to ride to Jersey so you can talk to Chet Joseph's family."

"And how do you propose I get that to happen?"

"You're pretty damn creative. You'll have an answer by morning."

I wasn't worried about an answer though. I worried about spending so much time in Jasen's company. What was the point of taking the time to avoid him if I now had to spend the whole day with him?

I tucked the folder under my arm and stalked off to my room, ready to read, pout and then plot against Raina.

CHAPTER FIFTEEN

We drove for a few blocks in total silence so I thought maybe Jasen would let me off the hook. That was too much to hope for though. By the time we reached Myrtle Avenue, he had struck up a conversation.

"You ever thought about confiding in me?" He said, glancing at me before turning back to the road.

I could have pretended not to understand. "Immortality is not something you confide, Jasen. You wouldn't have believed me, anyway."

"I thought you and I had developed a close friendship. You knew I had feelings for you, and I thought you felt the same."

"I did. Which mattered when I was eighteen and you were seventeen. It wouldn't have mattered twenty or thirty years later."

"For months, I asked myself what I had done to make you leave. My brothers teased me about it. I was hung up on some girl who had just vanished on me."

"Look, Jasen. I tried to tell you. It didn't work. I left. Now I'm back, and you won't get the closure you need. The sooner you realize that, the better off we will both be."

"I guess it's easier for you because you've done this multiple times."

"Maybe you're right. You can only live with a broken heart for so long," I shook my head. "Can I fill you in on Chet Joseph now? Sheree did a little research last night."

"That's the file that Aunt Liz asked for last night but was rather cryptic about. What does Chet Joseph have to do with my case?"

"You ever heard of Freedom Summer."

"If I say no would I be embarrassing myself?"

I shook my head even though I had no right to feel annoyed. He was like so many Americans who didn't understand what people had endured for America to somewhat live up to the promises laid out years ago in her Declaration and Constitution. Why would I expect Jasen to know his history?

"Freedom Summer," I began with some of the annoyance in my voice I couldn't hide. "Refers to the Mississippi Summer Project. You know of the three civil rights workers killed down in Mississippi?"

"Yes, Neema. Most people do."

I smiled because that just wasn't true. "They were a part of the Summer Project; they were three of hundreds of volunteers involved that summer."

"And let me guess, Chet Joseph was a volunteer."

"He wanted to be, and even though his mother didn't want to, she gave him permission to join the Project. Since he was under twenty-one, he needed her consent. Mississippi was terrifying back then." I took a deep breath as memories of the brutality swept over me. The last time I had gone down to Mississippi was in 1964. It was one of the few states I couldn't seem to visit even now.

"And how do you think he connects to Allison?"

"After Chet left New Jersey, his mother never saw him again. She reported him missing after a few days passed with no contact. But he's in a picture that Allison had." I reached in front of my chair and pulled an envelope from my bag. "I know you didn't think much of the pictures that Allison had, but I think they connect to her case." I pulled out the picture of smiling black and white faces. Chet's face had been circled.

"You think this young man went down to Mississippi?"

"I'm not sure, but I think he volunteered for the Mississippi Freedom Project. If he disappeared down in Mississippi, he wouldn't have been the only black man."

"Growing up, I remember hearing the story of Emmett Till," Jasen said, glancing at me as we drove out of the Holland Tunnel. "But I guess they weren't just stories to you. You were there."

I gazed out of the window, the sunlight much too bright for the memories tumbling around in my head.

THE SUMMER OF 1964 was tough for both me and Raina. Earl Ray, Raina's father, had come back from World War II a different man. I had seen the signs. He was twenty-years-old, still laughed and joked but his laughter had rung just a little too loud. His joking had seemed just a little too forced, but I was focused on my problems, my life. I had found traces of the Vodou, and I was obsessed with finding her. My obsession grew stronger the more she eluded me. Raina was born in 1945 and other children soon followed, but I didn't pay close attention to Ray. He worked by my side almost every day until one day he stopped working. The country was in an uproar. The boycott down in Montgomery, the murder of Emmett Till. I dragged Ray through the South with me, slaughtering demons he couldn't see.

He saw the despair in black faces though, families destroyed as I fought to break the hold the demons held in the Southern states. Did demons roam places like New York and Pennsylvania? Yes. But the South proved to be a breeding ground for hungry, angry demons. I hunted them without mercy, angry that the Vodou eluded me, angry that the demons had risen from hell in droves. I hunted them with a single vision, and all the while, Ray cracked under our burdens. Maybe before the war he would have been strong enough, but after the war, after the Jewish concentration camps, he struggled under the weight of a hellish America.

I didn't realize how much he relied on Raina until 1964. Raina came home from Howard, and Earl Ray said he couldn't travel with me anymore. When I looked at him, I saw what Alabama and Georgia and Mississippi and Louisiana had done to him. I wanted to stay by Ray's side like he had stayed by mine, but Raina had become determined to go down to Mississippi. I couldn't let her go alone, and Ray didn't want her to go alone.

Whenever thoughts of Mississippi slip through my defenses, I think of how hard it is to tell of the everyday atrocities that blacks faced down there. While the white folks sat in their plantations and lamented about losing the War, black folks labored in cotton fields like the slaves America claimed they no longer were. They lived in broken down shacks, averted their eyes lest they be considered uppity, stepped off sidewalks to let white folks pass them by, and Mississippi just kept on. Living that life on the few occasions I traveled down to Mississippi always took a toll on me. I struggled to hold my tongue as hatred spewed from the lips of poor white boys and rich Southern belles. My task was to destroy demons, but the humans and demons of Mississippi had become so intertwined that I struggled to keep them separate in my mind. I should have noticed when Ray faltered, and as much as I didn't want Raina in Mississippi, I could do nothing but follow her there.

When we arrived in Oxford, Ohio, I had spent the whole trip trying to talk Raina out of going down to Mississippi. How do you explain to a child of New York, a student at Howard University, what it would be like down in Mississippi? Mississippi had defied every federal law, denied blacks of every right the Courts had promised them. Mississippians murdered their black citizens under the sun and in the cover of darkness. I couldn't press upon this eager young woman that down in the South, the states didn't recognize federal law. They took the law into their own hands and called it states' rights. Black people were beaten into submission by domestic terrorists just as evil as those labeled international terrorists decades later. It wouldn't have mattered that Raina was a woman. The only thing that mattered was that Mississippi maintained control over her "Negroes", and any body who came in trying to change the status quo would be a target.

I will always believe Mississippi changed Raina too, that it strengthened her. She headed down to Mississippi a teenaged girl but came back with the steel in her spine that made her irreplaceable.

"We're almost there," Jasen said.

When I glanced at him, I recognized his patience as I became lost in my memories. He had been like that as a young man too. Sensitive to the need for silence.

"His mother passed away about fifteen years ago," I said, clearing my throat. "But his sister is still alive. The place where we're heading is her last known address."

We were in East Orange, close to Chet's childhood home in Newark, New Jersey. We stopped in front of a modest house with a well-kept garden. I was reluctant to get out of the SUV and ring the doorbell, but I couldn't let my memories impede solving Allison's murder.

"You know you aren't alone," Jasen said, touching my arm.

I glanced at him and shook my head. "Yeah, I know, but these visits are never easy." I slid out of the truck and followed him to the front door. We looked everywhere but at each other as we waited for someone to open the door.

A boy of about seventeen came to the door, annoyance on his face as he peered at us through the screen. "Can I help you?" he asked, polite but short.

"We're looking for Ernestine Jackson, formerly Joseph. Is this her home?" Jasen said, flashing his badge.

The boy gave us an alarmed look before turning away from the door, leaving it open a crack. When the door widened again, an older woman at in her seventies stood at the door. She had removed one gardening glove from her hand and tugged at the other. "May I help you?" she said, one brow raised as she took in first Jasen and then me.

Her skin was the same pecan tan as her brother but a little weathered with age. Of average height, her shoulders stooped and her thick, gray hair was pulled into a bun at the back of her head. A gardening hat was tucked beneath her arm. She shared the same almond-shaped light brown eyes as her brother, a broad nose and a wide mouth with full lips. The resemblance was like that of twins. If Chet had lived, it wasn't difficult to imagine that he would have been the masculine version of the woman before us.

"My name is Jasen Davis," Jasen said, showing his badge. "This is Neema. We wanted to ask you a few questions about your brother Chet."

Her gaze sharpened, and she placed one shaky hand on the knob of the screen door. "No one has asked about Chet in decades," she said, pushing the door open. "And the police have never cared." She stepped aside to allow us in, and Jasen waved me forward. "Before Momma died, the police would ask occasional questions to pacify her, keep her from making a trip down to the precinct. I didn't continue the trips after she died cause I knew what Mama refused to acknowledge. Chet died long time ago."

"What do you remember about that time?" Jasen said. "What did Chet tell you?"

"I was out back working in the garden," she said, leading us through the living room. "How about we go out back to have this conversation?" She led us to a beautiful porch off the kitchen. The table tucked into one corner overlooked a well-kept, perhaps even award-winning garden. She was a skilled horticulturist. A swing on the other side of the porch had bright cushions and pillows.

"Lemonade, tea or," she glanced at Jasen "something stronger."

"Tea would be great," Jasen said, pulling out a chair that allowed him to watch both the garden and the door. He pointed me to a chair near him and even though I hesitated for a moment, I sat down.

"Did I tell you that my oldest son just turned 21?" he said when the porch screen closed gently after Ernestine stepped back inside. He watched the door as he spoke.

"We have yet to discuss either your life or mine over the last 30 years."

"My oldest son is older than you."

"Older than I appear to be, you mean," I said, annoyed. "And what's your point?"

"This tea is my special recipe," Ernestine said, coming outside with a tray, a glass pitcher of tea and three tall glasses filled with ice. She had even added an assortment of bite size sweets. Raina would have arranged a tray like this for guests. Younger generations didn't entertain like this anymore.

"That time was tough for us," she said, sitting down. "Mama and her family moved to Jersey in the 1930's just so they could escape Mississippi. Mama didn't expect us to go back."

"So how did Chet convince her to give him permission to go?" I asked, popping a shortbread cookie in my mouth. I had to fight the desire to close my eyes and hum, the cookie was that delicious.

"He wore her down. Before that summer, SNCC had put out ads in the *Harper's Weekly* and the *New York Times*. Dick Gregory had gone down to Mississippi to bring them food and supplies when the white folks thought to starve them out of wanting change. So many eyes were on Mississippi but Mama and her brothers and sisters paid extra close attention since they still had kinfolks down in Mississippi."

"Is that why your brother wanted to head down there?"

"Oh no. Chet was in college learning all about SNCC. He liked Dr. King and even Malcolm X, but the thought of those college students entering Mississippi was something Chet admired more. Not even King and his SCLC were venturing into Mississippi. Then when James Baldwin talked about Mississippi that sealed the deal for Chet. James Baldwin was his favorite writer."

"Did Chet go down to Oxford for the training?"

Ernestine nodded her head. "He headed there for the June 14th training. Chet had worn Mama down with his relentless requests for permission. and he wouldn't give up. I had never seen Chet so determined. I think that's why Mama relented. He didn't change her mind. He showed a commitment we had never seen before."

"Did he drive alone?"

She smiled. "Chet didn't drive. He was driving down with some friends. The police and the FBI questioned them, but his friends don't know what happened to Chet after they arrived in Mississippi." Ernestine shook her head and reached for a tart on the tray. Her movements were absent, like she was just keeping occupied. "It was a long time ago, but I've never been able to forget Mama's fear. Back then, black men often disappeared without a trace. Black folks only traveled during the day cause the Klan ruled the night. When Mama was a little girl, her grandfather disappeared one night. He had always been one of the few black men who talked about rights and freedom. It wasn't until one of her brothers disappeared, though, that Mama's family packed up and left Mississippi.

"The thought of Chet going down there took a toll on her. She tried to impress upon him the dangers of Mississippi. She reminded him of Emmett Till. That most times the Klan was the law. That two men in her family had vanished. Mississippi liked her blacks destitute, uneducated and terrified. Why would Chet want to go down there? But Chet was determined to help. While the Civil Rights Movement had come to Georgia and Alabama and Florida, it had yet to penetrate Mississippi. Only CORE and SNCC were down in Mississippi, and they were recruiting college students." She shook her head. "The young and the foolish."

"I've always thought SNCC workers courageous for going down to Mississippi," I said. "I understand your mother's fear, but nothing was changing in Mississippi. CORE was doing work down there, but nobody was paying attention. SNCC got the rest of America to pay attention to Mississippi."

"But our children didn't have to die for it."

"You think Chet died down in Mississippi?" Jasen jumped in.

"The only reason people paid attention to the death of James Chaney was because he was killed with two white boys. If Chaney had died by himself, the world would have never cared. I think Chet died down in Mississippi that summer, and no one cared."

"But SNCC had a system for the volunteers. If any didn't return at a certain time or call in, volunteers would call jails. They phoned into main offices, contacted their police, their congressmen." I frowned. "If Chet were a SNCC volunteer, he couldn't have disappeared without an alarm being sounded."

"It never made sense to us either," Ernestine said, standing. "I want you to read some of the letters Chet wrote to us. He only wrote a few before he disappeared."

"SNCC may have had a bunch of college volunteers, Jasen," I said as soon as the door closed. "But SNCC workers were organized. There is no way a volunteer could become lost, and an alarm wasn't sounded. When Chaney and the others disappeared, they called around that same night. Black Mississippians might have vanished but not SNCC workers."

"What are you suggesting?" Jasen said.

"That something isn't adding up, and I can't be the first person who noticed. No way SNCC would have let Chet go missing."

"Please be careful with these," Ernestine said, coming back outside. "This is all I have left of Chet from that summer."

She placed a photo box in front of us and took the lid off. Inside were packets of letters tied together with a ribbon and neat stacks of photos. I took the letters while Jasen reached for the photographs.

"Chet was adamant about going down to Mississippi," Ernestine said. "So many young people were. But those that didn't live down South, didn't understand how to survive there. And as dangerous as the South was, no where was like Mississippi. Even Dr. King and his people thought Mississippi was too deadly to crack. Especially after Beckwith murdered Medgar Evers on his own doorstep and got away with it. Some Mississippians were gunning down black men like animals. I don't think kids like Chet understood what that meant. Just because they weren't from Mississippi didn't mean they were safe."

"But he wanted to go anyway," Jasen said.

Ernestine nodded her head. "There was no deterring him. He was determined to go down to Mississippi no matter the consequences. It was about them voting, yes, but Chet hated how black men were being killed down there. He was only ten when Emmett Till died, but I remember how much Till's death devastated him. Chet was like that, you know. This was personal on a level that my older brother and I couldn't understand. Mama understood though, and as much as she didn't want Chet to go down to Mississippi, she still gave him permission. But she never forgave herself for letting him go."

It had been like that for many parents who wanted to protect their idealistic children but didn't want to crush their desire to create change. Earl Ray had let Raina go, even made me promise to protect her. But only because he could no longer be trusted at my side. He had become a liability.

With unsteady hands, I reached for the packet of letters.

"THERE AREN'T MANY," Ernestine said as I untied the ribbon. "He wrote for a few weeks after he left, and when the letters stopped coming, we knew something was wrong."

"Can you retrace Chet's steps?" I said, unfolding a brief, handwritten note I withdrew from the envelope on top.

"The first group entering Mississippi was to report to Ohio by June 14th. Since Chet was driving to Ohio with a friend, they left on the 12th. He was home for the summer so he left from here. I remember how Mama was reluctant and scared for him to leave, but she packed up a basket full of food for him.

"Chet was always a playful, happy boy and he would tease Mama in ways that my older brother and I never felt comfortable doing. The last image I have of him is of the day he left. As Mama packed his basket, he kept teasing her, tried to tickle her, kept kissing her on the cheek until he made her laugh as she swatted him away. As strong as Mama felt about Chet not going down to Mississippi, something felt good, felt right about him leaving. He was the baby, but he was making the choice of a man."

Ernestine shook her head and reached for a picture in the box. She looked at it before she handed us a black and white photo of a woman and two men. She pointed at the man to the right of the young woman. "That's me in the center," she said, smiling. "I was a lot younger and a lot more hopeful then. That's my other brother Leonard and my younger brother Chet." She tapped the young man to the left.

I could see the boy she had described in his laughing eyes. In the picture, he was about fourteen years old and full of life. So optimistic that I couldn't imagine him down in the darkness of 1960's Mississippi. It would have changed him.

"Why do you think he made it down to Mississippi?"

"The last letter he sent us," she flipped through the small stack before she pulled a letter from the bottom. "He sent it the day after the Mississippi Project started. The first group headed down on June 21st, and the last letter we received from Chet was dated on the next day. By that time Chaney, Schwerner and Goodman were already missing. No one would notice a little black boy missing when those two young white men had gone missing the first day of the project. That summer, they pulled black men out of the river every week in Mississippi. Plenty of women were crying for husbands and brothers who just disappeared. Chet was just one more boy who disappeared."

I didn't want to insist again that the CORE and SNCC systems down in Mississippi would have never let her brother go missing without that story getting in the news somehow. Volunteers always had to report in by a specific time whenever they left their headquarters. SNCC workers were on the phone calling jails within an hour if any volunteer missed a report-in time. I couldn't see how this lone boy wouldn't have garnered the same treatment that every volunteer received. Chaney, Schwerner and Goodman disappeared on the first day of the Mississippi Project, so every volunteer was vigilant when they crossed the Mississippi border. Ernestine, though, had spent fifty-one years convinced that SNCC had let her brother die. Me challenging her beliefs was not about to change her mind. She wouldn't believe any other explanation.

Something else had happened to Chet after he left for Mississippi, and Allison Stevens had been trying to figure out what that was. Her interest, though, couldn't have been as simple as curiosity.

I picked up one of Chet's letters and studied it. "Who was the friend Chet went to Ohio with?"

"Boy named Benjamin. One of Chet's friends from New York. Benjamin was the one who alerted us when Chet went missing. I doubt anyone would have ever told us. I remember being so angry that summer. Angry at those SNCC students who arranged for our children to go down into the South and get killed. Black folks up here just didn't understand the South. They didn't know how to survive, how to keep their head down, how to stop from staring white folks in the eyes. Chet would have never understood the South, and when he got down there, somebody killed him."

"We found a new picture of Chet," Jasen said, reaching for the white envelope he had placed on the table. He pulled out the picture I had given him from Allison's collection and handed the picture to Ernestine. "We found this picture taken when he was down in Mississippi."

Ernestine took the picture from Jasen with shaky hands and stared at it for so long I wondered what she saw that we hadn't seen.

"Chet had this shirt on the day he left," Ernestine said. "Mama made this shirt for him for his birthday just a few months earlier. He liked to say the shirt gave him luck, so he wanted to wear the shirt when he headed to Ohio. It was his favorite shirt."

"He wore the shirt in Mississippi too," I said.

Ernestine shook her head. "Except that photo wasn't taken in Mississippi."

I sat up straighter, her words roaring in my head. Since the picture had been in the stack of photos that Allison had inherited from her uncle, I had assumed that the picture was taken down in Mississippi.

"I don't understand," Jasen said, reaching for the photo. "This picture was among several photos taken during Freedom Summer. We assumed that it was taken down in Mississippi."

Ernestine shook her head. "The boy standing next to Chet was the one who drove to Ohio with him. They were good friends or at least as good as they could be. Although the North wasn't as dangerous as the South, people up here had their own prejudices about a white boy and a black boy being friends. But that's not what I'm referring to." She pointed to a young white girl who stood behind Chet. The girl's reluctance to be photographed was clear.

"I didn't know the girl well," Ernestine said. "But she was a neighbor of Chet's friend, I think. Chet said she was always underfoot and wanted to join the Mississippi Project, but she was much too young. Maybe she was thirteen or fourteen when this picture was taken."

I drew the picture closer. I had been so focused on Chet that I hadn't looked at the young man standing next to him nor the girl standing in the background. Chet's shoulder shielded her face, but her dark coloring was striking. Allison had singled out Chet, but I was curious about the girl in the background. The 1960's had been a time when little white girls stayed far away from little black boys. I found it intriguing that she stood in the picture so close to the two men. And how she watched Chet was.... disturbing.

"Chet's friend died in a car accident about twenty years ago," Ernestine said, "but maybe you can talk to his family. They still live in New York, down in Long Island." She sat back. "The boy's last name was Goldstein if I remember right. His family owned a business, real estate, out in Long Island. Maybe you can find out more about the girl in the photo."

"Do you mind if I take pictures of these letters?" I asked, taking out my phone.

She pushed the letters toward me, and I scanned them as with my cell phone. I wanted to spend time with these letters. Study them. Learn who Chet Joseph had been and, perhaps, discover why Allison had drawn a neat pink circle around his face.

The only reason I had connected this photo with Mississippi was because of Allison's uncle, but I needed to know more about the other two people in the photograph. Allison, for whatever reason, wanted to know more about Chet. Maybe she had already discovered the identity of the girl in the photo.

Lost in thought on the ride home, I tried to move the pieces around in my head and determine how they all connected. Jasen, also quiet, didn't engage me in conversation, and I knew he was in detective mode. Long Island, for both of us, was next on the list.

CHAPTER SIXTEEN

When I arrived home, I found Baal's calling card in my bedroom. He liked to leave me little reminders of my time in slavery to let me know he wanted to speak with me. He didn't do it often, but he had left these "notes" a few times over the last two centuries. The awl he left me was one I remembered. My master had carried one like it. Frowning with annoyance, I knew he left this souvenir to remind me of my *specific* enslavement. Baal always knew just how to anger me. Walking my bike out of the garage, I hopped on and headed down to the African Burial Ground. The Burial Ground was the only place that Baal would meet me. He thought it unnerved me, but I was learning to appreciate the burying ground. They may have built lower Manhattan over the graves of African women, men and children, but at least we had once had a place to celebrate our homegoing services. We were the foundation of New York City, one of the most intriguing US cities. I would accept his attempts at cruelty, as unsuccessful as they were.

I sped my bike through the streets, crossing the Williamsburg Bridge into the city. When I reached the burial ground, the afternoon sun still beat overhead. Considering that Baal preferred night time meetings, I was rather surprised that he would summon me during the day. I left my bike in the back of the memorial and entered the other realm through the obelisk. Baal sat in a chair awaiting my arrival. He had propped his feet on an ottoman and watched the entryway. He wanted to appear relaxed, but he wasn't. His concern had intensified.

He unfolded his lanky frame and stood before me. The room's dullness made his orange ponytail even brighter. He had pulled his hair high atop his head and its length swung behind him when he moved.

"I'm working to find the girl's killer," I said.

"In the meantime, our world is in chaos."

"It takes time Baal."

"Time we don't have, Neema. A group of demons attacked one of the seven princes. We cannot allow another mutiny."

"Are we one less prince?"

"Don't sound so eager. You don't want to imagine what would happen if one of the seven dies. Demons on earth are a dangerous lot. Without us, they would go a little ....wild."

"And they don't already? They seem to be rather excited. At least, the ones who have faced me head on."

"Which you should find odd. Every demon knows to be wary of you."

"So why did you call me here?'

He stared at me before he stepped forward and placed an object in my hand. It was an arrow head. I sniffed it, recognizing the smell of holy water. Now this was interesting. How would a demon get an arrowhead formed with holy water? The arrowhead had a hollow spot in the center which meant the holy water had been placed inside the hollow.

Someone had wanted the demon prince to feel excruciating pain. Although the princes possessed more powerful than other demons, they weren't invincible. I took the arrowhead and slid it into the pocket of my jeans, eager to know its origin.

"What do you expect me to do with this arrowhead?"

"That was pulled from the body of Beelzebub."

I couldn't control my smile. Beelzebub had been my nemesis often: derailing slave rebellions in the 1700's, helping to destroy black families in the 1800's, fanning segregation in the twentieth century. He liked pain, and he loved to turn people against each other. I had hated those moments when the culprit proved to be Beelzebub. I knew whatever came my way would end with broken lives. I found it fitting he knew the sting of mortality. An arrowhead like the one in my pocket embedded itself in the body of its victim. And it would burn in a way that was almost impossible to escape.

All the suffering that Beelzebub had caused made it more difficult for me to sympathize with him. "Will he live?" I said.

Baal nodded. "Even though you may wish otherwise, Beelzebub will live. But I must know who made this arrow."

"You don't need me to make that discovery, Baal. You can find out on your own. The question is, why *do* you need me?" I tilted my head so I could study him. "You're trying to keep this mutiny from getting out, aren't you?"

Baal couldn't hide his annoyance with me. He needed my help, but he didn't want to deal with my curiosity. "Abaddon convinced us to ask for your help."

I drew in my breath. I had never had the pleasure of dealing with Abaddon but I had heard demons speak of her with an undeniable fear. She was the only demon strong enough to guard the abyss. Not the most powerful, just the most ruthless. I did not like that she knew me by name, but it was foolish of me not to realize she would. How many demons had begged me not to send them into the abyss?

"You seem to be missing a rather important point, Neema," he said, his eyes watching for my reaction, but I didn't know what reaction he desired. "You are still young, but you have walked the earth for almost three centuries. How many men, or women, can forge weapons from holy water? Who has made weapons this powerful?"

I could feel the sword sing with the knowledge of his words. The heat against my back wasn't painful, but it reminded me of just how powerful the sword at my back was. "I have only known of one man," I said. "Priest."

"Until now," Baal said.

"Until now." I pressed a hand against the pocket that held the arrowhead. "You think Priest trained another."

"I think I would like for you to find out."

"Because if another can forge weapons out of holy water, that would be a danger to you."

Baal smiled. "I would think you would like to discover whatever you can about your Priest. Every story about him you chased over the years has proven false, has it not?"

My face tightened, and I stepped back from him. "I will find out what I can," I said, turning away.

"There was also a ...." Baal hesitated. "A small rip in the abyss and a few demons might have escaped."

I turned back to face him, my eyes growing wide. "Did Legion escape hell?"

Baal looked at me, but he refused to answer. He, instead, thought to turn that charming smile on me, but I was not weak enough to be charmed by a demon. "You have always liked to assume the worst, Demon Hunter."

"I am sure I have made my feelings clear on that name. If there is nothing else then I should like to return home. Unless you have other business worth my while."

Baal gazed at me, his hatred burning bright between us. Rafael's interference in our first meeting was one he had never forgotten. I had been much weaker then, much easier to kill.

"In the chaos of the... uprising," he said, "A soulcatcher might have gone missing."

My eyes widened, and I did a cough laugh. "What the hell? You lost a soulcatcher? How many are there? Four?"

Baal cleared his throat. "You can sense our urgency. The soulcatcher can be a powerful weapon."

Which I knew well. I couldn't stop my hand from rubbing at the remembered pain in my right leg. It was a weapon I wanted to avoid at all cost. I had last seen two and been shot by one by the demon Alastor at Allison's wake. I didn't like the weapon being in the hands of any demon walking this earth.

"When did you notice it missing?" I said.

"Tonight. After the attack on Beelzebub. It is our most powerful weapon so we keep it guarded. You met one guard. You sent him back to earth when you first returned to New York."

While that explained how Alastor had access to the soul-catcher, it didn't explain why he had them. I wasn't egotistical enough to think he had them for me. "He caused two suicides down in Louisiana. I had to send him back."

"Well, you might have waited until he had gotten more information about the missing soulcatchers. But you have always been one to strike first."

"So now you need me to track down the soulcatcher?"

"I'm sure that whoever is behind this mutiny also has the soulcatcher." Baal smiled. "What better way to neutralize the Demon Hunter?"

"A soulcatcher can't stop me, Baal."

"But it can slow you down, Neema. And that might be just enough."

I didn't want to think about Baal's words on the drive home, but I worried about the soulcatcher more than the lesser demons. The soulcatcher worked on humans the same way as my iron manacles worked on demons. I had been overpowered by one a century ago and I never, ever wanted to repeat that experience. I had to find that soulcatcher, and I had to find Baal's rogue demon now.

WHEN I REACHED HOME, Jasen who should have been long gone was in my basement with Raina and his aunt Liz. They had spread out photographs and articles on the wall like they were in a police precinct. While I had been meeting with Baal, they had been busy trying to draw connections between Allison's death and Chet Joseph's disappearance. I didn't mind the extra help, and neither, based on her glowing face and laughter, did Raina. But I minded Jasen's presence in my home. It was nothing perverted. He was too old, too married, and my feelings for him were more like moments of nostalgia. But I didn't like being reminded of our long-ago friendship.

"Jasen was just telling us that the two of you are driving to Long Island tomorrow," Liz said as I came down the basement stairs.

"You shot out of here so fast," Raina said. "We didn't have time to talk about your visit to Chet's family. Jasen filled us in though."

I wrinkled my nose at her. "Baal left me a message," I said, noting the slight way she stiffened when I said his name. I knew that would get her attention. "You know how he gets if I leave him waiting."

"What did he want?" Raina asked, mindful of Jasen and Liz standing nearby.

"To warn me that a soulcatcher has gone missing." Although he had been just a little late with the warning.

"I found out a little about Chet's friend," Jasen said, turning from the photographs on the wall. "We're heading to Woodbury in the morning to talk to his family. The parents are no longer alive, but a younger brother still lives there. He said he would tell us everything he remembers."

"What I don't understand," Liz said. "Is how this boy Chet disappeared? If SNCC was as meticulous about its volunteers as you guys say, then how could this young man vanish on the way to Mississippi?"

"It seems like you guys are focusing more on Chet Joseph than Allison."

"We think the two deaths are related somehow."

Jasen's phone rang then, and he glanced at it before answering the phone and rushing up the stairs. I figured that it was either Kenneth or his wife, and I found myself curious about the latter. He had said nothing about his wife, and I was interested in the woman who had married Jasen. Or more like the woman that Jasen had married.

I wandered away from the others, slinking into my little corner of the room. I hadn't wanted Raina to notice, but she had spent the last fifty years of her life attuned to my every move. She would see me trying to escape.

"Maybe his presence in your life won't be such a bad thing, Neema," Raina said, handing me a Simply Ice.

"I'm adjusting to you leaving me Raina. You don't have to keep throwing people my way."

She smiled. "I don't know if I'm leaving you so much as changing roles," she gave Liz a tender look. "I've never seen her look so vibrant. She loves this line of work. She's been retired for several years now, but the love of a mystery is in her skin."

"Then I don't need..."

"Don't even think it," she said, pointing the tip of her bottled water toward me. "I'm 70 years old. Flipping off bikes and shooting arrows, while still plausible, is no longer smart. I don't have the reflexes I had in my younger days."

"Jasen isn't a young buck anymore either."

"But he can help you until I get Sheree trained. You can use him for now, Neema. Just to watch your back."

"If you remember that my home is your home, Raina."

She glanced around the basement. "I rather like our brownstone. They don't make buildings like this anymore. I'll stay Neema, but I can no longer follow you."

I nodded my head and took a sip of my drink, refusing to turn my head at the sound of Jasen's footsteps on the basement stairs. I would use him to solve Chet's and Allison's murders, but I wouldn't use him one minute longer.

CHAPTER SEVENTEEN

Our ride to Long Island was even quieter than our ride to Jersey. Jasen had left close to midnight and then returned almost nine the next morning. By that time, I resigned myself to having Raina's new love interest underfoot which also translated to continued contact with Jasen. I didn't know how to deal with an acquaintance, well a friend, thirty years later. The only folks I had kept in contact with throughout multiple decades were all related to Raina.

The home we stopped in front of was one of those towering homes that defined New York. It stretched three stories high and, I was sure, had a basement. The air around the house was unnaturally still and the block rather quiet for the time of day. I interpreted these as signs and withdrew my daggers. While my sword was strapped to my back, it was more difficult to maneuver a sword and avoid tripping over furniture at the same time.

The house was earth tone, blending in with the sedate colored houses that lined the block. Its bay windows watched us, as if there were something waiting in the house we should avoid.

Jasen glanced at the daggers in my hands and the seriousness of my face. "You expecting trouble?" he said, withdrawing his gun as he took the first step.

I placed my hand on his elbow. "Not the kind that a gun can fight."

Several steps led to a porch that jutted from a section of the house. A garage sat on one side, and a wide window sat on the other. Through a slit in the curtain, I could see a window seat and the corner of a book.

"Perhaps you should wait in the car." I said, when we reached the front door.

Jasen shook his head. "I've been a cop for a long time, Neema. I am not hiding behind you."

"Making sure you're safe is not hiding, Jasen."

Jasen ignored me, his hand wiggling the doorknob which was locked. He rapped on the door twice, but there was no answer.

"Do you feel it?" I said.

He looked at me puzzled before shaking his head. "I don't... I don't feel anything."

"But you do," I said. "That's why you're so tense. You can feel them."

"That's ridiculous. I don't—"

I put a finger to my lips and then reached for the knob. Twisting it toward Jasen, I felt the knob pop before it broke. When I pushed at the door, however, the dead bolt was still locked. I did nothing as fancy as kicking the door in. Besides the heavy oak would have given my leg a beating. Instead, I turned the knob and pushed at the door just enough to break the deadbolt.

"I guess that's your superhuman strength," Jasen said, looking at the broken door knob. "I'm assuming you had it back when we were dating."

"We never dated," I said. "And my strength has been like this for over two centuries. A side effect of my curse."

"I'm sure that superhuman strength is not a side effect," Jasen said, moving to enter the house before me.

Even though part of me wanted to leap in front of him, I also recognized that his ego dictated that he leads while I follow. I had to hope that nothing dangerous awaited us on the other side.

When I walked into the house, I realized that we had just entered a shitload of trouble. Demons had taken over this house.

The colors of the house, the vibrancy had muted. Every item inside from the floors to the walls had taken on a dull hue, like the entire house had faded from too many washings. The house had taken on the grays and browns of the demon realm, and I realized why the air had been so still and the street so quiet. While the house had seemed as if it still sat there on the street, the demon presence here had become so strong that it had sucked the house into the demon realm. This house, for lack of a better word, was possessed.

JASEN STOPPED AT THE bottom of the stairs and turned to glance first at the front door then at the open doorway that led to the living room.

"Neema!" he called out, his eyes searching for me in the gloom of the house.

I stood right beside him, but he couldn't see me. He still stood in the natural realm while whatever demon that had taken over this house was strong enough to have sucked me into the demon world. Jasen turned back toward the front door, but the door was sealed shut. For him, this house would seem haunted. Humans often mistook demon-possessed houses as haunted, but some parts of our world could fall so firmly under demon control they slipped into the darkness. Whatever had taken over this house had gotten a firm grip.

I slid my daggers back into their sheaths. They would be handy, but I needed a swifter weapon. I withdrew my sword, the blade ready to behead the first demon I saw. Jasen started downstairs first, walking through a living room at the front of the house, and I followed him. The unnatural stillness that had been present outside of the house was even creepier inside, and I felt a slight chill. I followed him into the kitchen and noted as he did, a tray of crackers on the counter. A plastic container of hummus sat next to the tray and a knife dipped inside as if someone had been preparing a snack. A pitcher of tea sat nearby, water condensed on the outside as it lost its coolness. The glass of ice had only been half-filled with tea.

Jasen touched the side of the pitcher which was still cool to the touch. Since the demon realm dulled human senses, I could only read Jasen's reactions as a gauge. I followed him from the kitchen into another sitting room, this one larger with a piano in one corner. The furniture in this room was more formal with French doors on the opposite side of the room. The doors led back to the foyer and I stood at the base of the stairs again, gazing at a front door that had fused with the frame.

"What the hell-" Jasen said, one hand touching the fused wood where the door frame should have been. He shook his head, annoyance on his face. "I don't know where you went off to Neema, but there will be hell to pay when I find you."

I followed him up the stairs knowing he would never find me. At least not without my help. We took the stairs, Jasen's gun leading us. I gripped my sword with both hands, ready too. No quarter. When we reached the landing, we turned left, heading down a rather lengthy hallway before we reached the first room. This, I knew, was the work of the damn demons. They sometimes distorted reality in ways that played with the human psyche. Jasen was no exception as he struggled to make sense of this impossibly long hallway.

He placed his hand on the doorknob, and I stood on his heels. When he opened the door, a freaking demon convention stood before us. Demons of all shades lounged across the bed and stretched across the floors. Demons—whether Sin demons, Death demons, Whisperers, Shape shifters or Hijackers—stayed with their own kind. There was a clear demon hierarchy. Even I had only met three of the seven princes. Demons didn't mingle with each other but in this room, Sin demons, Death demons and maybe even Shape shifters slithered together like one happy family. That spoke trouble for us.

They stopped moving, stopped talking, stopped everything and turned their heads toward us as one. Jasen couldn't see them, but I could see the fear in his eyes when he sensed that something was wrong.

"The Demon Hunter," one of them hissed, and I stepped forward with my outstretched blade. Every demon knew when it was in the same room with the sword the Exorcism.

They recoiled, but not with the same fear I often inspired in demons. They all—wrath, death, greed—seemed less afraid. And these were the lesser of the demons, less of a challenge.

"Times are a-changing, Hunter," one of them growled, before they all lunged toward me in some crazy choreographed move. I grabbed Jasen by the elbow and pushed him from the room, shutting the door on his look of shock and fear. He, who couldn't see anything happening around him, would be convinced that the house was haunted.

The demons charged me, surprising me with their attack. I was used to demons like these doing everything they could to avoid me. I was not used to them attacking me. At least not since I taught them to fear me. Gripping my sword, I was swift, the blade slicing through demons like paper. They almost ran into my blade. One fell onto the sword and as it sliced through its body, another attacked me from the side, forcing me to use my feet and my sword. I spun first right and then left, kicked with both feet, sliced with my sword before I realized that all of this, the demons, were just a diversion. A freaking diversion I had fallen for. Angry, I beheaded three in a row with lightening speed before I threw the door open and jumped into the hallway. Slamming the door shut behind me, I wasn't surprised to see that Jasen was gone.

Sword dripping with the dark blood of demons, I held the blade out to the side as I stalked down the hallway. My black New Edition t-shirt and soft blue jeans were no longer pristine. I had been splashed with the disgusting, putrid innards of dead demons and was glad I walked with proof of their demise. I hated when they tricked me.

THE HALLWAY ENDED ABRUPTLY, the smooth, unadorned wall reminding me I had lost Jasen, but I had learned much dealing with Baal over the last century and a half. Some walls were doors that humans couldn't see. Grim, I stepped through the wall and into a dungeon. The dungeon felt like prisons of long ago: Locked dungeons without light or hope. Jasen crouched against one side, chained to the floor like an animal. The shackles on his feet and manacle on his neck were those many slaves had known all too well. He wouldn't be able to stand, and he wouldn't be able to escape.

He looked at me, able to see me now, his eyes full of anger and despair. Time moved different in the demon world. I might have been in that room of demons for minutes, but he had been locked in here for weeks or even years. He looked as if he had taken a hell of a beating, with a swollen left eye and a split lip. Blood stained the tattered rags of his clothes, and he looked filthy. Even his hair had grown into a short Afro and he sported a full beard and mustache. His hair had matted and locked together. By the looks of him, I had been gone for months.

"I couldn't find you," he said, his voice hoarse, "But they said you would come for me."

"And I did," I said, my voice sharp. "This isn't real Jasen," I said, looking around. "None of this is real. The demons have a knack of screwing with the human mind. When they take over a house, they do everything in their power to distort reality."

He shook his head, but I knelt before him, my hand gripping his chin. "This isn't real Jasen. None of this is real. You have got to snap out of it."

His breathing slowed as he stared at me. "I think this house is haunted."

"It isn't," I said, "it's possessed. And that means something important happened here. You've got to snap out of it Jasen so we can find out what's going on."

"It feels real, Neema."

"I know. That's what makes the demons so damn good at this. They can make anything seem real. This is not real though, Jasen."

"None of this is real," he repeated.

"Not a single thing," I said, which was true. In part.

He nodded his head once and the room around us vanished. We sat on the floor of the living room we had first entered when we searched the house. We were sandwiched between a sofa and an end table. The lamp on the end table had toppled to the floor. Jasen looked about surprised, then looked down at his hands. The manacles and shackles had vanished. All his bruising, the blood, the wounds had vanished. He still wore the blue polo shirt and jeans he had worn this morning. With a trembling hand, he touched his bald head and the neat goatee he had sported upon entering this house. In, maybe just a few minutes of time, Jasen had faced horrors he wouldn't soon forget.

"What just happened, Neema?" he said, looking at the back of his hands.

"Well that was fun," a voice said above us.

I looked up to see Alastor standing over us, the soul-catcher clutched in his hands. "You were a real bitch to send me back to hell," he said, a smirk on his face. "But I'll forgive you since I caught a ride back."

"So you're the rogue."

He laughed. "Um, no. You think I'm brave enough or stupid enough to take on a demon prince. No, I'm just playing my part."

"And what is that part, Alastor?"

"To slow you down, Demon Hunter." He shrugged. "Maybe provide a distraction or two."

Jasen glanced from me to Alastor who had done little to make himself appear human. He didn't have scales or wings or any of the many looks that history attributed to demons. He looked like a young Korean man in his twenties, an ordinary man. The shapeshifters could do that, make themselves look human and, I guess, like other demons. But if one looked close enough, there was a slight point to the top of his ears and his teeth ended in short fangs. Each of them. The changing rim of his eyes, first yellow then red then a brilliant white revealed what I hadn't seen when I first captured him. He could be any demon he wanted to be. And in Louisiana, he had been a death demon. He had pulled his black hair in a neat topknot and his black jeans, black t-shirt, black-lined eyes spoke to a youth culture he played no part in. Like the blond-haired, blue-eyed boy he had been in Louisiana, he was just playing another part.

"What is he talking about Neema?" Jasen said.

"I thought you were a death demon," I said, recalling our run from Louisiana to New York.

Alastor smiled. "I know, dearest Neema. You figured you knew everything about demons, didn't you? You've only been hunting us for what, almost three centuries now. But there are things you missed."

"What is going on here?" Jasen said, rising to his feet. Jasen standing forced me to stand as well since I was not about to remain seated in their presence.

"You didn't tell him about the demon world, Neema. Been keeping secrets, have you?"

"What demon world?" Jasen said, stepping away from me. "What haven't you told me?"

"You realize that now is just not the best time for us to discuss this, Jasen."

I tried to keep my eyes on the soulcatcher and Jasen at the same time. While I didn't fear what the soulcatcher would do to me, I feared what the weapon would do to Jasen. I had yet to see a human survive an encounter with the soulcatcher.

"Why this house?" I said instead. "What's so special about who lives here?"

Alastor's face closed, and I knew this was the question he had tried to keep me from asking. Whose house were we in? And I didn't mean a name. I wanted to know what role they played in whatever battle was playing out. I tried to glance around the room while keeping one eye on him.

"Neema hunts demons," Alastor said, dropping onto the sofa and propping his feet up in the seat. "She's been doing it for almost three hundred years now. She didn't tell you?"

Jasen looked at me, frowning. "You didn't tell me about that when you talked about your immortality."

"Well, it's a little tough to fit immortality and demon hunting in a casual conversation. You couldn't handle both topics at the same time. But I promise to tell you all about it," I said. "Just not now."

"Have a seat," Alastor said, waving at the two chairs opposite him. The chairs stood on either side of the window, much too far apart. I guided Jasen to one chair and stood next to him, ready to protect him.

"So that's how you survived my blade?" I said. While the Exorcism killed the lesser demons like Wrath and Greed. It only sent the shapeshifters and higher demons back to hell. I had never tested the Exorcism or the Hwi on a prince.

"Let's talk about what you can do for us," Alastor said, his fingers tracing the barrel of the soulcatcher.

"There's no point since—"

He pointed the weapon toward Jasen. "I don't know, Demon Hunter. I think there is a point."

That was when I spotted it, a picture I couldn't believe I hadn't noticed when I first entered this room. The picture, about 8 by 11, was a replica of an image captured in the summer of '64. It sat on the end table near Alastor's head. I didn't want to stare, but I couldn't seem to stop myself.

I recognized Chet Joseph in the shirt that his sister had called his favorite. His laughing face shone with youth and hope. Again, I could see why he had wanted to join the movement. He exuded a fire that organizations like SNCC could have capitalized on. This picture was taken on the same day as the one that Ernestine had shown us. Chet with the friend who had died twenty years ago in the car accident. The friend's face was sharper in this image. His brown hair framing a face that reflected the same fire Chet showed. But it wasn't either of these young men who had caught my attention.

My attention was captured by the teenage girl in between them. She had been hidden in the picture Ernestine showed us, just a fuzzy image in the background. But in this picture, her animated face had been front and center, young maybe twelve or thirteen and so alive. She wore the same look that so many young people had worn during the movement. She had been a believer, young but down with the cause. And I recognized her.

I recognized her from a picture I had seen that night I went to Allison Stevens' house, the night Allison had died. The resemblance was uncanny, and it helped another piece fall into place. The young woman in the picture with Chet Joseph had been Allison's mother. Allison's mother who had killed herself almost thirty years later.

I tore my gaze away from the picture and looked at Alastor who had been watching me. I could see the moment he realized that I knew. I knew which of them had mattered, and I would connect the dots soon.

"Well that's not good," Alastor said, rising off the couch.

I dove across the room, grabbing his shoulders the moment he shot the soulcatcher. Its silver web twisted, hitting the wall above and next to Jasen before I slung us both back into the demon realm. A puzzled Jasen stared at the empty spot where we had just stood.

CHAPTER EIGHTEEN

Florida

1742

If immortals could grow stronger, then I surpassed human strength. My vision, sharper since those nights in Harlem, had become so sharp I could "see" with my eyes closed. My hearing, my strength, every one of my senses had grown stronger. Although I didn't fear this newer me, I kept my increasing power a secret. I did not want the women and men of this community to label me a witch. I felt safe here, a feeling that had escaped me since the night I woke up in the burial ground. I didn't want this freedom or safety to end. All around me were former slaves—women, men and children who had left the South Carolina and Georgia plantations to make a life for themselves. I felt at home here, and I didn't want to leave.

Most of the former slaves stayed close to the camp, but I ventured out further and further each day. I had learned movements from Dagon that resembled a strange dance more than a means of fighting. I didn't quite understand how effective these movements could be against the sword and the musket, but Dagon and Priest believed relying only on weapons was a disadvantage. So I learned this strange eastern dance from Dagon and swordplay from Priest. I had fought demons on instinct, but instinct was not enough.

A slight noise to the right caused me to string my arrow so fast that any human would have missed the movement. I didn't move; instead, I stilled. Pivoting, bow raised, I pointed my arrow at the man standing behind me.

"You've been here too long," he said, stepping closer.

I didn't move back, but I was watchful. He didn't glow like he had done last time, but I could see a hint of his wings. "What is too long?"

"You are the Demon Hunter." He looked around. "What demons do you see here?"

"But I feel safe." I said. I wasn't ready to venture out into a world where humans *and* demons wanted me dead.

"Remember the boy in South Carolina that you could not save," Rafael said. "How many more like him will exist before you realize your role in this war?"

His words struck their target. The boy still haunted me, and I did not want another boy to be taken by a demon because I hid in the woods. "I did not ask for this task," I said.

"We often perform tasks we don't ask for, Demon Hunter," he said. "But you have all you need to fight demons in this world. The only question is, what will you do?"

I blinked my eyes against the sudden light. Rafael had vanished, so I lowered the bow and arrow. I disliked being reminded that this place was not my destination, and it would be time to move on soon.

In the last several weeks, I had convinced myself that angels did not exist, that I had dreamt up the last visit by Rafael. I had even wondered if, perhaps, I had only imagined

South Carolina. I knew these thoughts were foolish. Jacob was dead, I was to blame, and hiding in the Florida swamps erased none of those facts.

MY STEPS WERE SILENT as I headed to the clearing by the stream. The place was secluded, hidden by a thick covering of trees, but Priest had let me into his sanctuary. It was where he taught me the sword and the dagger. When I climbed over the steep bed of rocks, he stood almost at the foot, his gaze turned to the babbling stream. In his hands was the sack I had hidden in my room. I could only wonder who had found it and given it to him.

He turned and showed me the shackles and the machete in his hands. "Why did you think you must hide these from me?" he said, his voice rough.

Priest and I had grown closer over the last few months as I healed, trained, and grew stronger. We had shared our experiences under slavery, and I had spoken about Cuffee. Most, I kept secret. Priest overwhelmed me with his presence and his watchful nature. Now, looking at the shackles and thinking of South Carolina, I didn't want to talk about Jacob.

"This is a Dahomean sword," he said, pushing the blade toward me. "The King's personal guards carried these weapons, and only women served in the guard. How did you come about one?"

I moved away from him. "My mother's mother was in the King's guard."

His nostrils flared with anger. "Impossible. The women in the King's guard were celibate. They weren't allowed to marry. No warrior woman had a child."

"I tell you only what my mother told me," I said.

"I despise a liar, Neema."

"As do I," I said. I had never had his cold anger directed at me, and it was not a good feeling. "But my mother never told me a lie. After she was captured from her village, she was sent to Elmina. From the Coast, she came to the Americas."

"And who was your mother? Was she a warrior?"

"My mother trained to be a priestess before she was captured."

"Is she the one who enchanted this blade?"

I stared at the blade in his hand, wondering again who had ventured into the room they had given me. I hadn't hidden the blade well, but I had hidden it to avoid answering the questions I was answering right now.

"How do you know the blade is enchanted?" I asked.

Priest edged closer until he stood so close I could see even the small scar at his brow. My sword rested at his side. I refused to let him see how much his proximity unnerved me. Cuffee, even as we fell in love with each other, hadn't touched me. Priest, though, had stood closer to me than any man, and each time, he raised uncomfortable feelings in me. Even in my slave state, my mother had sheltered me so I was untutored in the ways of men. But I was but one of the few women drawn to Priest. Priest, though, kept to himself, but he watched me with a gaze I had seen on the faces of many men in New York City. That look, more than anything, unnerved me.

"I can feel its power," he said. "But why would you need enchanted blades? What have you not told me Neema?"

"I told you that an angel sent me to you."

"You claimed he appeared to you in a dream. That his blessings helped you to heal." He lifted the blade, its sharp edge coming to rest against my throat. "But I doubt your honesty."

"Who dared to search my belongings?" I asked instead.

Priest backed me up, the blade still against my throat. I didn't fight back nor did I struggle. When my back hit a tree, I still refused to flinch or beg him. "Do you think I would betray you?" I said. "That I would tell anyone where you are."

"You have only been here a few months. I know not what you would do."

I was angry enough to shove him from me, but I controlled the desire. "Why does my blade matter so much to you?"

And that, I could see, was the right question. His hand lowered and the blade no longer pressed against my throat. He lifted his other hand and touched my neck with his finger. When he drew his hand away, I could see a little blood. "A blade like this one killed my father." When he stepped away enough, I no longer felt overwhelmed by his presence. "My village lost the battle, and I was captured and enslaved."

"How long were you enslaved?"

"Before they took me to the coast and sold me to white slavers? Perhaps a month or two." He looked at me in anger, but his anger was not directed at me. "I prefer to believe they would have made a different choice if they had known what awaited us on those slave ships and beyond."

I reached out a tentative hand, touching him on his arm to bring his attention back to me. "I did not intend to keep secrets, but to avoid questions. I prefer not to think about what happened in New York or what led me here."

He looked at my hand on his arm and then turned that intense gaze on me. He was an enigma, a man who led a handful of people who didn't know him or understand him. I had recognized the Africa in him. There was a difference between those born in Africa and those, like me, born on American soil. We didn't have Africa in our spirit like him or like my mother. We were a new breed of people.

The only way I could explain what happened next was that thoughts of him had distracted me. I saw the arrow first, its point heading for Priest. Pushing off the tree, I reached behind him and plucked the arrow out of mid-air before he could react. I had an arrow in my bow before I had completed the turn, aiming for the silhouette tucked behind the trees. The Seminoles had a talent for guerrilla warfare, and their ability to blend with nature had vanquished many a foe.

We had made peace with the Seminoles in our region, so I was surprised to find them here, fighting us. I had not yet learned to control my new ability to see demons so the sudden sight of white bodies shocked me. My bow faltered, and an arrow whizzed by my arm, nicking when I didn't move fast enough. Bright white bodies with long black hair snaked their way over the bronze skin of the Seminoles surrounding us. Even though I knew the Seminoles were being driven by an external force, I couldn't hold back. I either had to draw my bow to kill or Priest and I—well, Priest—would die.

Priest adjusted, but it was an ambush. They far outnumbered us and their fighting skills were legendary. We only had my bow and arrows and the Dahomean sword to defend ourselves. I had yet to reveal myself to Priest, but I had no choice now. I could either hide and protect my secrets or show what I had discovered: I could move faster than the human eye.

Arrow after arrow I drew and released, my feet stepping one over the other as I faced first one way then the next and picked off the Seminoles with their arrows pointed at us. Priest, though my blade rested in his hand, tried to follow me with his gaze but he wasn't fast enough. So, I fought and watched over him, my arrows steady and accurate. Protecting him proved a distraction, though, as the last Seminole fell but not before his arrow pierced my chest. I couldn't flinch or even scream before I dropped to the feet of the Priest, dead.

I WOKE UP TO MUFFLED songs of mourning as if I heard them through a barrier. Opening my eyes, I saw nothing but unrelieved darkness and reached up a hand, except my hand didn't go far. Sliding one hand up the front of my body, I touched wood. They had buried me in a pine box. Closing my eyes, I focused on remaining calm. I had only died once and had never been buried, but hysterics would do nothing to ease my situation. I had to focus on extricating myself from this coffin.

I had been dead long enough for Priest to bury me, and now they were mourning my death. I hoped they had not buried me too deep, but either way the dirt above me was freshly disturbed. Taking a deep breath and closing my eyes, I focused on the sounds above me. Soon their voices were more than just harmonious singing. I could hear the voice of Lily, leading the others as they sang for my safe passage to Heaven. Heaven, though, had already sent me back.

I could see Priest, standing apart from the others, shocked and at a loss. The time we had spent together had affected him as well. I didn't know how I felt about that when I felt like I betrayed Cuffee. Taking a deep breath, I drew strength from the human world and from a realm I had yet to enter. The singing stopped as the women and men above me looked around in fear. Only Priest looked about, alert and ready. He had one hand on the sword he had taken from me.

I could feel the strength in me grow and knew in this second death, I had returned to the human world with greater spiritual weapons. I reached out a hand just as the earth before me opened and the top of my coffin peeled back. It was as if giant hands had parted the earth above me like a curtain, and I could step through. When my hand touched open air, another hand closed over mine, and I gazed into the disbelieving but unsurprised eyes of Priest.

"You *are* the Demon Hunter," he said, as he pulled me from my grave. "And you are immortal."

"I wanted to explain everything to you," I said, "but you didn't seem ready to believe."

Those who stood around us moved away from me, their eyes registering a fear they had never shown me.

"The angel who came to you did not appear in a dream."

"No, he did not," I said. "And neither did the demons."

He moved away from me and raised his hand. "Go inside," he told those who had come to my burial. "And I will deal with this."

They needed no other words to leave us, some looking over their shoulders as if they feared that I might follow.

"You must have sensed what I was," I said. "You've been teaching me to fight."

"I saw it in a vision," he said. "I was tasked with training you."

"It was not a vision."

"Demons do not exist, Neema. They *cannot* exist. Neither can angels."

I narrowed my eyes as I looked at him. Concerned with my role in this battle, I had failed to consider his. What if he were more than a mere blacksmith? Rafael had sent me to him for a reason. "Who are you?" I asked, stepping closer to him. "Who were you before you were brought to America?"

He shook his head. "That question matters little, Neema. Not as much as your immortality. How did you come to be immortal?"

"I was cursed."

"By?"

"A woman my mother called the Vodou."

He drew in a deep breath and grabbed my arm. "You saw the Vodou?"

"She cursed me."

"The Vodou is neither woman nor man although it can appear in both human forms. The Vodou is also cruel. You must have been given either more or less than immortality."

"Only demons could kill me."

"You mean only demons could take your soul. No human could kill you, but any demon could have taken your soul. You would have been forever hunted." He nodded his head. "And that is why you saw the angel. So that your soul would not be taken. The question is why did the Vodou curse you?"

"She blamed me for destroying the lives of several slaves."

He shook his head. "Her curse would never be for such a simple reason. The Vodou seeks destruction and chaos. I heard the story of the slave trials of Manhattan. Those trials would have fed her hunger. Your curse was because of more than what happened in Manhattan." He looked down at the blade in his hand. "There is more at play here."

I didn't want to believe his words, but I didn't want to blame myself for the slave trials anymore. I wanted, no needed, to believe the trials had come from the irrational fear of white Manhattanites rather than my misspoken words.

"Priest," I said, closing my hand over the fist clenching my sword.

"I thought you were dead," he said, his gaze like a caress. "And I didn't like the feeling." He touched my face with his other hand. "I've never allowed myself to be close to a woman. I watched slavery destroy too many families and vowed that slavery would not destroy mine."

"We are no longer slaves."

He settled his hand against my neck and tilted my face before he kissed me on the lips. "You are not for me, Neema," he said. "You are the demon hunter. You are destined for bigger than this."

"Priest—"

He stepped away from me and placed my sword against my chest. "Your mother's enchantment is not strong enough to keep fighting demons. I will strengthen the power of this sword, and I will forge you another."

"I deserve more," I said in response.

"There are greater things in this world, Neema, than me and you, than us."

And he walked away. Leaving me to stand before an empty grave, my heart disrupted again. I did not want to be this demon hunter, to die only to live again. I wanted to stay in this hidden place, away from slavery, away from civilization. I wanted to lay my sword down and leave the demon hunting to others, but I could not ignore the warning I had received in the spiritual realm before I woke up. If I did not take up my sword, humanity would lose a war it did not know was being fought. And hell would reign on earth.

PRIEST DID NOT AVOID me, but he no longer sought me out for training sessions. He seemed to fear me. Not as the others did, but as a man determined to be rational rather than emotional. I continued to train without him and to discover more of what I could achieve. The others also stayed far away from me as if expecting me to curse them. One or two I overheard whispering, wondering if I were a witch. Since they had been whispering quite a distance from me, I wondered the same thing. What, but witches, could do as I do?

Dagon, who had left right before the Seminoles attacked us, had yet to return. She had taught me a great deal before she left, but only Priest possessed skills close to hers. With neither available to practice with me, I worried that my form would suffer. However, I trained alone as I waited for Priest to finish my weapons. I watched him from afar. Passing near the stable he used to create from metal, I cast long, considering glances his way. The strength in his arms caught my gaze, but the intensity in his face drew my interest. He was a man of power and grace and as human as he appeared, there was something other worldly in the way he listened to his surroundings.

He knew I watched him, but he never glanced toward the doorway as I passed. Yet Priest was as aware of me as I was of him. I felt an interest in him that, as he had said, could never bear fruit. That did not keep me from hoping that he would take months to forge my weapons, but he finished in two week's time.

I no longer ventured as far as the clearing where the Seminoles attacked us. but there was another area where I could prepare without interruption. I practiced with my bow and arrows, with a sword I took from Priest since he took mine, and with a set of daggers. I knew I would have to leave soon.

Even though I realized that Priest had completed my weapons, I waited for him to find me. I was reluctant to leave, so I would not rush my departure. I packed my belongings and lessened how often I passed near his stable. As much as I desired his attention, I wanted to prolong my stay. To my surprise, he allowed another week to pass after he had completed my weapons before he approached me.

I stood near the place where I had been buried, part of me hoping that Rafael would appear and explain what had become of my life. I was not afraid when I woke up in that coffin, but I had been confused. I had gone to a strange place when I died, and I needed to know what that place had been. I returned to my grave as if I would find answers there, but I sensed that Rafael held all the answers I needed.

"I had another vision last night," Priest said, his tread so soft that he would have surprised someone other than me.

I refused to ask about his vision because I already knew the time to leave had come. Not wanting him to see my sorrow or see his lack of sorrow, I did not turn around.

"The angel showed me the demon battles," he said. "Battles where demons fight for the souls of women, men and children. Especially those that have been set aside for a higher purpose. Too many of those battles are lost without your presence. It is time for you to take up your sword, Neema."

"I am not ready for this burden."

I flinched when his hand slid across my hip and an arm wrapped around my waist. He pulled me back until the length of his body rested against my own. His other arm came to rest atop my breasts, and I raised my hands to clutch his arm. He rested his cheek against the top of my head and held me in a way I had never been held before. The hardness of his body shocked me, but I felt protected.

Even though I knew better, I leaned against him a little. I knew this might be the last time I could lean against anyone.

"You are immortal, Neema. There is nothing for you to fear."

"Except for the burdens I will carry. I don't want the fate of someone's soul to rest in my hands."

"The Vodou chose you for a reason," he said, his voice filling me with warmth. "Some call her the Destroyer because she seeks to vanquish the seed of her greatest enemies. You say you are the daughter of a Priestess, the granddaughter of a Dahomey warrior. That matters. The Vodou wanted to punish you with a fate worse than death."

"I am no demon hunter, Priest," I said.

He stepped back, and I felt a coolness where his body had been. As I closed my eyes against the disappointment, he turned me to face him. "Neema, you are *the* demon hunter so you cannot stay here. You were chosen for this."

"I—"

"As much as I would like you to stay, the angel Rafael visited me last night in a dream. You must leave this place." His hands gripped my arms and moved me so close to him I could feel his breath against my lips. "I have forged weapons for you that every demon will come to fear."

I hadn't cried since they captured Cuffee, but I felt the need to cry now. Closing my eyes, I resigned myself to the decision he had made. He would let me go. The softest touch brushed my lips, and I opened my eyes to see his face so close to mine I blinked. He held my face still between his hands as he pressed his lips against mine and kissed me.

As the kiss deepened, I almost pulled away in shock. No man had ever been so intimate with me, touching his tongue to my lips then to my tongue. I didn't think I should feel this way so soon after losing Cuffee, but I stepped closer to him until my breasts brushed against his chest. I nearly jumped when his hand drifted against the skin at the small of my back. I couldn't explain the heat of my skin or the heaviness between my thighs, but my mother had told me enough for me to understand that Priest's nearness had awakened the woman in me. The feelings only confused me, made me wonder why I had never felt this with Cuffee.

When he released me, I felt a yearning for a touch I had never known. I didn't know how to explain my feelings. I didn't step away from him, but I didn't move closer either.

"Your purpose is greater than me," he said, "greater than this."

"Until I lose a soul or lose a life."

But he looked as if he didn't agree with me. As if his vision of me had revealed a different truth. Unlike him, I knew I was no protector. I could hunt demons, sure, but that did not mean I would save anyone's life. Priest looked at me with enough faith and hope I realized there would be a cost if I failed—a cost that others would pay. That others had already paid.

Sighing, I told him about the boy in South Carolina.

CHAPTER NINETEEN

When I released him, Alastor flew against the wall with a painful crunch. I landed on my hands and feet, ready to pounce on him if needed. The soulcatcher had fallen to the ground somewhere behind me. He would have to get through me to reach the weapon, and I didn't think he'd be interested in that. Standing, I drew my bow and shot three arrows in quick succession, pinning one of his arms to the wall.

"That's not very nice, Neema," he said. "I wanted to have a quick chat with you."

"You shot the soulcatcher at Jasen. That isn't a chat."

I walked over to him and pinned his other arm down with my foot. I gave into the temptation to cause a little pain since he had wasted my time by leading me on a chase designed to distract me.

"So, you caused that suicide down in Louisiana just to catch my attention."

"They wanted to do that stupid pact, anyway."

"Maybe they thought about it, but you egged them on. You made those feelings stronger just so you could get me to chase you." Just thinking about his callousness ticked me off further, and I added more pressure to the arm beneath my foot. I thought about crushing a bone or two.

"Don't you think you should get back to your friend," Alastor said. "It isn't wise to leave him in this house by himself."

I glanced over to see Jasen pacing in the living room and mumbling under his breath. He had his gun in hand even though he had to know by now that guns didn't mean a thing here.

"Did you lead the attack on Beelzebub?"

"And gain his attention? Not at all. Beelzebub is not to be trifled with."

"But you must have sided with someone powerful for you to chance stealing a soulcatcher, or rather two soulcatchers." I smiled. "You know Baal is looking for them, don't you? It's only a matter of time before he suspects you. Aren't you a guardian?"

Alastor looked terrified, which made little sense. He was making moves against the demon princes and princesses that could only be interpreted as hostile. So why did he still seem so afraid?

"Tell me what's happening?" I said, "maybe I can convince Baal to spare your life."

"In our wars, Demon Hunter, we never change sides. I've already made my choice."

"So then tell me about this house. Why here?"

"Didn't you already figure that out?"

"I only know the man who lived here was connected to Chet Joseph. That still doesn't tell me what happened to Chet or how any of this got Allison killed."

"You realize that these arrows are painful. I don't know how you expect a conversation to take place—"

I exchanged the bow and arrow for my sword, which still stank of demon blood, and placed the blade against his throat. "Do you feel more inspired now?"

"You'll only be sending me back to hell."

"With a note for Baal and maybe," I tilted my head. "Abaddon."

"Threatening demons with the abyss is a cruel move."

"Then inspire me to be nice."

Alastor gazed at me for a long moment before he sighed and lost some of his arrogance. "I'm not high enough on the totem pole to tell you anything of value," he said. "Your best chance is to find the brother, Elliot. He's still in this house. He's just amongst demons."

"Why him?"

"I've never taken you for an idiot. You should know the answer by now. To make sure you didn't talk to him. Elliot is a fount of information."

"As are you."

Alastor's face tightened. "Either way I'm screwed. Whether because I helped you or because I didn't. You made sure of that."

"And this demon war?"

"My advice to you is to stay out of it. You don't want to get caught in the middle." He tilted back his head, causing my blade to nick him. Gritting his teeth, he was silent as his skin bubbled. "Go ahead. Send me back. They'll kill me, anyway."

I didn't know if I could believe him since all demons lie, but I had to at least search for this Elliot. Wrenching my arrows from his arm, I ignored his howls as I dragged him from the demon realm and tossed him at Jasen's feet.

"You have got to stop disappearing," Jasen said, jumping when we appeared beside him.

"Can't be helped," I said, pulling off my arm bracelet. I could see Jasen's eyes grow big as the shackles and manacles were released. Alastor shook his head at me, but I didn't trust him with Jasen. These chains were better than any prison and none could free him since I was the only key. Priest's magic was one that still awed me. He had done what no human had done after him. Then I thought of the arrowhead in my pocket. At least, until now.

"You can't trust a demon, Jasen," I said.

"But shackles, Neema? Manacles?" Jasen shook his head. "These are symbols of slavery. Why—"

"I only wore these one time," I said to him, pulling out my mother's machete and handing it to Jasen. "And it was because of a demon. A blacksmith took the chains meant for my captivity and made them into a prison for demons. Believe me, he knew what the chains symbolized. He took what was meant for our defeat and turned it into one of my greatest weapons." I looked from Alastor to him. "Don't think the irony was lost on him. He knew what he was doing." I closed Jasen's hand around the hilt of the Hwi. "All demons lie. When his lies threaten to overwhelm you, the machete will help."

"I think we should talk about this more, Neema. I was aiming the soulcatcher at you, not your boyfriend here."

"Well, then your aim sucks because you missed me by a large margin." I shook my head. "Why don't you explain how to find this Elliot."

"If I told you he was in the basement, would you believe me?"

"You better hope for Abaddon's sake I do."

Alastor offered a sick laugh. "Then to the basement you go."

I gave him a quick nod and turned to leave the living room.

"Neema," Jasen said, grabbing my arm. "Perhaps you shouldn't go alone."

I looked back at him and shrugged. "I've always gone it alone, Jasen." I extricated my arm from his grip and headed downstairs, but I wasn't as flippant as my response suggested. I had always gone alone, but that wasn't something I could ever get used to. Even after two hundred and seventy-four years.

A DOOR IN THE KITCHEN led down to the basement, my least favorite part of other people's houses, particularly possessed houses. I sighed, sword ready. I had switched my weapons too many damn times since I entered this house. I needed to just stick to one and if I did, it might as well be the deadliest one.

I opened the door and flipped the switch to my left., because the moment seemed perfect, the light flickered before it faded into complete darkness. I flipped the switch at least twice and an extra time for good measure, but the light did not come on again. Descending the stairs, I waited for that creepy hand to reach out from below the steps, or the sudden, sure knowledge I was not alone. Instead, my eyes grew accustomed to the dark, and I peered into a basement that shone as if a soft light had flickered to life.

When I reached the bottom of the stairs, I could tell that the basement had settled into the demon realm. It was a finished basement with a washer and dryer shimmering in one corner. A couch sat opposite the stairs but I couldn't tell its color since it had taken on a grayish hue. I turned to the right and faced a wall of neatly arranged tools. In the corner, sandwiched between a row of cabinets and a long but narrow table was a thin figure clothed in tattered rags. I walked over, arm extended so I could remove the rags with the tips of my fingers.

Haunted brown eyes looked up at me from an emaciated face. Lank, dull hair plastered his head, and he looked and smelled awful. He may have been down here for only a day or two, but he looked as if he had been locked in this basement for years.

"He is ours," a voice said behind me.

I jerked back to see the glistening, golden skin of a death demon standing near me. She wore a long white skirt that fell to her feet, but only a pair of suspenders crossed her nipples. Demons amazed me with how they treated human clothes. It was as if they didn't understand how most clothing functioned so they wore pieces in ways that defied logic. She wore suspenders but no shirt. That made perfect sense.

"Not anymore," I said. "He's needed upstairs."

She tilted her head. "Alastor left me in charge, and you shouldn't be here."

"We could always fight for him," I said, tilting my sword toward her. "That should be loads of fun."

"I will call the others."

"That would be even better."

She stood there and stared at me, unsure of how to respond. She shook her head. "Alastor will punish me if I let you have him."

"Since Alastor's chained up that might be a little tough." I said, touching the sack of rags in the general area of where a shoulder should have been. "Elliot, it's time to leave."

Elliot looked up at me as if I had spoke in some complicated, foreign tongue.

I looked back at the demon who still seemed confused on whether she should fight or let me pass.

"I can simplify this for you," I said. "I've been killing demons since I entered this house, and Alastor will never break his chains. You can either waste time trying to fight me although it won't take me long to kill you. Or you can step aside. The wrong choice will be bad for you since you won't be sent back to hell. Demons like you don't come back. They get replaced."

"I don't want to go into the abyss," she said.

"Then I suggest you step aside and let me pass."

She made me wait longer than I appreciated before she stepped aside with her head bowed. I kept an eye on her as I lifted the bundle of rags. A head rolled from beneath a tattered shirt and feet seemed to come from nowhere as they touched the ground. I jerked back as the stench from his body drifted to my nose. He bore the smell of death, but I knew this wasn't real. None of it was real.

"They will kill me for allowing him to escape," she whispered when we reached her. I didn't sympathize enough to let him stay, but I felt sorry for her.

"I have Alastor chained upstairs," I said to comfort her.

She shook her head. "He is not the one I fear."

I didn't have time to dwell on her words or ask questions. I needed to return upstairs and into the human realm before demon reinforcements arrived. I looked at the man I had rescued as we reached the base of the stairs. Brown eyes stared at me from a thin face, their rapid blinking filled with amazement. I supported his body as we made our way to the stairs.

"My name is Neema," I said. "I'm taking you ho—, well, to another part of the house."

"I didn't think I would ever escape," a thin voice responded. "I was close to giving up."

As we took each stair, he grew stronger. His body became more erect and heavier. The stench surrounding him faded, and I could feel his rags shifting, becoming more solid. By the time we reached the top of the stairs, he was no longer the bag of bones he had been.

He was an older man, in his mid-sixties with silver hair and a physique that spoke to the muscular build of his younger years. About my height, he wore a pair of khakis and a hunter green polo shirt. I was a little surprised to see how good-looking he was, good-looking in the way Sean Connery was even as he aged. I helped him into the living room and into the chair across from Alastor. He didn't need my help anymore, but he seemed to draw strength from my proximity.

I helped him settle into the chair even as I watched Alastor. He looked both devastated and terrified. Whatever Elliot could tell me was something that Alastor didn't want me to hear.

"WHY IS HE SO DAMN IMPORTANT to you, Alastor?" I said, as I helped Elliot settle into a chair.

Jasen looked at me and shook his head. "Won't do you much good. He refuses to talk, to help."

"I can't afford to help you, Neema," Alastor said. "Not if I want to live."

"You act as if it matters. Whatever demon put you up to this will assume that you helped me, anyway. There's no other way you could have survived the *Demon Hunter*."

Alastor's face tightened as he yanked at his chains. "I can't help you, Neema. I'm—"

"I think I know why they are interested in me," Elliot said, his voice stronger. We had all recognized Alastor's fear and perhaps, Elliot, like me didn't want to face what that fear meant. "Last week, I was going through some of my family's old boxes, and I found some of my brother's things from that summer in 1964. Freedom Summer, people called it."

"That alone wouldn't—"

Elliot held up his finger. "Before I could go through the box, I was sucked into whatever was going on in my basement. I think those creatures didn't want me to see something in the box."

"Which," I said, rolling my eyes. "Is still in the basement, isn't it?"

"But the box reminded me of that summer. I was fourteen, much too young to head down to Mississippi but not too young to want to. Me and Esther both wanted to go to Mississippi that summer."

"And who was Esther?" Jasen asked.

I walked over to the side table and picked up the picture that had caught my attention earlier. Its black frame was chipped in one corner, but the photograph was undamaged. I looked again at Chet's smiling face, the only black man in the photograph. He wore a t-shirt and bell bottoms like the other two males wore, but he possessed a confidence they had yet to find. The younger of the two white males was Elliot, younger but good-looking.

"This is Esther," I said, studying the young girl in the picture with them before I passed him the frame. She had been about thirteen or fourteen then with her dark hair parted in the center and falling in full waves to her shoulders. Her dark, thick brows were neatly shaped, and she was rather beautiful. She and Elliot must have been a walking photo shoot.

Jasen took the picture from me and studied it. "So this was the girl in the other picture we saw. Except she was hiding her face. Who was she?"

"Esther," Elliot said again.

"Allison's mother," I answered, taking the picture and shoving it in Alastor's face. "Tell me why she matters, dammit. What was so important about the three of them? About Chet, Benjamin and Esther?"

"They're all dead now," Elliot said, as if he had just thought of that fact. "After Chet disappeared, my brother wasn't the same, and Esther and I drifted apart."

"You'll never figure it out, Demon Hunter," Alastor said. "You won't—"

"We need the box," I said, cutting him off. Alastor stopped then and eyed me with such hatred I felt even more determined. There was something he didn't want me to see. "Which one is it?" I said to Elliot.

"I wrote '64 on it," Elliot said. "The boxes are to the left of the stairs. Right at the bottom."

"Get up," I said, yanking the chains so that Alastor stumbled to his feet. I pulled him in front of me, the chains in my left hand and the sword in my right. He was at a perfect distance so my blade could reach his neck, and I communicated that fact.

"You should let this go, Neema," he said, as I headed back toward the kitchen. I tugged on the chains, making him stumble before we came to the door of the basement. I didn't expect trouble, but the demons seemed emboldened.

Pushing him down the stairs, I followed with my blade at his neck. This time I was prepared when the world went dull, the grays and browns even more depressing than usual. The demon who had guarded Elliot when I entered the basement the first time was still downstairs looking dejected, but this time two other demons joined her. These two demons were bright red, making me wonder again why the demons were forming such unusual alliances.

"I need a box," I said, when they moved closer to the stairs. "And I don't want trouble."

"We can't let you have it," the female said. She seemed bolder now with her reinforcements.

I pulled on Alastor's chain. The iron cutting into his skin would be painful.

"Let her have the box," he said.

The demons looked at me and looked at the chains gripped in my hands. "We're under strict orders," one of the male demons said.

"Let her get the damn box," Alastor said again. His voice deeper, filled with frustration and impatience. "Let us get the box and leave."

"You know what our punishment will be if we let the box out of this room."

"I'm not ready to face Baal in hell. You'll only die by her blade, but I'll suffer far worse. So just step aside and let her take the box. It will make our lives much easier."

"Only for now."

Alastor sighed. "For now, will be long enough for me."

I was a little surprised when the three of them stepped aside and let me take the box.

I HANDED ELLIOT A SMALL, cardboard box worth a lot more than I could see. Pulling the other chair closer to Elliot, I gripped the chains with one hand. I was ready to leave this house with demons just a floor below us, but I wanted to see what was in the box. I had carved a Chi-Rho on the basement door, the P with an X on top glowing before the lock settled in. The lesser demons couldn't break through.

Demons like Alastor required a stronger lock, but I didn't have time to cast one.

Elliot opened the box with a trembling hand, and I felt my anxiety rise. He pulled out photographs first, more photographs of the Summer of '64. I flipped through them, not sure what to look for. The pictures seemed to be a record of the preparation for Ohio. The photographs featured Chet and Elliot's brother, but a few pictures included Esther and Elliot. I pulled out a photograph that held a new face; a boy the same age as Chet and Elliot's brother stood at the edge of the photo. His presence didn't stand out as much as the intense stare he gave Chet and Benjamin. While they posed for the camera, he stood to the side gazing at them with enough malice it drifted from the photo.

I slid the photograph toward Elliot and pointed at the young man. "Who is he? Another one of your brother's friends?"

He took the picture from me and brought it closer to his face. "No, he was a neighbor, lived a few streets over from us. He believed Jews shouldn't live in the neighborhood and hated both my brother and Chet, and he did everything to show how much Chet's presence offended him. Chet was only here two days. The day he arrived, and the day they left, but that idiot," he flicked the picture, "gave them grief the entire time Chet was here."

Elliot pulled something else out of the box then and I jumped back, almost dropping my chains. Alastor and I glanced at each other, and I realized that Alastor had been telling the truth. He didn't know much. Sometimes demons could be like mindless drones. The shapeshifters like Alastor though were more independent in their thinking. I shook my head and kept a wary eye on the object that lay in Elliot's hand.

"Is that your brother's?" I said.

Elliot shrugged. "I don't remember seeing it, but then I was the younger brother. Benjamin kept me out of many aspects of his life."

The object could fit in the palm of his hand. Two small sticks were bound with what looked like brown string. The tips were painted red with letters on each stick. Depending on how you held it, it could have been a cross or an X.

"That isn't a language I've seen before," Jasen said.

"Because it isn't a language for humans," Alastor said with disgust. "It's a language of angels, both the chosen and the fallen," he said, "this is a beacon, and you can only make one if you capture a demon."

"I've never seen one of these before," I said, frowning, and I had seen a lot in almost three hundred years.

"Well you've never needed one," Alastor said. "You pass from the human to the spiritual realm with ease. Most humans would prefer not to interact with us, but whoever owned that piece wanted to call forth a demon."

"What does this have to do with capturing a demon?" Jasen asked.

"That beacon," Alastor spat, "is made of the bone and hair of a demon."

Elliot dropped it to the ground and rubbed his hand against his clothes. "Why would someone want to make that?"

"I've already told you," Alastor said. "To call a demon. And you only use that beacon if you want a powerful demon. A shapeshifter, a hitchhiker or one of the demon royalty."

"But why would my brother want to call a demon," Elliot said, puzzled. "He only wanted to go to Mississippi to be part of the SNCC project. What would he need with a demon?"

"Assuming it was his," I said, pulling the picture toward me that had caught my attention earlier. There was something about the boy at the edge of the frame that troubled me.

"When do you think Chet went missing?" I asked Elliot.

"The volunteers were due in Oxford by June 21st and Ben and Chet wanted to make sure they left in plenty of time," Elliot shook his head. "I will never forget that day. They left two days before, excited, ready to go down to Mississippi."

"But Chet didn't make it to Ohio?"

Elliot shook his head. "Neither did Benjamin. Something happened on the way there. The police brought him back, and he was never the same."

"So how did Chet's mother get a letter dated for June 22nd if Chet was already dead?"

Elliot looked away from us, but not before I saw the guilt in his eyes. "It was Esther's idea. We couldn't get anything out of Benjamin. He was, gone, you know. For a month after he came home. He wouldn't talk, wouldn't do anything. We didn't know what to tell Chet's mother so—."

"You lied," Jasen said.

"Not a lie. More of a reprieve. For us."

"But then you never told her the truth. You let her think her son disappeared down in Mississippi."

"So, what about when Benjamin started talking?"

Elliot shook his head. "He never spoke about that. A month and a half after he came back, he snapped out of the trance as if nothing had happened."

"The demons took over your house for a reason, Elliot," I said, pulling the box toward me. "And amnesia is not the reason. We've missed something, and no one's getting rest," I looked at Alastor, "until I find out what the hell it is."

Alastor looked at me annoyed, but I cared so little I didn't acknowledge him. I was missing part of the story and I felt Alastor and Eliot knew those parts. The problem was that I had Jasen, a novice to this world, as my only backup.

Since time didn't pass the same in the human world, we had lost all the afternoon. The sun had set and even though Jasen and I should have been heading home, it was time to bring in real help. Taking out my phone, I, with some guilt, called Raina.

CHAPTER TWENTY

"This better be worth me leaving a wonderful date," Raina said, as she pushed past me. "I had to convince Liz that I would be safe before she would let me leave. And trust me that wasn't easy."

She came in like the Amazon that only Raina could be. She had dressed in one of her breezy jumpsuits, its tawny color glowing against her skin. Her makeup, as always, was flawless, and she made seventy look damn good. She had brought her bow gun, strapped at her side but ready.

"You can feel the demon presence when you step on the lawn," she said. "And it's dark and gloomy around the house, like it's midnight rather than twilight."

"You know I would only call you if it were an emergency," I said.

"No, you wouldn't. You'd call me if you needed me, emergency or not." She stepped into the room, her quick eyes taking in Elliot seated in the chair, Jasen standing by the mantle, and Alastor chained on the floor. She shook her head and looked back at me.

"He's Korean now," she said. "But isn't that the same demon we were chasing in Louisiana? The one who made those teenagers commit suicide."

"How can you tell?" Alastor said. "You aren't the Demon Hunter."

"Well, if I told you that then I might as well take out a sign for the whole demon world to know." She said, not bothering to look at him. "Why do you have him chained to the couch? Just send his ass back to hell."

"He isn't a death demon," I said. "He wanted me to think he was. He's a shapeshifter and my distraction."

"From what?" Raina asked.

"Great question. I haven't been able to get an answer out of him. Claims he doesn't know but I'm sure it's connected to this rogue demon."

She looked at Alastor. "You can convince him to answer you. You have a way of convincing demons." Alastor moved back when she walked further into the room. Raina had a knack of intimidating even demons. "So, let me see this box," Raina said, sitting on the couch. She pulled the box toward her, glancing down at the beacon on the floor. "Why do you have a beacon?"

I tossed my hands up. "How do you know what that thing is, but I didn't know?"

"You never needed or wanted to know. It was always my job to know the human things. Your focus has always been the demons." She nudged the beacon with a toe. "Was this in the box?"

"Yes," Jasen said. "It belonged to Elliot's brother."

She glanced at Elliot before she looked around the room. Her eyes fell on the picture on the couch next to her. The same picture that drew my gaze. "No, it didn't," she said, lifting the picture so she could get a closer look. She drew her glasses from the top of her head and peered at the image. "No, this beacon belongs to the young man standing at the edge of the photograph."

"How do you know this?" Elliot said.

"I walk with the Demon Hunter," Raina responded. "She has her gifts and," she smiled. "I have mine." She opened the box and set items aside. A book. An advertisement for the Mississippi Summer Project. An article about the disappearance of James Chaney, Michael Schwerner and Andrew Goodman.

The next withdrawal was slower than the rest, and her hand shook. She pulled out a folded white cloth, a handkerchief. She unfolded the handkerchief, but didn't touch the items on the cloth. I couldn't read the singed paper, but I had seen enough witches and demons to know this did not bode well. "This is for a spell," Raina said, wariness in her voice. "It's connected to that beacon and didn't find its way into your brother's things by accident." She looked at Elliot. "Do you remember where this was found?"

Elliot shook his head. "I can't tell you for sure. It might have been in his car. Some of those items were in his car. Like that menorah," Elliot took the leather necklace with the small wooden menorah at the end. "Benjamin was never one to parade his Jewish heritage, but sometimes he would have these little symbols here and there. College had changed him a lot, you know. Not that he stopped believing, but he stopped practicing."

"Well someone summoned a demon for your brother. And that someone is right here." She picked up the photograph. "What do you remember about the young man in this picture?"

"I remember that he and Benjamin never got along. I was always underfoot, so I was often around when he bothered Benjamin."

"Who is he?" Jasen said, impatience in his voice.

"Our neighbor. He lived a few blocks over from us when we were children." Elliot shook his head. "Our parents moved to Long Island when Benjamin was a senior in high school. It was tough for him. Long Island neighborhoods didn't welcome Jews. Benjamin had a tough time at the high school, tougher than he ever told my parents about, but he couldn't hide much from me."

"You remember the two of them ever getting physical?" I asked.

Eliot shook his head. "Benjamin wasn't that kid. Twice the neighbor, Winston, got physical with him. Benjamin never touched him though, that would have only made things harder for him, but he argued back. Their arguments got so bad that the hatred between them seemed visible."

"What did they argue about?" Jasen asked.

"You must remember that the 1960's were a confusing time for white people like Winston. Their world was changing. Blacks in the South were challenging laws, and blacks in the North were trying to leave their acceptable place. Blacks could live in the rundown neighborhoods in Brooklyn, but they weren't supposed to leave. When my parents moved to Long Island, people like Winston figured that it would just be a matter of time before African Americans moved in too. I think that's what pushed Winston over the edge that summer. Chet being in our house was just too much, and Chet stayed overnight."

"I have a hard time believing integration would be so divisive for them." Jasen said. "They were just kids."

"In battleground states, no one was a kid," Raina said. "The country was volatile. There was the Vietnam War, civil rights, women's rights. The assassination of Kennedy in November of '63. The unrest affected the young and the old. Anybody old enough to remember the '60's, believe me, did not escape unscathed."

"When Chet arrived that day, several of our neighbors came by the house. A few of them warned my parents in their condescending way. I remember overhearing a few and was shocked at that side of them. The thought of Chet in our house angered our neighbors, but none more than Winston. In fact, his reaction made Benjamin leave early that next morning before the sun rose."

"You people are no closer to discovering the truth," Alastor said, rattling his chains. "And, if you ask me, none of this matter. The only important questions are—what did this boy Winston ask of the demon? And what did the demon demand in return?"

RAINA PUT EACH ITEM back into the box while Alastor's words rang in the surrounding air. He was right about the questions, but he wasn't right about that day. Whatever made Benjamin and Chet leave before sunrise was important to understanding Allison's murder. Raina used the edge of the handkerchief to pick up the beacon and drop it into the box.

"When Benjamin came out of his trance?" Raina said. "How did he act?"

"Like the last two months hadn't happened. He didn't ask about Chet, and he never mentioned Freedom Summer again."

"Do you think he forgot what happened?"

"I always wondered about that, you know. Sometimes I thought he had forgotten, but sometimes he would get quiet and seemed troubled. He had a hard time after that. Right until he died."

"And Winston?"

Elliot shrugged. "His family moved that winter. Wanted a neighborhood for white families only."

Raina and I looked at each other. She reached into the bag and brought out the blessed oil I had asked her to bring. "We have to leave, Elliot," I said, "but Raina and I can shield your house until you call in a rabbi or a priest."

"Will that keep me safe?"

"No. The only thing that will keep you safe is if we find the demon who was after you. It will give you better protection though."

Raina picked up the box and handed it to Jasen. "Do you mind if I take the box?" she said, turning away from Elliot before he could answer.

We sprinkled oil on every door frame of the house before we left. Jasen followed us, eyeing us like we had gone insane. Since holy water was harder to get, I used blessed oil to keep out demons. It didn't burn them like the holy water, but it made it impossible for them to cross thresholds. That would have to be enough for now.

"You have got to find out what happened to Chet Joseph," Raina said, when we stepped outside.

"That's a little difficult since Chet and Benjamin are dead."

"But it doesn't mean this Winston is," Raina said. "He would be about my age now." She reached for the box, which Jasen handed to her. "And if that fails, you'll just have to ask Chet or Benjamin."

"But they're dead." Jasen said.

Raina smiled. "And you think that would stop Neema?" She gave us both a little wave before she walked down the driveway and got in her car, leaving me with a curious Jasen. I shoved Alastor into the back seat of the car and considered taping his mouth shut.

"Explain," Jasen said when we got in the car.

"We find Winston Merrill first."

I waited while he called the precinct to have one of his colleagues to track down an address for Winston Merrill. I could have done it much faster with Sheree, but I was already having challenges with Jasen. I didn't want to flaunt my illegal methods in his face.

"Now answer the question," he said, hanging up the phone and starting the car. "I'm going through a drive-thru real quick while we wait for the address."

I shrugged. "Sometimes I can call spirits, but I prefer not to disturb the dead. It's... not the wisest decision."

"But you can call Chet or Benjamin?"

"And they don't have to answer. But you must be careful when you delve into the spirit realm because sometimes other beings like to hitch a ride. That's why I don't like to call a spirit back to earth."

"But you're a demon hunter. Couldn't you send whatever it is back?"

"Sometimes they move too fast. They can attach themselves to people nearby, and once a demon digs themselves into a human soul, it's tough to break that tie."

"She's trying to tell you she doesn't want to risk you or anyone else," Alastor said. "If she calls forth a spirit, every demon will race to the door she's opened and try to jump through. If one gets through, she won't be able to control where it goes."

"But if—"

"We try another way first, Jasen. Trust me, this is something you don't want to dabble in. Too much can go wrong. Let's find Winston Merrill, see if he remembers that day."

"You better hope that his feelings toward black people have changed." Alastor said.

Our conversation paused as we ordered our food. I was starving after the battle at Elliot's house. It had been a long time since I had faced so many demons at once.

"What is a demon hunter?" Jasen asked when we were on our way to Winston Merrill's house.

"A nuisance," Alastor said.

I threw an annoyed look over my shoulder before looking back at Jasen. "Wars, catastrophes, assassinations—every major event that has changed the course of human history can be traced back to spiritual warfare. What most humans don't understand is that heaven and hell are in constant battle, the divine and the fallen. The fallen have three hierarchical levels. The lowest, the ones I call the Sin Demons, are the ones I most often face."

"Are those the demons that make us sin?" Jasen asked.

Alastor sucked his teeth. "First, demons can't *make* humans sin. The whole devil made me do it is bullshit. We can, however, take advantage of what's already there. If someone is already angry enough to kill, it may not take much to push them over the edge."

"That's sickening," Jasen said.

"It's nourishing," Alastor said, his voice rapturous. One would have thought he was feeding.

I reached behind me to tap his leg. "None of that in the car," I said. "Demons feed on the chaos and confusion their meddling brings. When you're angry, a wrath demon will try to stoke that anger and then feed off it."

"Is that what happened to Kenneth?"

"No, a Whisperer influenced Kenneth. Whisperers are in the second tier of demons, and they're more dangerous than the Sin Demons. The Hijacker and Shapeshifters belong in that group. Our buddy back there is a Shapeshifter. He's a Korean man now, but he has played other roles."

"And what's the highest tier?"

"The Demon princes," Alastor said.

"And princesses," I added. "There are seven. And all seven are dangerous as hell, but they are less likely to come to earth. When they battle, they battle the divine warriors, the angels that stand next to God."

"So that's where you come in." Jasen said, nodding his head. "And have you ever had to face a demon prince?"

I could feel Alastor's gaze burning into my back, but I was saved from answering Jasen's question as he slowed down to turn onto Merrill's street. The man lived in Hicksville, a town in Long Island's Nassau County.

JASEN STOPPED IN FRONT of a house in the middle of the street. A sprawling two story with a wrap around porch and a well-maintained lawn. I took in the neat front lawn and the tree that shadowed one corner of the porch.

"Stay in the car," I said to Alastor as I slid out.

"And just where do you think I'm going when you've got me chained up," he said, rattling the chains.

I adjusted the scabbard on my back, hoping I wouldn't need to use my sword and followed Jasen up the stairs.

"I feel it here too," Jasen said. "Does that mean demons—"

"No, but no demon possession doesn't mean that this house is demon-free."

Jasen looked annoyed, but my skin felt clammy. I rubbed at the sudden ache in my belly. Jasen knocked on the door and stood aside as we waited for someone to answer.

We waited for about three minutes before a middle-aged woman came to the door. She wore a nurse's uniform, her blond hair pulled in a neat bun. Her skin was pale and her features thin. She looked exhausted and irritated and when she saw us her lips pursed with impatience.

"He won't want to see you," she said, the screen door a barrier between us.

Jasen and I looked at each other. "Who won't want to see us?" Jasen said.

"Winston," she shook her head. "He doesn't like black people. And he's mean about it."

"We wanted to ask him about an old neighbor of his, Benjamin Goldstein."

The nurse shook her head. "I can't promise you he'll talk to you. Maybe you can get his sister to talk to him for you. Let me see if I can invite you inside."

She left the door cracked, and Jasen and I both shook our heads. He walked over to the railing of the porch and leaned against it while I stayed in front of the door. I tried to peek through the crack in the door, but I couldn't see much.

After a five-minute wait, the nurse came back to the door and opened it wider. She unlatched the screen and stepped aside so that Jasen and I could enter.

"Winston is not too happy about you being here, but his sister has agreed to talk to you. He's gotten a lot more difficult over the years and," her voice dropped, "more of a bigot so..."

She led us to a parlor, their version of the room that Raina had set aside for unwanted guests I was sure.

"Ridiculous," Jasen said when she left the room. "Are we not in the twenty-first century?"

"Just because the times have changed, doesn't mean the thinking has."

He cocked his head sideways as he looked at me. "Tell me about your world some time. I was so angry at you for a long time after you left, and I never would have imagined," he waved a hand toward me. "This. I want to understand what this—" He halted at the click of heels across the floor.

We stood silent as Winston's sister entered the room, and I didn't have to look at Jasen. I could feel his shock like the slightest pressure on my chest. I wasn't sure what I had expected, but it had not been Helen, Allison's aunt. She, however, wasn't surprised to see us and only tilted her head toward us.

"I hoped you wouldn't be led to my brother," she said.

"What made you think we would be?" answered Jasen.

I only stood there and stared at her, trying to draw connections that weren't clear yet.

"Please," she waved a hand toward a settee that looked like it had been transported from the 19th century. While I was struck by the formal ambiance of the room, I had not looked at the furniture. This room was styled after a parlor from 19th century America. I had spent too many moments of my life in rooms just like this one.

I moved toward the settee and sat down. This seat had seen almost as much of slavery as I had. Jasen settled next to me, and Helen sank in the armchair across from us. A maid came in with a tray and set it on the coffee table.

"I'm not sure if you need a drink," Helen said. "But I do." She poured a generous glass of brandy and took a healthy sip. "When Allison went down to Mississippi, I expected trouble to come back. Her uncle Joseph was always seeing things and hearing things that were better left alone."

"Allison came to you about those photos, didn't she?" I said.

"I was just a child during '64. I wasn't old enough to be a part of the movement. My parents would have never allowed me to be involved, anyway."

I thought about Denise McNair, Carole Robertson, Cynthia Wesley and Addie May Collins. They had been just fourteen and one was eleven years old when they were killed in the Sixteenth Street church bombing in '63. They hadn't been allowed to be young, to opt out of the Civil Rights Movement. I wanted to, but didn't say this to Helen. She did not deserve my anger. Yet.

"I was fourteen-years-old that summer," she said, "Same age as Esther and Elliot. I didn't know much."

"But Winston did. Did Allison ask to talk to your brother?"

Helen looked away from us. "It would've just been a matter of time. Allison came back from Mississippi excited. She had hundreds of photographs from Joseph's collection. She wanted someone to help her go through the pictures."

"So she asked Peter, your husband, her uncle."

"But what would Peter know," she poured her second glass of straight brandy. "He was nine, maybe ten in '64. She left the photographs with him."

"And you saw them."

"I saw the one with Chet Joseph, his face circled either by her or her uncle Joseph."

"And a picture of Chet caught your brother in the background."

Helen polished off that second glass and poured herself another. "I didn't recognize Chet at first but—"

"But I did," a voice said from the doorway.

CHAPTER TWENTY-ONE

The man in the doorway sat in a wheelchair which emphasized the air of danger surrounding him. He looked to be in his late seventies maybe early eighties but he was the same age as Raina. His full, silver hair framed bright blue eyes that studied us. He didn't have the good looks that Elliot still claimed, but he had been good-looking as a younger man. The anger and hatred that shone from his youthful face in the picture had settled in the permanent lines and creases in his face. This man's life had been defined and shaped by darkness.

"I thought I made my wishes clear regarding visitors," he said, addressing Helen, but keeping an eye on both me and Jasen.

"They were interested in Ben Goldstein," Helen said. "I thought it best to let them in."

"You've come over here for nothing," he said. "I won't tell you a thing."

"Not even how you killed Chet Joseph."

He turned toward me when I spoke. His eyes steady and seeking. I could smell the demon scent on him, a clear sign of his long and intimate relationship with the demon world. No demons filled this room, but the stench of demons had entered the room with him.

"What demon did you make a pact with?"

He gave me his full attention and smiled at me. "I did not kill Chet Joseph."

"Then tell me what happened to Ben and Chet on the way to Ohio."

"They got lost." Winston shrugged. "I warned him against traveling with that nig—Negro, a black man. I warned him. Just because we were in the North didn't mean race didn't matter. Ben chose not to listen."

"So you taught him a lesson."

"I exposed him to the truth, yes." Winston Merrill waved a hand at us. "You aren't welcome here—."

"We can always make this visit official," Jasen said.

Winston laughed. "You could try, but that might be difficult since you're a New York City cop, and this is Long Island."

"Just cooperate with them, Winston," Helen said. "Allison was my niece, and if Chet Joseph's murder has anything to do with her death, then I want the truth."

Winston stared at us before he made a decision. "I warned Benjamin Goldstein about riding to Ohio with that boy. It was bad enough that Ben was Jewish. Traveling with that Negro—black—African American boy would have only made matters worse. So, I warned him."

"How charitable of you," I said.

"I won't allow the likes of you to mock me," Winston said, his face tightening. "I only answer you because Helen wishes I do so."

"Then tell us what happened to Ben and Chet on the way to Ohio," Jasen interjected.

Winston studied me, but I met his gaze. When he realized that I would not cower before him, he turned back to Jasen. His intimacy with demons was enough that he recognized me subconsciously, but he could never put his unease into words.

When he talked, I could see the darkness rising inside him like a storm cloud moving beneath the surface of his skin. The story he told was one he had practiced for years, equipped with pauses, emphasis and just the right hint of emotion.

He and Ben had argued the night before Chet Joseph arrived. Over the years, they had developed an odd relationship—he and Benjamin Goldstein. They were enemies: they had to be. Ben was Jewish, and Jews were not welcome in his neighborhood. But Ben was also the same age as he, and they had similar interests. They both liked Elvis Presley, but then most folks their age did. It was their interest in rock-and-roll that had underscored their awkward bonding. Benjamin leaned toward artists like Chuck Berry, but Winston preferred the Beatles. At least in public. In private, he was also interested in the new Motown music. Only Ben knew of his secret interest.

Their arguments often stemmed from this paradox. How can you listen to the Miracles but not see the value of the boycotts and sit-ins? Ben would say. You can't acknowledge certain aspects of Negro life as acceptable and ignore others. Music is different, Winston would say in response. It's not about color. Ben would put on the Sam Cooke song then and shake his head. A life of experience is in that song that you know nothing about. There's color in the music, man, color in the damn music. They were seventeen then.

Soon, their arguments became about what divided them. Benjamin talked about the death of Medgar Evers. Winston, though, didn't know who Medgar Evers was or why he mattered. While Benjamin spent weeks angry about the death of a man he called "a fallen soldier," Winston didn't understand how Evers could equate with men who fought for their country. There was no war happening in America.

He didn't understand why men like Benjamin thought their world needed to change. Science had proven that Negroes were inferior. Because of their smaller brains, their child-like tendencies, their inclination toward violence, they needed policing that white men just didn't require. Keeping them in separate neighborhoods and schools and even hospitals was necessary to preserve the white race. Once we allow them into our neighborhoods, he would tell Benjamin, they will want to enter our homes. Then they will murder our men and rape our women. Segregation made sense.

Ben though, with his naïve nature, saw a different world. How has science, he said, proven the inferiority of the Negro? Have you ever heard of W.E.B Dubois or seen the paintings of Jacob Lawrence? Have you not heard of the bravery of Rosa Parks? The only violent ones in the boycotts and the protests are the white people who spit and kick and berate Negroes for standing up for themselves. Is that the beauty of the white race you want to preserve?

The arguments would spin in circles, grow heated, fill with angry statements from both sides. Sometimes, sometimes, there would be name-calling. Mostly from him, but what tolerance they felt for one another deteriorated. By the time Benjamin Goldstein came home from college that spring break with his application for the Mississippi Summer Project, Winston had developed a distinct distaste for Benjamin and the entire Negro movement.

Their arguments devolved into Winston confronting and agitating Benjamin and Benjamin refusing to argue back or even debate Winston's concerns. They lived in Long Island, in New York. What business did Benjamin have in Mississippi? What happened in the South was the business of the South. Besides, this fight for voting wasn't their concern. Benjamin, being Benjamin, refused to listen. What affects one state affects all of America, Benjamin would say in response. This is the *United* States of America, so voting rights in Mississippi are very much a concern for New Yorkers.

Winston had heard about the Mississippi summer project at Harvard and found it ridiculous that any student would sign up. To him, Mississippi was in some backwoods part of the country that didn't deserve their attention. Besides, he didn't believe Negroes should vote. The country had ushered in thirty-five presidents without Negro approval and America had been stronger for it. To join this ridiculous summer project would be an unnecessary headache.

He expressed as much to Benjamin who considered the comments ridiculous. So over two centuries of brutal slavery and dehumanizing segregation is your idea of a strong country? was Ben's incredulous response. Where is your fucking humanity, man? When Benjamin received his acceptance letter that May, he waved it in Winston's face. I have to be in Oxford by June 14th, he said, his excitement fueling Winston's anger. They argued about voting rights, about equality, about Negroes right until the moment the Negro arrived.

He had been passing by the Goldstein house when he saw the Negro inside, sitting right in front of the living room window, like he belonged there. Winston stood and stared at them for so long that Benjamin had enough time to bring the Negro to the door.

Winston didn't believe Ben would bring the Negro over to him until he did. He refused to shake Chet Joseph's hand, refused to respond to the bright, friendly smile, refused to even say hello. Without a word, he spun on his heel and went straight home. He realized that he now had no other choice but to save Benjamin Goldstein from himself. Benjamin didn't understand that Jews and Negroes had nothing in common. And even though Winston understood that Benjamin's Jewishness made him different, at least he wasn't as different as a Negro. The Jews could become a part of America. The Negroes could never be. So, Winston decided that he would be charitable and save Benjamin.

From his grandmother, Winston had inherited an ability to call the dead. It was an ability she had warned him to keep a secret from his mother. Even as a child, his mother had never understood this strange ability. As an adult, wife to a minister, she had become even less tolerable of her mother's strange ways. Because of this, she would have hated this quality in her oldest child and only son. The few weeks a year that Winston visited with his grandmother were spent learning her secrets. The most powerful was, in his opinion, calling spirits and demanding them to do her bidding. Winston had not done this often growing up. Sometimes, sometimes, when he wanted things to go his way, he called on the spirits. He demanded that they haunt or that they possess.

On the night that Benjamin and Chet packed to leave for Oxford, Ohio, he was in the shed in the back of his house, the private space he had convinced his parents he needed. With three younger sisters, a boy, his father agreed, needed his space. He built a shrine, and in that shrine, he called forth his familiar. His familiar was Alastor, a spirit who looked so much like him they could have been brothers. Occasionally, he had asked Alastor to help him with small things. When he wanted to make the baseball team in junior high, when he wanted to be senior class president in high school, when his mediocre grades almost cost him Harvard. He had asked for minor favors to help him be more successful in life. Didn't they say the Kennedy's had done the same?

He asked Alastor to help him stop Benjamin and Chet. He didn't want them to make it to Ohio. Didn't want Benjamin to go any further down that road. He believed if Benjamin went down to Mississippi, he would come back a different man. Why did he care so much? Winston never allowed himself to answer that question. He wasn't a thinker. He was a man of action, and action demanded that he keep Benjamin and the Negro boy from arriving in Ohio. This, he felt, would be a way of saving Benjamin.

HE PARKED AT THE CORNER the morning that Benjamin and Chet left. He didn't know what time they planned to leave, so he waited outside in his car starting at about one in the morning. A few times he fell asleep, but he didn't sleep long because he planned to follow them. They came outside about four in the morning, joking and laughing. He could see their excitement even from the end of the street. Their lights turned the corner before he started his car. He had never followed someone before so he may have traveled just a little too close. They, young and unaware like him, never noticed.

The drive was the longest that he had ever taken, and he had to fight not to fall asleep. He could have met them in Ohio, but he felt a sense of urgency. If they reached Ohio, Ben would be lost. He didn't consider in what ways Benjamin would be lost.

Ben and Chet stopped in Pennsylvania for gas, and he stopped as well. It was only then he heard the banging on his trunk. He should have known from the way she had been watching him for the last few days that she was up to something. He dragged her out of the trunk and dumped her on the ground.

You even think about leaving me, Winston Merrill, she said, and I will go straight to your parents. He didn't know what she planned to say to his parents, but it didn't matter. His father and mother would interfere with his plans. He considered tying her up somewhere and hiding her so he could collect her later, but he didn't know how soon he could get back to her. So that was how he ended up driving those next few hours with a fourteen-year-old Esther sitting next to him. She thought he was going to Western College to be part of that summer project. She didn't realize that he didn't plan on any of them reaching Ohio. They also wouldn't allow a kid to be part of the project. She didn't seem to care, thought she could lie her way to Mississippi.

She tried to talk to him as they sped toward Ohio, but he was not interested in conversation. He was trying to determine when to stop Benjamin. That decision was made for him when Ben and Chet pulled off the highway after they left Pennsylvania. Chet laid a map out on the hood of the car while Benjamin stretched his legs. Winston could see them as he drew closer to their car. The two men exchanged words with an easy camaraderie that Winston and Ben had never achieved. He drove just a little past them before he decided that this was the moment. Moving the gearstick into reverse, he pulled up right in front of Benjamin's Chevelle.

Both men looked up at his car in surprise until Winston got out. Ben grew serious, the annoyance on his face causing Winston to flush with embarrassment. The embarrassment made him angry.

What the hell, man. Did you follow me? Benjamin had stepped toward him. You're making a mistake, Winston told him. You shouldn't go down to Mississippi. Benjamin and Chet exchanged a look that Winston understood all too well. They might question his sanity, but of the three of them, Winston knew he was right. He couldn't allow them to continue to Ohio.

Look, Chet said, but Winston refused to acknowledge him. Why don't you go back to New York, and Benjamin and I will just continue on our way? We'll forget that you followed us.

Benjamin, Winston tried again, the need to convince him was overwhelming. We must go back now. He could see that his words weren't swaying Benjamin. They made him even more determined. Ben just shook his head and turned back toward the car, and that was when Winston felt the familiar pull that meant Alastor was coming.

At least, that was what he thought at first until the surrounding wind picked up speed spinning sand into the air. The dust storm was light at first, but the small rocks picked up by the wind stung their skin—even his. That pull, often beginning like butterflies in his stomach, was instead a sharp pain.

He struggled to ignore the clenching of his stomach as he stared into Benjamin's startled gaze and Chet's worried one. The wind had picked up pace, and the sky had darkened like a sunset. He hadn't known Alastor to be one for theatrics, but if the theatrics made Benjamin return home, then so be it. He could see Esther peeking at them from the front of the car, and he wondered how they appeared to her.

What's happening, Winston, Benjamin said, his voice touched by fear and Winston felt pleased at the sound of his fear. He opened his mouth to answer, to tell Benjamin to go back home, but instead he spoke to Chet. You have been chosen, he said. At least he knew he had spoken, but the voice did not sound like his. It was guttural, deep. Chet only stared at him, eyes wide.

Winston felt strange, different. Not like himself at all. And Benjamin and Chet stared at him with such fear he wondered if he had also changed physically. What the hell is wrong with you, man? Benjamin said, backing away from him. He tried to move forward, but the pain had become more intense. He clenched his teeth to fight back the scream, but he wasn't strong enough to drown the pain. It burst from his stomach and traveled to his head and feet at once, bringing him to his knees. When the pain burst in his head, he screamed and passed out.

When he came to, it was to the sounds of Esther screaming at him. Benjamin won't snap out of it, she said. She must have said it more than once. He looked around slowly, at her and then at Benjamin. He didn't see Chet and feared what that might mean. Esther had gotten them both into the car and drove a short distance back the way they had come. She had pulled the car to the side of the road once her hands shook too much for her to drive.

Everything went crazy back there, she whispered. You and Benjamin and Chet. It happened so fast. I—I didn't know what to do. Benjamin won't speak, and Chet's dead. Now that shocked him. He couldn't remember what had happened, but he and Esther and even Benjamin were covered in blood.

SILENCE FILLED THE room as Winston's voice faded. Jasen and I looked at each other while Helen sat in the chair, stunned.

"I need another drink," she said, tottering a little as she got to her feet. The only sound was her heels against the tile and then the liquid hitting glass as she poured brandy.

"What did you do Winston?" she said.

Winston shook his head. "I am neither foolish enough nor stupid enough to answer that question, Helen."

"And there is no statute of limitations on murder," Jasen said.

I laid a palm on Jasen's arm. "How is all of this connected to Allison's death?"

Winston didn't answer me, just watched us. "She discovered your secret, didn't she?" I said. "When she got those pictures from her uncle, she somehow stumbled onto Chet Joseph's story. Did she come to see you? Ask questions?"

"I think you should leave now," Winston said.

Jasen shook his head. "Not until—"

I squeezed Jasen's arm and stood up. "If we have any more questions, Mr. Merrill, we'll be back," I said.

Neither Helen nor Winston Merrill moved to escort us out, so I led Jasen to the door.

"What's next?" he was saying as I snatched the back door of his car open. I didn't register Alastor's wide-eyed gaze before I swung into the back seat and settled across his lap, my knees resting on either side of his hips. I closed the door on Jasen's puzzled face as I whipped out my dagger and placed it tight enough against Alastor's skin I drew blood. His skin bubbled where my blade touched him.

"You seem a little upset," Alastor said, trying not to move his throat against my blade.

"What in the hell are you doing, Neema?" Jasen said as he opened the car door and slid behind the wheel.

"Just drive me to a secluded spot," I said, smiling at Alastor. "Some place that won't draw nosy onlookers."

"Don't you dare," Alastor said.

I shrugged. "We can always go to the African Burial Ground instead. I'm sure that Baal will—"

"A secluded spot works for me. And we can talk about why that blade is against my skin."

"You kept out parts of the story, Alastor."

"I didn't think it was important."

"While we were trying to figure out how demons connected to Benjamin Goldstein's family, you didn't think mentioning that you were Winston Merrill's freakin' familiar was important?"

"Neema—"

"Winston Merrill thought he was calling spirits, but he never realized that he was calling demons, did he? You let him dabble in the demon world so you could have an easy way back to earth."

"Neema, you've got to listen," Alastor said, his neck had grown black with blood, but I refused to back down. "I was only doing what I was told."

"And you were told to act as Winston's familiar. I find that hard to believe."

"That's because you still think every demon acts alone, but sometimes we don't." Bitterness crept into his voice. "You fall on the wrong side of a battle, and you might not find a way out."

"I hope you don't think I feel sorry for you. One, you're a demon. Two, those suicides in Louisiana. Three, I don't give a damn."

"You have to believe—"

"I don't give two shits about anything you're saying Alastor unless it's about Chet Joseph." I tilted my head and stared down at him. With demons, the question was never what or why. Why demons did what they did, was always the same:

their anger and hatred for God and angels. So that didn't matter. What mattered was the who. They chose their victims in search of a chosen one. "Who was Chet Joseph?" I whispered. "Why did he matter so much?"

The truck stopped then, but Alastor and I were focused on each other. He watched me, studied me, perhaps saw something that only he understood because he drooped against the seat, the bravado gone.

"Winston comes from a long line of necromancers. His grandmother and her mother and so on had an ability to summon the dead. This trait passed to the women in the family, but Winston's mother never developed this ability. We believe the ability was present in one of his mother's sisters, but the sister died at a young age."

The back door opened, and Jasen stood there watching me, a warning look on his face. "What's going on Neema?"

Alastor snorted. "What does it look like? Torture."

"Neema—"

"Don't mettle Jasen."

"I don't think you have to do this."

"Don't make the mistake of thinking he's human." I turned to look at Jasen. "He wouldn't think twice about destroying you."

"May I speak to you for a moment?" Jasen said.

Annoyed, I looked back at Alastor who thought he was about to get a reprieve. This was why I kept no humans in my life except descendants of Quaco. Only they, with their lives intertwined with mine, understood the true nature of demons. I climbed off Alastor and stepped out of the car, slamming the door in anger.

"Is this necessary?" Jasen said.

"This," I pointed toward Alastor. "Is a world that has no room for humanity. No room for weakness. If you can't stomach this, then you and I can part ways."

Jasen, arms across his chest, looked away from me, but I could see in the hardening of his jaw he didn't care for either choice. "I'm just asking you to back down."

"Have you forgotten what happened to you down in that basement?" I maneuvered my body so he had no choice but to face me. "That was courtesy of Alastor because that is how demons work. If you're struggling with my methods, go home, and I'll handle this alone. If not," I moved closer to Jasen. "Then step aside and let me work."

I gave him a final disgusted look I knew he didn't deserve before I opened the door and climbed back in. Alastor, with his human form, would fool most humans, but there was nothing human about him.

I slid across Alastor's lap and sat against the opposite door. If not for the manacles attaching his wrist to the hook behind the seat, our conversation would be friendly. Well, if not for that and my dagger.

I waved the hand that didn't hold the knife, gesturing for him to continue. "So, Winston can call the dead. How did you enter the picture Alastor?"

Alastor sighed and shook his head. "You already know there is a thin line between calling the dead and calling a demon, Neema. When Winston called his first spirit, I took its place."

"But why? What was it about Winston Merrill that made you pretend to be the spirit of someone dead?" Instead of answering my question, Alastor gazed at me. I lowered the dagger and sat back, my legs settling on his knees as I peered at his face. "It was all about Chet Joseph, wasn't it? Even back then. So why was Chet so important, Alastor?"

"I don't know everything Neema. I'm—"

"Just a pawn." I nodded my head. "I know that's what you want me to believe, except all demons lie. And that," I poked at his chest with the dagger, "includes you."

Alastor sighed and closed his eyes. "You'll get me killed or worse."

"Talk, Alastor."

He sighed. "Despite what you think, I'm not privy to every aspect of this plan. You remember the demon wars of the 1960's."

One more war I wanted to forget. "Yes, I remember," I said. "It was bad down in Mississippi."

"All that anger and hatred was..."

"Intoxicating," I said.

"I can't tell you why Chet was chosen, but my task was to keep him from going down to Mississippi."

"And killing him was an option."

"Killing him was the only option."

"What happened on the way to Ohio, Alastor?"

"I came when Winston Merrill called me."

The front door opened then, and Jasen slid behind the wheel. He and I exchanged a look, but neither of us said a word about our earlier conversation.

"You killed Chet?" I said

"There was no need when Winston was happy to do the job. The Whisperers didn't even have to push hard for him to kill Chet."

"But then you owned his soul."

"Not me, no. But any demon would love to have a necromancer at their command."

"So what demon commands Winston Merrill?"

"I am not that foolish Neema, Daughter of the Priestess, Isoke. Granddaughter to the Fon Warrior." Alastor offered his neck. "Send me back now so that I might know the cost of my betrayal."

"Tell me about Esther."

"She witnessed what happened that day Winston killed Chet. At first, Winston tried to convince Ben to go back home, but Ben wouldn't listen."

"Winston says he blacked out. That he doesn't remember what happened."

"It's easier for Winston that way, but he wanted Chet dead the moment Chet arrived at Ben's home. For Winston, it was a personal affront. He believed Chet had stepped out of his place."

"You didn't help him?"

"I didn't say that. You wanted to know if Winston was hijacked, and he wasn't. He housed no demon when he killed Chet Joseph. And one cut, one stab in the right place would have done the job, but Winston was... well, the man he is now."

"But there is no way we can connect Chet's murder to Winston," Jasen said.

Alastor looked smug. "Not unless you find the body."

"It's buried somewhere between Pennsylvania and Ohio. Under foundation and concrete by now."

"I'm sure I could find it for you," Alastor said.

I scoffed at him. "In exchange for what?"

"The protection of the Demon Hunter."

"I don't protect demons. But you can tell me about Esther. Did she kill herself?"

"In a way. For years, Esther had difficulty dealing with what she saw that day. She struggled as a teen and as an adult. Even though she knew Winston killed Chet, she never said a word." He shrugged. "Only Esther knows why she kept his secret. When they got back to Long Island, she kept up the pretense. She sent a few letters to Chet's mother. She never told Elliot what happened and kept everything from Benjamin once he... snapped out of his shock."

"But she couldn't handle this secret. She went to Winston, didn't she? Told him she wanted to come forward."

"Esther was an addict by that time, Neema. She imploded. Winston knew it was just a matter of time."

"So, he called on you."

"He didn't need me for Esther. She was already on the edge. It didn't take much to push her over. One or two whisperers was enough."

Jasen started the car as I sat there ruminating over what Alastor had told me. I wasn't surprised to discover that demons were all over Chet Joseph's murder. But I had one more question for him. "And Allison?"

Alastor drew back then, his face shuttered. His accommodating attitude gone. He was silent as we sped down the Southern State Parkway back to Brooklyn. I could see in his eyes he wouldn't answer any more questions, which meant I didn't need him anymore. But I didn't want to kill him in front of Jasen. Even though I knew full well what I was dealing with, Jasen struggled to adjust to this new world.

I DIDN'T BRING DEMONS into my sanctified home so when Jasen parked his car behind mine in the driveway, I dragged Alastor around the house and into the backyard. I had him strapped to a chair and was moving around a few items in the tool shed for his stay when Raina stepped outside to join us.

"Still don't understand why he's still alive," she said, as she stood over Alastor. "Those kids in Louisiana hadn't even lived life yet. One of them, the girl, was scheduled to attend Xavier in the fall."

"He doesn't care about that," I said, from inside the shed. "They were just a means to an end for him. What we need to find out from him is who killed Allison. I'm guessing it wasn't Winston Merrill since he's confined to a wheelchair."

"Winston's creative," Alastor said.

"Not that creative," I stepped to the door of the tool shed so I could look at him. "And you will help me find Chet Joseph. We're bringing him back to his family."

"Sorry I offered."

"Be glad you offered, or you'd be facing Baal right now."

I hadn't used the shed in a while, but the iron chair bolted to the floor wasn't going anywhere. I settled Alastor in its clutches while Raina stood in the door way watching me.

"This is rather cruel," Alastor said. "You can't leave me out here."

"You may look human, but we both know your body does not function like that of a human being. You'll be fine out here. Besides, you didn't think I'd let you in my home, did you? Not so you can summon your demon friends and dirty my place with your presence."

"I don't think dirty is the right word Neema." He tilted his head back so he could see me as the last lock clicked into place. With his wrists and ankles attached to the chair, Alastor wasn't going anywhere.

"Stay here," I said, "while I figure out what happened between Allison and Winston, and behave." I tapped his head. "Draw a mental map so I can find Chet Joseph's body and pray that I don't come back with Baal."

"You would never do such a thing."

"You hope." I locked the tool shed and looped the key through a thin chain I drew around my waist. I tugged my shirt over the chain and followed Raina inside. She stopped me right inside the door, her hand clutching my upper arm.

"I went through that box," she said. "The one we got from Elliot Goldstein."

"Find anything useful?"

"I need you to take me to Allison's apartment."

"And how do you propose that we leave here with a house full of people?"

She gave me a pointed look until I shook my head. "No, Raina. I am not walking through the spirit world with you. I won't take that chance."

"We need to get into that apartment, Neema."

"Didn't you bring Sheree up here for just these moments?"

"Is she the one you called tonight when you needed help?"

"No but—"

"Because she isn't ready and doesn't know what to look for. Trust me, Neema. If I could send her instead I would, but she doesn't know what to look for yet."

"And you do?"

"Well, *I'll* know when I see it."

I shook my head because the idea was a bad one, but I didn't want to go back out with Jasen. I'd rather have Raina at my back, anyway. I squeezed her hand. "Then we have to leave now."

"I know. And no matter what happens, I won't let go." We didn't need to discuss what could happen if she did. Taking a deep breath, I crossed into the spirit world, holding Raina at my side.

Time and space operated different here. The browns and grays of the demon realm were always a shock, but they were the first clue we had left behind the human world. I hurried us through the house and into the street because I didn't want to be caught here with Raina. Once outside, several houses down, I slipped back into the human realm, my heart thundering. No one's safety meant more than Raina's.

We walked to my car, parked at the end of the street. We slid inside and pulled off. "Liz worries about me," Raina said. "She thinks I'm too old to be doing this."

"So, do you."

"If it were up to me, Neema. I would be by your side for many more years, but I'll be seventy-two on my next birthday. And I know what you will say. I'm fit and healthy. But I'm just not able to keep up with you anymore."

"I know that Raina, but I don't like it."

"You'll be fighting demons long after I'm gone, Neema."

And that was the crux of the situation, wasn't it? I had been fighting demons for almost three hundred years, and was no end in sight. Raina, Ray, and even Sheree would find their way out, but I would still be the Demon Hunter.

Before the self-pity settled in, I pulled onto Allison's street. The entire block was eerily quiet as I drove by her brownstone. I parked several doors down and grabbed my sword from the back seat. Raina grabbed the bow and arrows before we headed up the dark and quiet street.

CHAPTER TWENTY-TWO

Florida

1743

The Dahomean Sword vibrated in my hands, its power so intense that it felt alive. Priest had graced the sword with enough holy water that any demon would sense its power before it even drew near me. The strap that hung from my hip had a hilt for the sword, and I slid the sword inside. The longer sword he had forged was strapped across my back, its power burning against my skin. He had designed these blades to exorcize demons with a single blow. The language he had used to bless the blades was unlike any language I knew, but the words were etched into the steel.

The daggers and bow and arrows were secondary weapons I hoped would not be necessary. I preferred to be swift when dealing with demons. I slid on the arm bracelet he had shaped from the shackles I brought from South Carolina. This bracelet was beyond anything I had imagined and made me wonder who Priest was. A deceptive piece of jewelry, the bracelet reformed into manacles, acting as a prison for demons I wanted to capture rather than kill. I thought the idea rather clever and appreciated Priest's innovation. The bracelet also scared me since he had performed a magic that was not human.

I stood alone in the room they had given me, my meager belongings wrapped in a sack at my feet. The others steered clear of me since I had walked out of that grave, and I couldn't fault them. A dead woman coming back from the grave would terrify anyone. Ready to move on, I packed while they all slept.

Once I strapped on my weapons, I grabbed my sack. My sudden disappearance would be best for us all.

"You would consider leaving without speaking with me first." I glanced at the doorway to see Priest staring at me.

"You've been avoiding me since the Seminoles attacked us, since you kissed me."

He looked away from me, but when he turned back his look was intense. "None but a thief need sneak out at night."

"It is best I go silently."

"I was wrong to avoid you, but there is no future for us. You cannot hunt demons and stay by my side."

"You could always join me," I said.

"And be a burden to you?" He shook his head. "That is neither my decision nor yours."

I pulled the strap over one shoulder and knotted it crossways under my breast. I tried to slide past him, my face averted, but he didn't move.

"You know I must leave," I said. "I can't risk more demons coming here to hunt me. That puts you and everything you have built in danger."

"I never thought I could care for another woman."

"And you've clarified that neither of our feelings matter."

"The first and only woman I loved was taken from me and sold deeper South. By the time I got to South Carolina, she was already dead."

"My condolences."

"I took care of the men responsible for her death."

"I am sure you did."

"And I promised that I would never allow myself to fall for another woman. Not while slave or fugitive."

I understood how he felt. I had vowed the same when Cuffee died. That our lives were not our own was difficult to withstand. I looked up at him standing over me and tried to memorize every line of his face. Whatever we said or did in this moment did not change what was about to happen. I had to leave.

"I'm scared, Priest."

He placed one hand against my chest, right above my breasts. My breathing slowed as I felt a calmness fill me. I could see my feelings reflected in his eyes, and I wondered how I could feel anything after Cuffee. Cuffee had died just a year ago, and here I yearned for another man. He touched the puckered skin on my chest that had begun to fade, the scar a reminder of when I had dropped dead at his feet. Like all my scars, this too would disappear.

"I dreamed of you just now," he said. his eyes focused on the fingers that had traced a line down one breast. "In my dream, you no longer walked alone."

"Did you walk with me?"

He shook his head. "The dead man, Quaco, had children from a slave woman. One is a son. He will be your companion." He moved away from me, and I felt the loss of his touch.

"I cannot die, Priest. I will always walk alone."

"His children will belong to you and you to them."

"Come with me," I said, drawing closer to him. I put one hand on his forearm, and his muscles tensed at my touch.

"This place is a refuge, Neema, and I need to remain here until..."

"Until when? Until slavers find you? Hunt you down? I can keep you safe."

"I am not the one who needs your protection," he said. I could feel him drawing away from me, and I didn't want that to happen. I could not leave with distance between us. I would have rather left in the silence of the night.

I didn't know what to do, so I pressed against him until his back bumped the wall behind us. My breasts rested against his chest, my hips to his hips. He could only move if he pushed me away. I pressed close and placed my hands on either side of the wall above his shoulders. The beauty of being a woman my height was that we almost stood eye to eye. He watched me, but his hands remained clenched by his side.

I lowered my lids as my eyes combed his face, determined to remember every feature. Perhaps I felt too soon after Cuffee. Perhaps not. All I knew was that Priest woke something in me that was both strange and familiar. My mother had protected me against the interests of slave and free men, of white men and black, but I had never been a foolish woman. I understood what happened between a woman and a man even if I had never experienced it myself.

"Do you understand what you ask me for?" Priest said, dragging my attention from his rapidly moving throat to his narrowed eyes. "Do you understand?"

He lifted me in his arms like a woman much shorter and lighter than he before I could shake my head no. My weapons tumbled around us, and I couldn't catch my breath before my shirt followed. I had never bared myself before a man, but I had no time for modesty before his hands and mouth drew a fever from me. I felt overwhelmed, a little afraid because I did not know this was what we had been dancing toward. What Cuffee and I had never known.

I had no time to be ashamed of my nakedness or to cover myself before him because he was like a man untamed. He touched and took and never allowed me to take a deep breath. I was unsure but never surer of anything in my short life. I had died before knowing a man's touch, a husband's love and if that first touch came from Priest, then that was how it would be. He spoke in a familiar tongue but not in the language I knew. The sounds were guttural, a bold and strong sound I held onto as he touched me. It seemed right, fated that I found myself in the arms of Priest. I had been sent to him for salvation, and his spirit had called to mine long before our physical joining. We fit together as nature intended, but our connection was deeper than that. My spirit recognized him as part of my past, present, and future. He was meant for me, and I for him and in our joining, I knew we would be forever bonded.

"Stay with me a little while," he said, lying on his back beside me but with his hand resting against my hip. "Another hour or two won't hurt."

I still waited for my heart to settle, my breath to return. I had never, in my eighteen years of life, felt so connected to another human being. "Don't make this harder," I said.

"No need to wake me when you leave," he said. "But let us lie together for a moment before you go."

I hesitated, but I knew what my answer would be. There was no other answer once he had touched me. He turned on his back, shifting our bodies, so I draped over him. I liked the thought of protecting him as he, in forging my weapons, had protected me. Settling my arms around him, I wanted to spend these last moments as close to him as possible. But this memory would have to hold me until I made my way back to him because I didn't know how long that would be.

IT WAS STILL DARK OUT when I left the Priest. I buried my reluctance, strapped on my weapons, and slid from the room. I felt different from the woman who had left Manhattan so many months ago, different from even the woman I had been in South Carolina. Whatever innocence I had still had in slavery was gone, and I had become someone I didn't recognize.

I hurried away from the small community that the fugitive women and men had built and moved deeper in the woods. It wasn't until I had walked a mile I realized that someone followed me. I didn't slow down or falter in my steps, but I removed the machete at my waist. Considering my enhanced abilities, if anyone could follow me without my knowledge, I had to be distracted. That and the careful tread meant whoever followed me did not want to be discovered.

I slowed down, wanting the person to reveal themselves. It didn't take long.

With about two miles between us and the fugitive community, Dagon stepped into the sunlight. I sighed with relief when I realized that she had been the one following me. I wasn't prepared to fight in the aftermath of my time with Priest. I wanted to savor that moment as long as I could.

"I thought you might slip out when everyone was sleeping." Dagon said.

"When did you return?"

"Last night but you were... occupied."

She wore strips of cloth across her breasts and lower body, and I understood why her dress was not traditional tribal wear. She dressed for ease of movement. For the sensibilities of the Europeans, Dagon covered her body, but she did so only in ways that would help her hunt and protect. The only clothing she needed was the bow and arrows strapped to her back. And she didn't need them because her legs and hands were lethal.

Her hair had been separated into two braids draped over her shoulders and bound them with leather. The moccasins on her feet helped her to sneak up on her prey. She was a beautiful woman with her copper skin and black hair, and her tattoos only enhanced her beauty. I gazed at her with curiosity. She wasn't the savage the Europeans always called them, and the more time I spent with Dagon, the more curious I became.

"I am not ashamed of what occurred between me and Priest."

"Nor should you be," she said, smiling. "I was shocked to discover that you and Priest had drawn so close in my absence, however."

"But you have returned as you left, with no word."

She acknowledged my statement with a nod. "I heard of the Seminole attack. You saved Priest's life."

She had my full attention then. It wasn't what she said. Her tone sparked my curiosity.

"Lily told me you were killed protecting Priest. That you were dead when they buried you."

"But that would be impossible."

Dagon smiled. "Only for those who have never heard of the Vodou."

I stepped back, an arrow in my bow and pointed at her as the final syllable died. "What do you know of the Vodou?"

She smiled. "Did you have the same reaction when Priest told you of the Vodou?"

I wasn't ready to trust her with my secrets so I said, "We never spoke of the Vodou."

"You should have. He has had his own encounters with the creature."

I hid my surprise well. He had mentioned the Vodou but had not said he interacted with her. I hoped that I would one day be able to confront him over his reticence.

"Put away your bow and arrows," Dagon said, amusement in her voice. "I mean you no harm. In fact, I will help you find the Vodou."

"How do I know that you will take me to her?"

"Because I have searched for her myself," Dagon said. "And I know where she is."

I lowered my bow with some reluctance. The doubt that had marked me in South Carolina came rushing back. Whatever peace I had found in the refuge that Priest and his people had built was gone. I didn't want to trust Dagon, but my desire to find the Vodou outweighed my distrust. So. I followed her anyway.

WE TRAVELED FOR SO long I almost suggested we go our separate ways. My desire to find the Vodou had lessened by the time we entered Pensacola.

"Before the Spaniards came and claimed this land," Dagon said. "It belonged to the Panzacola Indians. Another tribe like mine that numbered many before the white man brought his disease and wars."

I was not interested in one of her tales at that point. We had traveled through swamps and untamed land, avoiding panthers and alligators, hunting deer and rabbits. This lifestyle was far from the one I had known in New York. Helping to take care of a household had not prepared me for primitive, outdoor living. Even though I had traveled from New York to South Carolina, I didn't think I would ever get used to living in the natural world. I much preferred to look up at the sky and see a roof instead.

We were also less than clean. We bathed in streams and scrubbed our clothes with a crude version of a soap I had learned to make from my mother, but I still didn't feel clean enough. I was excited when we arrived in Pensacola. Food and cleanliness outweighed my desire to see the Vodou.

"Pensacola, like St. Augustine, belongs to the Spaniards," Dagon said. "They will not bother you here. Not like the British."

"So, they offer slaves haven?"

"As well as they can with British colonies nearby."

"And how do you know the Vodou is here?"

Dagon smiled. "I just do."

I followed her to a tavern on a busy street. The curious looks cast our way didn't possess the danger that had followed me from New York to South Carolina. Perhaps I was as safe as I could be amid slavery. I had paid little attention to the wars between the European nations, but I found myself glad that Spain rather than Britain claimed Florida. For a little while, I could catch my breath.

Dagon walked to a corner furthest from the door and settled down at a table across from an Indian man. His skin was copper like hers, but he belonged to another tribe.

"You are far from home, Timucua," he said to Dagon, not bothering to glance my way as I sat in a chair between them.

"And you sound well schooled in the ways of the Spaniards, not the Apalachee."

He sat back, his stoic face belied by the clenching of his hands. "To live among them, we must adopt their ways."

She inclined her head in acknowledgment. "They change much with their presence. I too have learned the ways of the English."

His lip curved a little. "They seek to tame our people like wild horses."

"I come searching for a..." she paused, "Spiritual being."

"There are no elders here to guide you on a vision quest."

"You misunderstand me." Her voice lowered. "You have heard the Africans speak of the Vodou."

"I have heard of this African religion. The African slaves, the ones new to our land, often speak of the spiritual world."

"There is a—a—" she paused again. "A powerful being that calls herself the Vodou. She's black as night and stands taller than most humans."

He moved back as if she had struck him. "You should not speak of her. The Africans fear her. They call her a witch."

"Where can I find her?"

"I cannot help you," he shook his head. "You are venturing into treacherous ground. Go see the African witch doctor. She is banned from the city so she lives an hour's walk from here."

An hour's walk? I groaned. I desired food and a bed. The order they came in mattered little.

"We go to this witch doctor," Dagon said.

"Perhaps we should leave it be."

The Apalachee man looked as if he agreed with me. "You should go back the way you came."

Dagon smiled. "I came from too far away to turn back now. Come, Neema. There is a shaman we must see."

Not only was I less sure of finding the Vodou, but this quest had seemed more like Dagon's than mine. She also seemed to be searching for the Vodou. So even though I wanted a bath and some sleep, curiosity made me follow her out the door.

I EXPECTED A HOVEL, but the witch doctor lived in a sturdy one-room house on the edge of town. She was far enough away so the people would not feel threatened by her, but near enough that she could travel into town for any goods she needed. A pen with two pigs stood at the side of the house, and a goat was tethered to a bar at the front of the house. It bleated upon our approach.

Cautious, I strung an arrow. Dagon glanced down at my hands, frowned, and stepped closer to the doorway.

"You are not welcome here!" a strong, mature voice said from inside the house. The woman we sought was an older woman.

"We only want to ask a question," I said.

"You, perhaps, but not the one with you. That one is here for other reasons."

I tried again. "We only want to find the Vodou."

"Oh, I am sure that one with you wants to find the Vodou."

"Do not listen to her, Neema. She has been out here by herself for far too long."

The door opened, and the woman stepped through the doorway. She was much shorter than I had expected, but the power she exuded made her seem tall. Her hair, thick and silver, was braided in a ring around her head. And her skin was a light brown. Even her features, keen, spoke of a European influence. The light brown of her eyes was striking.

"You are not African," I said, my bow and arrow forgotten at my side.

She frowned. "Am I not? Look closer, daughter of Benin. The Europeans left much in Africa too. We all are more than what we appear to be." She looked again at Dagon. "Including this one. I know what you are."

"You know nothing."

"I felt your coming many days ago. You will fail, princess. Angels protect the one with you."

Dagon drew her arrow; its point aimed at the woman's heart.

"What are you doing, Dagon?" I asked, unsure of what was unfolding before me.

"She's working with the Vodou," Dagon said.

"The Vodou works alone," the witch doctor said, the sudden movement of her hand distracting me so I didn't move quick enough to stop Dagon's arrow before it struck the woman's chest.

The surrounding air swirled as if a storm brewed, but this magic came from the woman who had dropped at our feet. I moved to see if she were dead, but the air had turned into a dense cloud, and I couldn't even see my hands in front of my face.

Afraid to move, afraid to take the wrong step, I stilled my body until the world around me paused as if waiting too.

"Neema!" a familiar voice called, and I opened my eyes to see my mother standing before me.

The cloud, the house, everything around me disappeared, and I stood on the Commons in Manhattan.

"What is this?" I said, looking about in surprise.

"The witch doctor knew you would not heed her warnings, so she sent for me, my daughter."

"I am here to find the Vodou."

"The Vodou will not be found until she wants to be found. What Dagon has told you is wrong."

"But I don't want this curse, Mama. I want to come home."

She rested her hands on my shoulders and shook me. "Enough, Neema! You have the blood of a warrior, of a priestess pumping through your veins. My mother, left for dead in one of the King's battles, was one of the greatest woman warriors who ever lived. You will stand strong. You *will* be the Demon Hunter that heaven will respect, and hell will fear."

"But—"

"I have no time for your cries, daughter. I came to tell you that Dagon is neither friend nor ally." Mama halted and looked over her shoulder. "Take out the blade that the priest fashioned for you, my daughter. She strikes you from behind."

Without hesitation, I withdrew my sword from its scabbard and pivoted at the same time a sword came flashing through the cloud.

"What are you doing, Dagon?" I growled, standing hilt to hilt, chest to chest. The sword hummed as the Priest said it would at the scent of a demon.

Dagon's hand pushed into my chest, shoving me so hard that I stumbled back several feet before standing with my blade drawn in front of me.

"You are not worthy to hunt demons," she said. "And the old woman is wrong. I want you to find the Vodou." She cocked her head to the side as she stared at me. "Or rather, I wanted the Vodou to come to you."

"But you helped train me." I sounded close to tears.

"Why would I care if you learn to fight or not? I don't fear you. Less than a year ago you were a silly slave girl. How could you be a danger to any of us? I only wanted you so I could get to the Vodou but..." Her feet glided across the ground as she brought her sword down toward my neck.

I countered, our blades clanging against each other. Her blade flashed as she drove her sword toward my neck again. I blocked her with the flat of my sword, but I couldn't do much more than defend myself as her blade swung down from the right, up from the left. I stumbled back as I parried each thrust, realizing that I was no real match for her.

"How could you betray Priest?" I panted when she took a break from pummeling me with her sword and circled me instead.

She smiled. "Neema. I don't think he will care."

Dread overcame me, but I asked anyway. "What did you do, Dagon?"

"What do you think I did, Neema? Your Priest can't care about anyone. Anymore."

"Did you—did you kill them all?"

"Left not one standing," she smiled. "Perhaps if you had recognized me, you might have saved one of them."

I couldn't even scream or cry as I thought about Priest. Anger burning inside me, I gripped the hilt of my sword with both hands and brought it down on her with all my strength.

She lifted her sword to counter my strike, and I brought my foot down on her knee. The hilt of my sword hit the back of her head when she dropped to her knees. I pressed her chest to the ground with my foot while the side of my sword rested against her throat. She tried to move, and I let the sharp side of my blade nick her skin. She stopped struggling as her skin bubbled.

"Priest made your sword," Dagon said, adjusting so the blade wouldn't dig into her skin.

"I won't talk to you about Priest."

"Look Neema, there's no reason for you to get involved, to die because the Vodou cursed you without sanction. You can join me. Let me protect you, and we can make our own rules."

"Why?" I asked.

"Pay attention," Dagon said, she turned so she could look at me and I, because I wanted to see her face, let her. "Don't you understand what's happening here. You were in New York when the law murdered slaves because of a supposed plot. You were in South Carolina and saw how they punished slaves after the rebellion at Stono. You saw what the British did to Fort Mose, what happens when my kind get involved. There are battles fought every day that humans just don't see, battles between those who follow the Creator and those who follow Lucifer. But who says Lucifer should rule or be deemed equal to the Creator. He, like us, is one of the Fallen."

"You're putting me in the middle of a foolish demon war..."

"I am Lucifer's equal."

"So, take his place. This is not my concern. And it was not the concern of Priest."

"But it is," she grabbed the point of my blade with both hands and pushed the sword away even as her hands dripped blood and her skin bubbled. "You are the Demon Hunter and whoever controls the Demon Hunter can rule the demons."

"I can't allow you to roam free on earth, Dagon."

"And who said it's your call to make, Demon Hunter?"

I froze at the sound of a familiar voice and felt overwhelmed and outnumbered. I couldn't deal with one demon, much less two.

"Step back," Baal said, towering over me and Dagon. I remembered that day in Hughson's Tavern when I shivered in fear as he stood across the room from me. I had come far from that terrified slave girl, but I hadn't come far enough.

"She killed Priest," I said, pulling a dagger from the strap on my shin and driving it toward her chest. Baal grabbed my wrist before my blade touched her skin and squeezed until I dropped the knife next to Dagon. With his other hand, he lifted Dagon under one of her arms and pulled her from under me. The bindings he latched around her wrist looked as thin as thread, but they zapped whatever strength she had. She fell against him, but he took no notice of her weight.

"Dagon is a demon princess," he said. "Or a prince if she deems it necessary. She is for Lucifer to handle."

"She must pay—"

"I realize that it would be beneath me to battle you now. You are not..." he tilted his head to look at me, his red-gold locks swinging to the side. "A worthy opponent. At least not yet."

He smiled then, and the ground opened beneath his feet. But I knew it was only for my benefit. Wherever demons came from, they did not live underground. His tactic was still terrifying though. The earth formed a dark cloud around them, and they both vanished. But not before I saw the anger and hatred in Dagon's eyes.

The woman at my feet groaned, and I knelt beside her. The arrow that had protruded from her chest lay next to her. She gripped my arm as she struggled to a seated position. "Demons are dangerous enemies to have, Neema, daughter of Isoke. But you have powerful magic inside you. You need only to learn how to use it."

"My mother—"

The shaman shook her head. "Isoke says you can never return to this New York, at least not for years to come, but she has blessed my teachings. I will help strengthen you."

I helped the shaman to her feet, wanting to get her inside so I could go somewhere alone and grieve for the death of Priest. As angry as I felt over Dagon's betrayal, I was even more aggrieved that I would never see Priest again.

The shaman turned as we stood at the front door of her cottage and laid both hands on my shoulders. "One day you will discover the power you hold from your mother's blood *and* your father's. When you do, Demon Hunter, even the Vodou will regret what she has done to you."

She left me to stand there and wonder how I would ever discover the story of my parents. My father remained on an island in the Caribbean after my mother was sold to a slave merchant and taken to New York. Because of the mass hysteria that had resulted in slaves being killed or sold, I would never see my mother again. Anger at losing her, at losing Priest, built inside me and I embraced the emotion. Everything that had happened lay at the feet of demons. This much I knew. I welcomed being the Demon Hunter, and I vowed that every *single demon* would come to fear my presence.

CHAPTER TWENTY-THREE

I didn't want to walk through the demon realm to get inside so I had Raina keep watch while I jimmied the lock. The locks for these brownstones were sturdy, so I took longer to get inside. Three minutes later, Raina and I slipped inside the foyer. The landlord hadn't returned yet so the entire house was pitch black and still.

"The demon scent is still strong," I said, taking the stairs up to Allison's apartment.

"Did Alastor tell you why she was killed?"

"I think," I said, popping the lock to Allison's upstairs apartment. "That it was all about Chet Joseph."

An object flew out of the dark, hitting me on my shoulder before I could move. I didn't allow it to fall again, wrenching it out of the hand of my attacker and reaching for his throat. Or rather, once my eyes adjusted to the dark, her throat.

Annoyed, I shoved her away from me and tossed the bat across the room. "Why would you attack first? You could have hurt either me or Raina." I pulled Raina inside and shut the door before I turned on my flashlight.

Maria rubbed her throat and watched me. "I haven't felt safe since Ms. Stevens died."

"So, you came to the place where she was killed. Was that supposed to make you feel safer?"

"I don't know what else to do," Maria slumped against the desk. "I don't understand why anyone would want to kill her. I thought maybe if I came here, found something to explain why she's dead, I could go to the police and..."

"Help solve Allison's murder?"

"I know it's foolish of me but..." Maria looked at me. "You said you work with your dad, and you're the same age I am."

Raina and I exchanged looks before she grabbed the girl's arm. "Neema and I need to look around for a few minutes. I'd prefer it if you waited for us in the car." She placed her cell phone in Maria's hand. "You can even keep this so you can call her phone if you see anyone coming. Don't tell Neema this, but you don't have to bypass a PIN or passcode."

"Raina," I groaned. "How many times—"

"Go," Raina said, pushing the girl toward the door. "And don't disappear. I'd like to chat with you when we're done."

I locked the door behind Maria, shaking my head. Going over to the window, I pressed the remote key, and the car lights flashed. I waited until Maria climbed into the car before I turned back to Raina.

"She was lying," Raina said. "She was here looking for something."

I nodded my head. "Yeah, let's hope we come across that something."

"You look around out here," Raina said. "And I'll take the bedroom."

"And whatever we need will jump out at us, right?" I muttered, even though Raina had already left the room. I walked over to Allison's desk. My initial visit had been quick, so I wanted to be thorough this time.

Examining a person's life, particularly someone like Allison who died young, could feel invasive. I had poked my way through plenty of lives, and it still troubled me. Sitting behind the desk, I pointed my flashlight toward her desk drawer so I could take a closer, more thorough peek. I saw nothing different: pens, pencils, paper clips, erasers, the usual. Two envelopes turned out to be tickets of a showing for the Lion King next month and a notice for traffic court for next year, a product of New York's massive ticketing culture.

I placed the envelopes back and dropped to my knees to look for any clasp envelopes taped under the desk drawer or false bottoms. I knew I was thinking about what I'd seen on television, but sometimes television influenced the ones doing the hiding too. Grabbing the back of the desk, I pulled it from the wall and shined my flashlight on the back.

We called each other at the same time. "I found a beacon," Raina said, a piece of cloth in her hand. "It was in a corner of the closet. Allison wouldn't have noticed unless she was about to spring clean."

"And I found a hexagram," I said, pulling the desk further from the wall.

"Somebody was aiming some powerful demon trouble at our girl Allison," Raina looked down at the beacon.

"And it had to be someone who had access to her apartment long enough to paint the hexagram and leave the beacon."

"I don't understand why anyone would dabble with demons," Raina said, shaking her head. She looked at the beacon again. "You know, Neema, I'm sure that this is identical to the beacon we found in the box at Elliot's house."

"Is that significant?"

"The only way beacons are identical—same demon skin, same bindings, even the way it's wrapped—is if it's made by the same person."

WHEN WE OPENED THE car door, Maria sat in the back seat, arms wrapped around her knees. Her fear filled the car.

"What happened to you?" I said, turning to face her after I slid into the car.

She shook her head, and Raina and I exchanged looks. "Did something happen while we were inside?" Raina said.

Maria looked up at us. "I've been seeing things. These... these glimpses at the edge of my vision. Like something is watching me, following me."

"Since when?"

Her voice dropped even lower. "Since... since the night Allison, Ms. Stevens died. At first, I thought maybe it was her. Like she was trying to tell me something. That's why I came back here tonight. To see if maybe it would help me understand her more, but I... I don't think it's Allison, Ms. Stevens. I... I guess I never believed it was her."

"What is it you're seeing?"

"Shadows. Something that's not human." She shook her head. "I don't know what I'm seeing. I know it started the night she died."

I glanced at Raina before turning back to Maria. "Where were you the night Allison died, Maria?"

"I don't..."

"How did you get those photos?"

Maria rubbed her upper arms and rocked back and forth before she answered. "After Ms. Stevens came back from Mississippi, she was different. Subdued. She even missed work more. She was distracted in class, and stopped letting me eat lunch in her classroom. Said she had to work on something private."

"Did she tell you what it was?"

"Yeah, one day. I left school early and saw her in her car crying. Weeping. Like somebody had died or broken her heart. At first, I thought it might have been her boyfriend, but it wasn't."

"She had figured out what happened to Chet Joseph, hadn't she?"

"The guy in the photograph?" Maria nodded her head. "Her family was mixed up in his disappearance somehow, and Allison was afraid that her uncle, the one who gave her the pictures, was involved."

"But he wasn't. It was her aunt's family, no relation to Allison at all."

"But it was, you know. Allison had grown up seeing Winston Merrill as her uncle. She didn't want to think he was involved. That was why she went to see him that week before she died."

"Was she planning to turn him in, Maria?"

"I know that she was torn, but I know her. She had... she had taken me under wing. Offered me a place to stay when—" Maria stopped, her widened gaze settling on us.

"You were here that night, weren't you?" Raina said.

"I saw nothing. Allison had grown nervous since the day she visited her uncle. She was worried, didn't want to be alone. Even though my mother allowed me to return home, I stayed with Allison for a few days that week. Just to make sure she was okay."

"Did you see who visited her that night?"

Maria shook her head. "It was like she knew something was wrong the moment she heard the doorbell ringing. She gave me the photos, made me hide in a crawlspace in the roof of the house. She told me that no matter what, I was not to come out. I was not to scream or bring any attention to myself. She made me a promise. Told me if I broke my promise, she would never speak to me again."

"So, you were in the crawl space when Allison was killed."

A sob escaped before she clamped a hand over her mouth. "I could have helped her."

"You would have died," I said. "You couldn't have helped her."

"Neema," Raina said, smacking my arm.

"It's not as if I'm lying. As soon as that beacon was placed in Allison's apartment, she was dead, Maria. You're lucky they didn't kill you too."

"But I'm being hunted."

"No." I shook my head. "If they had wanted you dead, you would have been dead that night. Did you see anything? Hear anything."

"Just a woman's voice."

"Not," Raina said, looking at me, "a man's?"

"No, the person who came to see Allison that night was a woman. Of that, I'm sure. I hid in that crawl space until after the police left. I was... I was terrified."

Maria's words turned over in my head as I started the car. The demons had noticed her presence, but she hadn't been the target of their interest.

"So why would you come back here tonight?" Raina said. "And by yourself no less. That makes no sense."

"I know it was stupid of me, but I thought coming back here might help me remember details of that night. I didn't tell the police I was in Ms. Stevens' house that night, and I can't help but wonder if I should have. I owe her, you know. When my mom put me out of the house earlier this year, Ms. Stevens looked out for me. I wanted to look out for her."

"And that's it, Maria? You're telling us all you know?"

"I'm in way over my head, Neema. I'm scared. I think someone is following me, and I don't want to die. So yeah, I've told you everything I know."

Raina, still turned in her seat, patted Maria on the hand before she turned back to the front, but I was less inclined to offer comfort. I didn't quite trust the girl, and I did not believe she had told us everything.

OUR STREET WAS ALSO quiet when we turned the corner. Even though the hour was late, this quiet held the stillness that always told me when demons were present. I felt like I was driving back to Elliot's house. I passed the house and parked at the end of the block.

"You feel it," I said to Raina, my voice tight.

Raina nodded her head. "It's rather strong."

"What's rather strong?" Maria said.

I was reminded again of just how different Raina was from most humans. They all were, these women and men tasked with walking with me since that year long ago when their fate became entwined with mine.

"You stay here," I said to Maria. "I'll lock the door and put on the alarm, but you have to keep your head down."

"I don't want to stay in here alone."

"Listen," I faced her, the intensity of my voice causing her eyes to widen. "You're safer in here alone with the doors locked than you would be inside that house with me. Keep your head down and don't bring attention to yourself. And whatever happens, do not panic and leave this car."

"I got it," she said.

"I sure hope so."

Raina and I exited the car at the same time and as much as I wanted her to stay in the car, I knew it would be useless. We had left Jasen, Sheree and Liz in that house. I handed her the bow and arrows while I unsheathed the sword. We rushed toward the house, not wanting any of the neighbors to peek outside and see us walking down the street with weapons.

I led the way to the back of the house first, wanting to check on Alastor. The house had been demon-proofed years ago so if demons had somehow entered my home, I wanted to know how. When I opened the door to the shed, Alastor was slumped over the chair unconscious and still shackled. Raina and I entered the shed and closed the door. I used the light from my phone to be less noticeable.

"Alastor wake up," I commanded, and he came awake, arms stopped short by the shackles before he could thrash them around. "What happened?" I said.

He blinked before his dazed eyes settled on me. "The demons. They tried to bypass your protections." He struggled to swallow. "What did you use to bless this place?"

"I wouldn't be much of a demon hunter if I didn't know how to protect my home now, would I? You don't spend almost three hundred years as one of the most hated demon enemies without a haven," I sighed. "Now what did you see or hear?"

"Unchain me first."

"Not a chance. I can't have you loose in my backyard when I don't know what I'm walking into. Tell me what you saw."

"How can I see anything from a shed in the back of your house?"

"You're a demon. You're creative. Walls and doors have never stopped you from seeing inside."

"When the demons realized that they couldn't enter, the human went inside. Well, at least one went in, but two came out."

Raina and I exchanged looks, and she slid an arrow into the bow. "Let's not waste anymore time, Neema. We go now."

"Loosen me first," Alastor said, but we already closed the door to the shed.

I led the way up through the back door and towards the basement. The light didn't come on when I flicked the switch, but I still carried my cellphone. I switched on my flashlight app and guided us down the stairs and toward the silent computer station. I stumbled over a body and almost went down on one knee. When I shone the flashlight, Raina gasped but two fingers against her neck told me that Sheree was still alive.

"Help me," I whispered to Raina. I pulled Sheree onto the chair that Raina had rolled over, and I left her to wake up Sheree while I went to the fuse box to turn the lights back on. When light flooded into the basement, Sheree blinked her eyes open and rubbed her head while Raina took in the destruction to our property. The pictures we had taped to the walls had been torn down and ripped to shreds.

"Where's Jasen and Liz?" Raina said, shaking Sheree.

"It happened too fast, Aunt Raina. They overwhelmed us, and we had no time to react."

"What happened to Jasen and Liz?"

"I got knocked out, but I think they were taken upstairs."

"Did you see who took them?"

"I'm not... I'm not sure. I was knocked unconscious before I could see or hear much."

"Let's go upstairs," I said. "Alastor said only one human came in here, but I don't see how one person could have done so much damage."

"Well, remember that demons lie." Raina's anger showed in her quick, sure steps as she led the way up the stairs.

I stayed close behind her as we walked through the kitchen and into the living room. Raina, hesitant, grew more worried as we walked through each room. I didn't blame her. I didn't want to find either Liz or Jasen, but I didn't want to not find them either. When we entered the small office off the dining room, we found Liz.

"Honey," Raina said, dropping the bow and arrow and sliding to the ground next to Liz. She still seemed so young, so strong until I wondered if she could stay with me another year or two. Then Liz came to, sitting up with one hand pressed against her head. Raina kissed her on the lips before she checked Liz for any wounds.

"It happened so fast," Liz was saying. "We were downstairs with Sheree. Jasen had just come into the basement to tell us that the two of you had left. Which you know not to do Raina. We've discussed this. You let me know where you'll be so I won't worry."

"It was my fault," I said, clearing my throat. "I made Raina leave without even coming back in the house."

"Aren't you eighteen? Nineteen? How can you...?"

"You're right, ma'am. Something needed our immediate attention."

"And as much as you want to fuss at Neema we have other things to worry about. Like where's Jasen?"

"He's not in the house?"

"No, Liz. He's not—"

My cell phone rang then. Unknown number. I whipped it out.

"By now you know we've got your good friend Jasen."

"Who is this?"

"Does it matter?"

"Winston's nurse? Helen? Who is this?"

"I'm texting you an address. Come now."

The sudden silence left me with no other choice. I had to leave. By now, Jasen had to be ready to quit. First, his capture at Elliot's house and now, kidnapped from my home. What if this proved too much for him, and he cracked under pressure?

"Who was that, Neema?"

I turned to see both women watching me. "That was whoever has Jasen. I have to go."

"Neema..."

"I have to go," I said, rushing from the room, leaving the two women hugging and kissing.

THE ADDRESS BELONGED to an abandoned building out in Queens, a borough I rarely frequented. Anything located outside of Brooklyn was an on-occasion place. Even my knowledge of Manhattan mostly comprised of the African Burial Ground Museum. I may not have wanted to admit it, but my memories made New York City a difficult place to be.

I parked my car one street over and drew a deep breath. I had dropped Maria off at home and dragged Alastor along with me. It had been a long time since I had felt fear regarding demons, so I might have gotten a little cocky.

"I could be of much better use if you freed me from these shackles," he said, rattling the chains.

"I already told you, I'm trading you."

"It will be a bad trade, Neema. Any demon would think I'm worthless since I'm your captive. It would have been better if you had sent me back to hell."

"Forgive me if I think you're lying." I gripped the chains and dragged him down the street. "Tell me what I'm facing."

He stopped, causing me to bump into him. He drew in a deep breath with his eyes closed before he turned. "The Sin Demons are inside," he said. "All seven."

I looked at him. The Sin Demons were hardly ever in the same place. Even I had only seen Wrath and Greed Demons while trying to determine what happened to Allison Stevens. For all of them to be present in that building did not bode well for me or Jasen.

"Take these off, Neema," Alastor said, holding up his wrists. "You don't trust me, and I get that. But if you take me in there with these chains, you'll leave me helpless, and I'd prefer not to be helpless."

I gazed at him for a long moment before I removed his chains. "You cross me, and I'll banish you, first."

"I've been banished before."

"But not on the wrong side of a demon war. I've already told you. I'll be more than happy to reveal your role in this war to Baal if you cross me."

Alastor turned his nose up at me before we turned toward the building. He ducked behind me as I walked up the stairs toward the front doors.

"Shouldn't you be leading the charge?" I said, shaking his hand from my elbow.

"The safest place in a battle with demons is behind the Demon Hunter," he pushed me toward the front door.

I turned the knob, ready to unsheathe the sword at my back in a moment's notice. The demon presence was so strong that my hand shook as I pushed the door open and stepped inside.

"You sure you want to go into any more buildings," Alastor said.

"This place isn't possessed like Elliot's house."

"Maybe not but it's still dangerous."

The lighting was dim, just enough that we could see a few feet in front of us, but the light cast shadows on the walls. I didn't like open spaces like this one because you had to watch too many areas at once. Shadows flickered around us for a moment before they solidified into solid shapes: demons. There were so many around us, their green, red, yellow, blue, white, gray, brown and gold skins like a palette. They didn't move toward me though, only stood still and stared.

"What are they doing?" I whispered to Alastor who had placed a little distance between the two of us.

"Waiting."

"Bring me Jasen," I said, my eyes panning the room as I turned in a circle to see each entrance and exit. I couldn't tell who was in charge so I spoke to the room at large. "Bring him and tell me what you want."

"I want you to go away," a familiar female voice said. The anger built inside me before she came out of an office and down a few steps. Two shapeshifter demons came in behind her, dragging an unconscious Jasen by his arms. His head dangled so I couldn't see his face, and his body stretched out behind them.

"So, I guess the whole grieving relative bit was fake."

Cindy smiled. "Not all of it. I miss Allison a little."

She no longer looked pale and fragile. She looked dangerous.

CHAPTER TWENTY-FOUR

Cindy walked toward me, her look so different that I almost didn't recognize her. Her red gold hair, pulled into a topknot at Allison's wake fell loose around her shoulders in full, deep waves. Her makeup, flawless, had been applied with a light hand. She dressed like we were on a dinner date. Her wraparound dress with its bold teal and white design said she did not intend to get her hands dirty. Her strappy heels did not say girl fight, but then, a woman in a wedding dress had fought me before so her dress wasn't a perfect indicator.

"You expected my uncle Winston, didn't you?" Cindy said, smiling. "Or perhaps my mother?"

"That would have been less surprising, yes."

Cindy shrugged. "Unlike Uncle Winston and I, my mother is not a necromancer. She knows nothing of that world."

"And let me guess, your uncle taught you everything you know?"

"I've learned that there is much power in calling the dead."

"You mean demons. You've both been fooled into thinking you call the dead."

"Does it matter? Demon? Dead human? As long as I get what I want."

I couldn't keep the disgust from my face and voice as I looked at her. "You've known they were demons all along, haven't you?"

"My uncle should have figured it out, but he sees what he wants to see. I have to protect him."

"Is that why—"

"Do you think I want to answer all of your stupid questions? I only brought you here for an exchange."

"And what do I have that you want?"

Cindy tilted her head and looked as if she wanted to touch me, but she wasn't foolish enough to get that close. Much to my disappointment. "Just you," she said.

"Because you're what she wants to exchange," Alastor said.

She drew back as if offended. "Did I ask you to speak Alastor? I called you to serve me. You speak when I tell you to speak."

The surrounding demons had drawn closer, the Wrath demons glowing from Cindy's rage while death demons sniffed at the smell of death coming. But it wouldn't be enough to feed so many demons. She wasn't enough to control them.

"Why did you kill Allison?" I called out when she was about to walk away from me.

"I don't want to answer your questions."

"It's the least you can do before you hand me over to whatever demon controls you."

"No demon controls me," she said, turning back toward me with an awkward twist of her body. The Wrath demons moved closer as her anger grew brighter.

"Then tell me about Allison. She was your cousin. What could she have done to justify her murder?"

"Believe it or not, I didn't want to kill her. I wanted her to stop digging into the past, stop seeking answers. She received that box from her uncle down south, her father's brother, and she became obsessed. Allison wouldn't let it go, wouldn't stop going on about that damn Chet Joseph. When she went out to Ohio and Long Island, she kept asking her questions. She even wanted to go to New Jersey."

"But she didn't."

"No, I talked her out of that one. Even growing up, Allison was always this save the world type. Wanting to always make shit right. A bleeding heart. She wanted to do right by Chet Joseph. Even came by Uncle Winston's home demanding that he confess, that he sacrifice what's left of his life. It was stupid. He's an old man in a wheelchair. Why should he have to spend the rest of his life in jail for trying to protect a friend?"

"Maybe because he killed someone."

"And that's why Allison had to die. She wouldn't let that tiny little detail go. She came over the night before she died you know. Came to Uncle Winston's house and accused him of killing Chet Joseph, even of killing her mother who—the entire family knows—killed herself when we were twelve. She was threatening to ruin our family, threatening to break my mother's heart. I had to protect them."

"So, you killed her."

"So, I killed her."

"Even though she told the truth."

"Uncle Winston only killed Chet—"

"I mean her mother, Cindy. Your uncle killed Allison's mother too."

This time her anger brought her too close. "You're a lying bitch," she hissed. "My aunt killed herself."

It was my turn to smile. "So, Uncle Winston didn't tell you that part. The part where he called demons to drive Allison's mother to her death. Did he tell you that Esther was in the car that day he followed Benjamin and Chet to Ohio?"

"That's not true."

"Guess uncle didn't show you everything did he? Didn't *tell* you everything."

"I. Don't. Believe. You." She turned to Alastor. "Shut her up."

Alastor looked at me then turned back to Cindy. "She'll kill me."

"I fucking summoned you. You will obey me now."

The Wrath Demons lost control then and swarmed all around her, their glowing white skin and ebony hair swirling around Cindy as they fed off her rage. They seemed determined to drain her of every ounce of anger. They weren't meant to be in this enclosed space with only a single source of wrath.

"I suggest you calm down," I said, taking out my sword. "You're making matters worse."

"Allison was lying. Allison—"

"Was telling the truth, Cindy."

She took a deep breath. "Which doesn't matter. It doesn't change what I want, what I deserve to get." Cindy shook her head. "Allison, Aunt Esther, sometimes sacrifices have to be made." She shrugged.

"And what do you deserve to get, Cindy?"

"The usual. Fame and Fortune." She waved her hand. "What does it matter, anyway?"

"Your aunt wanted to come forward. She wanted to go to the police about the night Chet died. Your uncle couldn't let that happen so he killed her."

"A small sacrifice, Neema. I understand that and so did my uncle."

I nodded my head. "You've traveled too far down this path for me to save you so why don't you lead me to your little demon partner so I can finish a job."

"And that's always been your problem hasn't it," a voice said from the doorway behind us. "Always in a hurry."

AND THAT WAS WHY SHE hadn't sat right with me from the beginning.

She leaned against the door frame, watching me. She being Maria who I had left outside her freaking house on my way to this little rendezvous. She smiled at me, grinned and bowed before she walked just a little toward me. "No need for applause. But tell me, how is it that a demon hunter with almost three hundred years of experience can be so... clueless. It was so easy to send you in circles it was almost boring."

"I'm glad I could offer you some form of amusement even if you almost lost interest," I responded, trying to puzzle out who she was even as my brain resisted the answer before me.

"I guess I didn't teach you well," she said, her face seeming to melt and flatten until a familiar, much hated face appeared before me. I hadn't seen her since Baal came for her outside of the witch doctor's hut when she and I traveled to Pensacola, but I remembered every moment of our time together like it was yesterday.

She had taught me to hunt those months when we traveled from the woods near St. Augustine to the Spanish settlement in Pensacola. I had learned how to survive in the harsh lands of a wild, untamed Florida. Traveling from New York to South Carolina, I saw the land as an enemy, a thing to subdue, a beast to fear. The land had fought me and I, angry at the Manhattan slave conspiracy trials, had fought back. After losing Jacob, I had fought even harder, had gone to war. Dagon, though, had shown me how to embrace the world around me, and if not for her guidance, I would have gone mad after I left St. Augustine. I owed her my life.

Yet, she had been toying with me. She had played me then, and she played me now. My demon sense had not even recognized her presence, and that knowledge worried me.

"Don't feel bad, Neema," Dagon said. "I've been plotting this for years Since you betrayed me, in fact."

"I... betrayed... you. Did you lose your mind in the abyss? Because I remember how you tried to use me to call the Vodou."

Her smile dropped. "Don't mention the abyss. I was in the abyss for centuries before Alastor here helped me find a way out."

Alastor glanced at me. "I promise you it wasn't like that. I had no other choice."

"Look, I'm sure that this reunion is special," Cindy said. "But I'm not interested in observing it. I've delivered the demon hunter to you as promised. Now it's time for you to uphold your end of the bargain."

I attempted to shield Cindy from Dagon's annoyance, but my effort wasn't heartfelt. Dagon smiled and let her arm drift back down to her side. "Still the same Neema," she said. "You move to protect someone willing to sacrifice you."

"Why did you want Allison dead?" I said, "and Chet Joseph?"

"You heard Cindy."

"But I know you. You always have your own reasons."

Dagon tilted her head and studied me a little before she spoke. "You know like I do that there was a war happening in Mississippi. All those little college kids coming out of Ohio were foot soldiers walking into a project that was Bob Moses' brainchild."

"I know. I was there."

"And Chet Joseph would have been too. He was marked by an angel. The Summer Project would have made him into a force. A leader as great as Dr. King, as strong as Fannie Lou Hamer. Maybe even more. He would tap into young people in a way that the Movement had yet to do."

"So, you killed him."

"I prefer to think I eliminated a threat. We were winning the battle down there, Neema. Humanity was on our side. Do you know how much they despised black people? How many black men had disappeared into the waters of the Mississippi? We were winning the damn war, and Chet Joseph would have interfered with that. He would have changed too many minds, built too many warriors."

"You stopped nothing, Dagon. There was still Stokely Carmichael, Bobby Seale. Hell, the Black Panthers."

Dagon shook her head. "Chet was different. He would have weakened us, weakened our hold, and I couldn't let that happen. Lucifer, Baal, Beelzebub, Abaddon, me, we were all created equal. We were angels, heavenly soldiers banished together, cursed together. But somehow Lucifer appointed himself our ruler. But he was distracted by those idiotic segregation wars, which was my chance to—"

"To what, Dagon? Possess humans? Take their souls? And how would that have helped you with Lucifer?"

She smiled and waved a hand around the room. "I don't need humans when I have my demons."

I had been so focused on her I hadn't noticed the number of demons that had filled the room. Hundreds of demons surrounded us, their stares unblinking, and their bodies still. Although I knew I could hold my own with them, I was at a disadvantage because of the sheer numbers. They would be a distraction, which Dagon wanted right now.

"At some point," Cindy said. "You must stop explaining yourself to her and just kill her."

"Did you do that to Allison?" I told her. "Hand her over to Dagon?"

"Allison didn't know when to stop meddling, when to stop asking questions. She would have sacrificed her entire family, every single one of us, for some boy who died fifty years ago." Cindy said, moving toward us. "I couldn't let my uncle, my mother, pay for Allison's misguided desire to right what she considered a wrong. What happened to Chet Joseph just didn't matter anymore. I couldn't let her ruin our family because of him."

"So you struck a deal with Dagon, a demon princess?"

"See, Neema," Dagon said. "Whoever rules the human world holds a great deal of power. I don't see why that ruler must be Lucifer. So I tipped the balance in my favor."

For Dagon, Mississippi and even the death of Allison Stevens had never been about humans. It had been about gaining control over demons. She had gloried in the rage and cruelty of the human world because the demons could then gorge on human vices. "To gain more followers for your foolish bid for power, you promised demons unlimited access to humanity, didn't you?" I looked around at the demons standing so still all around us. "That's how you convinced them to follow you."

"No, Neema. Humanity, with all its hatred and jealousy and cruelty did a much better job of convincing them than I ever could."

She nodded her head then, and the demons moved as one.

I HAD TO TUNE OUT CINDY'S screams because I couldn't help her. I had my hands full of demons. So, so many demons. I had never been overpowered before, never had to test the limits of my abilities. My sword flashed, glowing as I beheaded first one then another demon, the air filling with the stench of burning flesh. The blessed blade tore through them, merciless as demons screamed in anger, pain and fear. I leaped into the air to avoid the sharp nails of one demon, my body twisting so I landed on both feet facing the opposite direction, but another demon, her white skin glowing, lashed out with both hands and tore into my t-shirt. Blood soaked the front of my shirt, but I didn't have time to even wince from the pain. I had forgotten just how much damage a demon could do.

Bringing up my blade, in anger I must admit, I sliced the demon in half, the sword cutting from the smoothness between her legs to the top of her head. I couldn't stop to savor her surprise as the halves of her body crumbled to the ground burning from the inside. I had not used so much of my strength on one demon in over a century. Another demon dropped from mid-air, and I raised my sword. Impaling him mid-flight, my blade sank into his mid-section as I stumbled under the weight of his body. I realized then he had sacrificed himself. He was stuck on my blade, and I was surrounded by demons.

As I struggled to shake his burning body loose from my sword, the demons surrounding me moved quicker, spying my dilemma. I placed a foot against the waist of the demon caught on my sword and yanked the sword free but not before another demon caught me on my thigh, his nails tearing through my jeans and piercing my flesh. I twisted loose, swinging the sword with my left hand. The blade cut into the neck of the demon, but the swing was too weak to behead him.

My arms drooped with fatigue, but the pile of ash forming from the bodies burned by my sword didn't slow down the horde of demons still running toward me. And I realized that Dagon knew that while the demons by the few may have been powerless against me over the years, the hundreds of demons that followed her would wear me down. I couldn't allow myself to be weak in front of her though. I didn't want to think about what she would do to me.

I gripped the hilt of my sword with both hands, but I struggled to swing my blade with the same force with which I had begun. Demons were getting past my defenses and tearing my flesh. Losing blood weakened me, and I needed to go somewhere soon to rest and heal. I brought up my sword one more time, ready to kill another demon when the room filled with a blinding light.

As the light swept the room, demons fell to the ground. Their mouths twisted in screams that didn't have the chance to form. By the time the light vanished, every Sin demon and Death demon in the room had dropped into a pile of ash and only Alastor, Dagon and I remained standing. The brightness faded and the room once again settled into the dim light that had kept us from complete darkness. My sword dropped to my side as the last bodies turned to ash, and I couldn't stand another moment. Dropping to my knees, I blinked away the blood that covered my face, taking in Dagon's stunned look. Cindy lay only a few feet from me, but I couldn't tell if she were dead or just unconscious.

Alastor gazed at me in abject fear. He had chosen the wrong side of this war.

"What the hell—" Dagon mouthed.

"Hell is right," a familiar voice I had never been so relieved to hear seemed to fill the room. Baal looked taller somehow, blacker, brighter. His red-gold locks were piled high on top of his head but still brushed the small of his back. He wasn't dressed in one of his usual suits. Instead, he wore a traditional, African dashiki and black trousers. He looked comfortable and clean amid the carnage that surrounded us. Beautiful to a fault, Baal was also terrifying. I could sense his anger even though his face and voice appeared calm.

"How did you find me?" Dagon said.

"You didn't think you could bring this many demons to the surface and not attract attention, did you? You left a scent."

"I covered it up."

Baal smiled. "Did you? Cause I found you anyway."

"You could always join me."

"You, dearest Dagon, have never interested me. You lack the... charm that Lucifer has always had." Baal turned to me and shook his head. "And you, Demon Hunter, you disappoint me. I always thought you were stronger."

With the tip of my sword digging into the ground, I struggled to my feet. Teetering a little once I stood at full height. I wanted to fall to the ground, but I refused to kneel before them. It took every ounce of strength I possessed to lift that sword before me and point it at Baal.

"I'm strong enough to kill you," I mumbled.

"Relax, Demon Hunter," Baal said, the smirk on his face showing that he saw through my bravado. "I'm not here for you. I only want Dagon, and you found her as promised. You and I can battle another day."

threats, I knew I needed to remain on guard. She had found her way out of a demon prison—rumored to be inescapable—and back into my life. I couldn't allow that to happen again, but I had another pressing concern.

"What of Alastor?" I said, feeling a little sorry for him as he stood silent, awaiting punishment.

Baal glanced at Alastor who shook with fear. "You chose the wrong side, shapeshifter. You understand that now, do you not?"

"Why didn't he turn to ash like the others?" I said.

Baal smiled. "I still need the soulcatchers, don't I?"

"But what happens to him now?"

Baal beckoned with a hand, and Alastor stood up. "We will determine his fate,"

"But I need him a little longer." I said. "I have to deliver Chet Joseph back to his family and only Alastor knows where his body is buried. And like you said, the soulcatchers are still missing. Who better than a guardian to help me find them?"

Baal gazed at me in annoyance before tossing back his head. "Deliver the shapeshifter in a week's time."

"And you will close the doorway that Cindy opened? We don't want her calling any demons."

"The demons were a little overzealous in their feeding so your human, if she wakes, won't be calling anything for a long time."

BAAL SHIFTED, AND I lifted my sword again.

He nodded his head, and demons I had not notic
folded from the shadows. Dagon only noticed them v
did, and her panicked sounds caused my heart to race.

"Please, Baal," she said, her voice filled with a fear .
shocked to hear. I could see a trace of the woman that
fooled me into thinking she was human all those years ⟨
Peering at the shadow demons again, I found myself curic
at beings that could strike fear in such a powerful demon
Dagon. "I can't go back into the abyss," she said. "Abaddo
will kill me."

"She may still be angry at what you did to escape, but I'm
sure she won't kill you. Abaddon is not that... simple."

"Baal—"

"Enough Dagon," Baal said. "You've caused us enough
trouble." The two shadow demons stood on either side of
Dagon. At a nod from Baal, each grabbed her by an arm,
and she screamed in pain as her flesh melted into theirs. It
was an efficient shackle she couldn't escape. They would free
her, I was sure, once they delivered her to the demon prison.
When Baal flicked his wrist, the ground beneath them soft-
ened and stretched, closing around their feet like liquid.
Dagon and the shadow demons sank as if they were being
swallowed by quicksand.

"I'm not done with you, Neema," Dagon screamed as
she struggled without success against their hold. She called
for my head, my heart, my life before the ground covered
her, and she vanished. Another special effect since Baal and
I both knew demons came from the spiritual realm, not
the freaking earth. His entrances and exits, though, were always colorful. While I felt no immediate fear over Dagon's

He shook his head. "I told you I'm not interested in you right now. Besides, if I hadn't stepped in," he said. "Dagon would have killed you."

"Dagon can't kill me."

"In a manner of speaking. You can't be killed Neema but *this* weak, you can be... controlled. I'm sure Dagon knew that when she gathered all those demons against you."

I didn't betray my surprise at his words. "Controlled by whom, you?" I said, gripping my sword with a renewed strength.

"Any demon prince," he said, smiling, "But I have no interest in controlling you—yet."

He tilted his head to the left, and I looked to see a groaning Jasen coming to, one hand gripping the side of his head. "I woke up your little human friend," he said.

"And I thank you."

He lifted his hands as if to open a new door into the spiritual world, but then he hesitated. "Did you find out anything about the arrowhead?"

"I was a little busy with your rogue demon, so no, I didn't have time to search for the soulcatcher or for the maker of the arrowhead. But I know of only one person who used that incantation on a weapon."

"Precisely my point Neema," Baal said, smiling. "When you're ready to chat, you know where to find me." Then he vanished as quickly as he had come.

I stared after him, stunned. When he had first given me the arrowhead, I hadn't allowed myself to think about what it might mean. But... but. Could Priest *still be alive*?

"What have you gotten me into, Neema?" Jasen said jerking me back to the present. As I helped him to his feet, he touched my face with a shaky hand. "And what is this stuff all over you?"

"Demon blood," Alastor said, one eye on the unconscious Cindy. "And what are you planning to do with her?"

"Let the police pick her up," I said, wrapping an arm around Jasen's waist, half-dragging, half-leaning on him as we limped across the fading ash. "Her and her uncle."

I was silent as we left the building, tuning out both Alastor and Jasen as I kept coming back to what Baal had suggested.

If Priest was still alive then what happened in that maroon community? And *where in the hell has he been for the last two hundred and seventy-five years?*

Author's Note

While I have taken some creative liberties with the New York Slave Conspiracy of 1741, the supposed slave plot is a part of New York's history. By the 1700's, New York had become the slave capital of the Northern colonies. Its role in slavery was only rivaled by that of South Carolina.

In the spring of 1741, New Yorkers feared a slave rebellion and began arresting slaves along with the whites believed to be aiding them. The arrests and trials, led by Judge Daniel Horsmanden, resulted in numerous slaves being executed or deported.

Although Neema's part in this story is borne of a vivid imagination, the trials are real events and its victims are real people whose stories should never be forgotten. You can find further information regarding the Slave Conspiracy trials from New York Court archives and multiple websites. Jill Lepore's book *New York Burning* also provides a detailed accounting of the supposed plot.

Neema's story also includes other aspects of America's slave past. The African Burial Ground in Manhattan, the Stono Rebellion in South Carolina and even Ft. Mose in Florida are all part of the rich history of Africans in America. Her story, however, does not begin in America.

I turned to Africa's past for Neema's origin story. The women warriors of Dahomey were fierce, powerful, and very real. For more information, there are multiple websites that can be researched, but *Amazons of Black Sparta* by Stanley Alpern offers great insight into this all-female regiment.

With so much rich and wonderful history to mine, it should come as no surprise that this is just the first book in Neema's immortal life.

L.L. Farmer

October 2017

Don't miss the next book in the series!
Black Ghost

On sale April 2018
Neema would much rather deal with demons of any kind than a human ghost, especially the ones that can't seem to let sh** go. That's probably why she should have sent Jasen's call straight to voicemail. And she should have *never* gone to that house in Queens.

Did you love *Black Borne*? Then you should read *Secret Fantasy* by L.L. Farmer!

Sojourner Truth Davidson reluctantly returns to her hometown when her grandmother dies, and she has every intention of leaving immediately after the funeral. But when Collectibles, the store that she has just inherited, is vandalized; her search for the culprit leads her on a journey to unlock Golsboro's secrets. Naturally, she seeks help from the town's delectable Sheriff. If only she can keep her lips...and hands...and well, everything else to herself.

Mike Soyinka, Goldsboro's Sheriff, has crushed on Sojo since he was 12 years old, but as his best friend's older sister, she's always been off-limits. But when she needs his help to fulfill her grandmother's final request, he jumps at the chance to satisfy her every...need.

As Sojo and Mike work together to discover the truth about Goldsboro, they soon realize that sometimes childhood crushes lead to adulthood touches, even when it's not part of the plan.

Read more at www.llfarmer.com.

Also by L.L. Farmer

Warrior Slave
Black Borne
Black Witch

Watch for more at www.llfarmer.com.

About the Author

A native Floridian, L.L. Farmer is the author of the stand-alone novel *Slave Ship Rising, and No Mammies Here,* the first novella in a post-apocalyptic novella series.

She is also the author of *Black Borne, Black Ghost, Black Saint,* and *Black Witch* the first four novels in the Warrior Slave series. She is currently working on book five, *Black Gods.* Her most recent publication is a series set in the fictional, all-Black town of Goldsboro, Florida, where magic is real.

L.L. is a die-hard fan of Octavia Butler and hopes to fuse her love of African American history with urban fantasy and the paranormal. L.L. Farmer currently resides in the metro Atlanta area with her daughter.

Read more at www.llfarmer.com.

Made in the USA
Las Vegas, NV
28 July 2022

52292280R00208